The voi

Aye, a soft voice said. *Get out of the wind and cold. Find shelter. You've drifted a long time.*

The dark unicorn blinked. No speaker met his eye. The windswept beach lay empty, deserted. Strange. The words had seemed to come from within. Feverchills danced along his ribs and limbs. Still muddled, he shook his head.

"Water first," he croaked. "Then . . . find the others."

He remembered companions vaguely: unicorns like himself. What were their names and whence had they come? Somehow he knew the golden, cliff-lined strand he recalled was not their home. Yet neither was this flat expanse of silvery shore.

Find the fire, the inner voice said clearly.

Glimmers of warmth and tremors of cold gusted through him. The dark unicorn shook his head.

"Fire?" he muttered.

He had forgotten his own name. . . .

☾

FIREBIRD
WHERE FANTASY TAKES FLIGHT™

Dark Moon

Meredith Ann Pierce

FIREBIRD

AN IMPRINT OF PENGUIN GROUP (USA) INC.

FIREBIRD
Published by Penguin Group
Penguin Group (USA) Inc., 345 Hudson Street, New York, New York 10014, U.S.A.
Penguin Books Ltd, 80 Strand, London WC2R ORL, England
Penguin Books Australia Ltd, 250 Camberwell Road, Camberwell, Victoria 3124, Australia
Penguin Books Canada Ltd, 10 Alcorn Avenue, Toronto, Ontario, Canada M4V 3B2
Penguin Books (N.Z.) Ltd, 182-190 Wairau Road, Auckland 10, New Zealand

First published in the United States of America by Little, Brown and Company, 1993
Published by Firebird, an imprint of Penguin Group (USA) Inc., 2003

1 3 5 7 9 10 8 6 4 2

LIBRARY OF CONGRESS CATALOGING-IN-PUBLICATION DATA

Pierce, Meredith Ann.
Dark moon / Meredith Ann Pierce.
p. cm.—(Firebringer trilogy; v 2)
Originally published: Boston: Joy Street Books, 1993
Sequel to: Birth of the firebringer.
Sequel: The son of summer stars.
Summary: Jan, the prince of the unicorns, pursues his destiny to save his kind from
their enemies by seeking fire in a distant land of two-footed creatures.
ISBN 0-14-250057-7
[1. Unicorns—Fiction. 2. Fantasy.] I. Title.
PZ7.P61453Dar 2003 [Fic]—dc21 2002043948

Printed in the United States of America

For P.G., in the hope of things to come

Contents

Dark Moon

Before

☽

He was the youngest prince the unicorns had ever known, and his name meant Dark Moon. Aljan son-of-Korr was swart as the well of a weasel's eye, the night-dark son of a night-dark sire, with keen, cloven hooves and a lithe, dancer's frame, a long horn sharper than any thorn, and a mane like black cornsilk blowing. While still counted among the colts, young Jan had won himself a place in the Ring of Warriors. Upon the death of his royal grandsire, Jan had seen his own father declared the king and himself — barely half-grown — made battle-prince.

During time of peace, Korr the king would have ruled the herd, but because the unicorns considered themselves at war, it was to Jan, their prince, that the Law gave leadership. His people's bitterest enemies, the wyverns, dwelt far to the north, in sacred hills stolen from the unicorns many generations past. Vengeful gryphons held the eastern south, barely a day's flight from the great Vale in which the exiled herd now made its home. And hostile goat-footed pans inhabited the dense woodlands bordering the Vale.

Such were the uneasy times during which this young prince came to power. I am his chronicler, and yestereve I spoke of his warrior's initiation, during which the goddess Alma marked him, tracing a slim silver crescent upon his brow and setting a white star on one heel in token *that one day he must become her Firebringer, long prophesied to end his people's exile and lead them triumphant back to the Hallow Hills.*

Tonight, I resume my tale little more than a year after Jan's accession: it was the afternoon of Summer's Eve. The morrow would be Solstice Day, when thriving spring verged into summer. Jan stood on a lookout knoll high above the Vale, rump to the rolling valley below, black eyes scanning the Pan Woods spilling green-dark to the far horizon, beyond which the Gryphon Mountains rose, flanking the Summer Sea.

Solstice

) 1 (

Cloudless sky soared overhead, blue as the sweep of a gryphon's wing. Breeze snuffed and gusted through the dark unicorn's mane, warm with the scent of cedars sprawling the slope below. Sun hung westering. Jan shifted one cloven heel and sighed. He was not on watch — no sentries needed this time of year: gryphons never raided past first spring. But the herd's losses had been heavy that season in fillies and foals carried off by formels — the great blue gryphon females — to feed their ravenous newly hatched young.

Brooding, the prince of the unicorns surveyed the folds of the Pan Woods before him. It was not the number of recent raids which troubled him most, but their manner. Always in springs past, wingcats had come singly, at most in mated pairs. This year, though, many of the raids had included more than two gryphons. A few had even consisted solely of tercels — male gryphons — no female at all. Jan snorted: clearly at least some of the spring's forays had had little to do with a formel's need to feed her chicks.

"Alma," the young prince whispered, and the wind stole the name of the goddess from his teeth. "Alma, tell me what I must do to defend my people."

Only silence replied. Jan's skin twitched. With his long fly-whisk tail, he lashed at the sweatsipper that had alighted on his withers. Vivid memory came to him of how, only the year before, the goddess had marked him with fire, granted him the barest glimpse of his destiny — and spoken not a word to him since. Standing alone on the lookout knoll, he felt doubt chill him to the bone. He wondered now if the voice of Alma and her vision had been nothing but a dream.

A twig snapped in the undergrowth behind him. Jan wheeled to spot a half-grown warrior emerging from the trees. Pale dusty yellow with dapples of grey, the other shook himself, head up, horn high. Jan backed and sidled. Like a fiercely burning eye, the copper sun floated closer to the distant horizon. The other snorted, ramped, then whistled a challenge, and the prince sprang to meet him. Horns clattered in the stillness as they fenced. A few more furious strokes, then the pair of them broke off. Jan tossed his head. Grinning, the dappled half-grown shouldered against him. The prince eyed his battle-companion Dagg.

"Peace!" Dagg panted. "What brings you brooding up onto the steeps so close to dusk?"

Jan shook himself and nickered, not happily.

"Gryphons."

Again his shoulder-friend snorted, as though the very thought of gryphons stank.

"Bad weather to them," Dagg muttered. "Broken wings and ill fortune — praise Alma spring's past now and we're done with them for another year."

Jan nodded, champing. Dusk wind lifted the long forelock out of his eyes, exposing the thin silver crescent upon his brow. Gloomily, he picked at the pine-straw underhoof with his white-starred hind heel. Beside him, Dagg shifted, favoring one foreleg.

"How's your shank?" Jan asked him.

The dappled warrior blinked grey mane from his eyes and slapped at a humming gnat ghosting one flank. He flexed the joint.

"Stiff yet, but the break's well knit. Teki the healer knows his craft."

Behind them, the Gryphon Mountains stood misty with distance. The reddened sun above the Pan Woods had nearly touched the rim of the world. Lightly, Jan nipped his shoulder-friend.

"Come," he told him. "Sun's fair down."

Dagg shook him off and fell in alongside as they started through the evergreens that forested the Vale's inner slopes. Amber sunlight streamed through the canopy. Just ahead, a pied form moved among the treeboles. Jan halted, startled, felt Dagg beside him half shy. A moment later, he recognized the young warrior mare Tek. Her oddly patterned coat, pale rose and black, blended into the long, many-stranded shadows.

"Ho, prince," she called, "and Dagg, make haste! Moondance begins."

Jan bounded forward with a glad shout, reaching to nip at the pied mare's neck, but light as a deer, she dodged away. Tek nickered, shook her mane, back-stepping, laughing still. The young prince snorted, pawing the ground. The next instant, he charged. This time, the pied mare reared to meet him, and the two of them smote at one another with their forehooves, like colts. Tek was a lithe, strapping mare, strong-built but lean, a year Jan's senior — though the young prince was at last catching up to his mentor in size. They were of a common height and heft now, very evenly matched. He loved the quickness of her, her sleek, slim energy parrying his every lunge and pressing him hard. With Tek, he need never hold back.

"So, prince," she taunted, feinting and thrusting. The clash of their horns reverberated in the dusky stillness. "Is this the best my pupil can do? Fence so lackadaisical this summer by the Sea and you'll never win a mate!"

Jan locked his teeth, redoubled his efforts. On the morrow, he knew, he, Tek, and Dagg — and all the other unpaired young warriors — must depart upon their yearly trek to the Summer shore, there to laze and court and spar till season's turn at equinox, when most would pledge their mates before the journey home.

Tek clipped and pricked him. Jan glimpsed Dagg standing off, absently scrubbing a flybite against the rough bark of a fir, and whistled his shoulder-friend to join in the game — but just then, more quick than Jan could blink, the young mare lunged to champ his shoulder, taunting him with her wild green eyes. In a flash, he was after her. Jan heard Dagg's distant, startled shout at being left behind as the young prince plunged breakneck down-slope through treeboles and shadows. The last rays of red sunlight faded. Moments later, he burst from the trees onto the Vale's grassy lower slope.

The hour was later than he had reckoned, the round-bellied moon not yet visible beyond the Vale's far steep, but turning the deep blue evening sky to gleaming slate in the east. On the valley floor below, the herd already formed a rudimentary circle. Ahead of him, the pied mare pitched abruptly to a halt. Lock-kneed, snorting, Jan followed suit. Korr, the king, stood on the hillside just below them. Jan tensed as his massive sire advanced through the gathering gloom.

"Greetings, healer's daughter," Korr rumbled.

"Greetings, my king," Tek answered boldly. "A fine night for Moondance, is it not?"

Jan felt himself stiffen at the black king's nod. He barely glanced at Jan.

"It is that," Korr agreed, "and a fine eve to precede your court-ing trek." The healer's daughter laughed. Pale stars pricked the heavens. The unseen moon was washing the dark sky lighter and yet more light. "Faith, young mare," Korr added in a moment, "I'd thought to see you pledged long before now."

Jan felt apprehension chill him. He had always dreaded Tek's inevitable choosing of a mate. The prospect of losing her com-pany to another filled the young prince with a nameless disquiet — the pied mare would doubtless be long and happily paired by the time such a raw and untried young stallion as he ever won a mate. Restless, he pawed the turf, and his companion glanced back at him with her green, green gryphon's eyes.

"Fleet to be made warrior, but slow to wed, I fear," she an-swered Korr. "Perhaps this year, my king."

The eastern sky turned burning silver above the far, high crest of the Vale.

"But I will leave you," she continued, "for plainly you did not wait upon this slope to treat with me."

Tek shook herself. Korr acknowledged her bow with a grave nod as she kicked into a gallop for the hillside's base. Still paces apart, Jan and his sire watched the healer's daughter join the milling herd below.

"A fine young mare," murmured Korr. "Let us trust this season she accepts a mate."

Jan felt a simmering rush. "Perhaps I'll join her," he said impulsively.

Korr's gaze flicked to him. "You're green yet to think of pledging."

Jan shrugged, defiant, eyes still on Tek. "I was green, too, to succeed you as prince," he answered evenly. "But perhaps I shall be Tek's opposite: slow to be made warrior, yet quick to wed."

The sky in the east gleamed near-white above the far slope. Korr's expression darkened. "Have a care, my son," he warned. "You've years yet to make your choice."

The young prince bristled. Behind them, Dagg cantered from the trees and halted, plainly taken by surprise. He glanced from Korr to Jan, then bowed hastily to the king before continuing downslope. The young prince snorted, lashing his tail. The king's eyes pricked him like a burr.

"Be sure I will choose when I know myself ready," he told Korr curtly and started after Dagg.

His sire took a sudden step toward him, blocking his path.

"If it be this year, my son," he warned, "then look to those born in the same year as you. Fillies your own age."

Astonished, Jan nearly halted. By Law, not even the unicorns' king might command their battle-prince. Angrily, he brushed past Korr. "Do you deem your son a colt still, to be pairing with fillies?" he snapped. "A bearded warrior, I'll choose a *mare* after my own heart."

He did not look back. White moonlight spilled over the valley

floor as the herd before him began to sway, the great Ring shifting first one way, then the other over the trampled grass. Jan's
eyes found his mother, Ses, among the crowd. Beside the pale
cream mare with mane of flame frisked his amber-colored sister,
Lell: barely a year old, her horn no more than a nub upon her
nursling's brow. Korr cantered angrily past Jan, veering to join
his mate and daughter as the dancers found their rhythm, began
to turn steadily deasil.

Jan hung back. Dagg's sire and dam moved past: Tas, Korr's
shoulder-companion, like his son a flaxen dun dappling into grey;
Leerah, white with murrey spots, danced beside her mate. Jan
spied his granddam Sa farther back among the dancers. Dark grey
with a milky mane, the widowed mate of the late king Khraa
whickered and nodded to her grandson in passing, placing her
pale hooves neatly as a doe's. Jan dipped his neck to her, but still
he did not join the Ring.

Other celebrants swirled by, frolicking, high-stepping, sporting
in praise of Alma under the new-risen moon. The circling herd
gained momentum, drawing strength from the moonstuff show-
ering all around; the white fire that burned in the bones and
teeth, in the hooves and horns of all unicorns, placed there by
the goddess when, in fashioning her creatures at the making of
the world, she had dubbed the unicorns, as favored sons and
daughters, "children-of-the-moon."

Tek swept into view, pivoting beside the healer Teki. The black
and rose in her coat flashed in the moonlight beside the jet and
alabaster of her sire. Tek's riant eyes met Jan's, and she tossed
her mane, teasing, her keen hooves cutting the trampled turf,
daring him to join her. Daring him.

In a bound, the young prince sprang to enter the Ring. Bowing, Teki gave ground to let Jan dance beside his daughter.
The two half-growns circled, paths crossing and crisscrossing.
Dagg drifted near, chivvying Jan's flank. Jan gave a whistle,
and the two of them mock-battled, feinting and shoulder-
wrestling.

Tek's eyes flashed a warning. Jan turned to catch Korr's disapproving glare. Reflexively, the young prince pulled up. Then, blood burning beneath the skin, Jan shook himself, putting even more vigor into his step. Moondance might have been a staid and stately trudge during his father's princely reign — but not during his own! Dancers chased and circled past him in the flowing recurve of the Ring. He found his grandmother beside him suddenly, matching him turn for turn.

"Don't mind your father's glower." The grey mare chuckled. "It nettles him that it is you now, not he, who leads the dance."

Jan whinnied, prancing, and the grey mare nickered, pacing him. They gamboled loping through the ranks of revelers until, far too soon, the ringdance ended. Moon had mounted well up into the sky. All around, unicorns threw themselves panting to the soft, trampled ground, or else stood tearing hungrily at the sweet-tasting turf. Fillies rolled to scrub their backs. Dams licked their colts. Foals suckled. Stallions nipped their mates, who kicked at them. Jan nuzzled his grandmother, then vaulted onto the rocky rise that lay at the Circle's heart.

"Come," he cried. "Come into the Ring, all who would join me on the courting trek."

Eagerly, the unpaired half-growns bounded into the open space surrounding the rise. Behind them, their fellows sidled to close the gaps their absence left, that the Circle might remain whole, unbroken under the moon. Jan marked Tek and Dagg entering the center with the rest.

"Tonight is Summer's Eve," he cried. "The morrow will be Solstice Day. Before first light, as is the Law, all unpaired warriors must depart the Vale for the Summer Sea, there to dance court and seek our mates. There, too, must we treat with the dust-blue herons, our allies of old, who succored our ancestors long ago. But mine is not to sing that tale. One far more skilled than I will tell you of it. Singer, come forth. Let the story be sung!"

Jan descended the council rise as the healer Teki rose to take his place. The singer's black-encircled eyes, set in a bone-white face, seemed never to blink. Jan threw himself down beside Dagg as the pied stallion began to chant.

"Hark now and heed. I'll sing you a tale of when red princess Halla ruled over the unicorns. . . ."

Restlessly, Jan cast about him, searching for Tek. He spotted her at last, nearly directly in front of him, eyes on her sire. Contentedly, Jan settled down to listen to the singer's fine, sonorous voice tell of the defeated unicorns' wandering across the Great Grass Plain. After months, Halla's ragged band stumbled onto the shores of the Summer Sea, watched over by wind-soaring seaherons with wings of dusty blue.

"So Halla, princess of the unicorns, made parley with these herons, to treat with them and plead her people's case," Teki sang, turning slowly to encompass all the Ring beneath his ghostly gaze.

"'These strands are ours,' the herons said. 'And though the browse here may seem good in summer, little that is edible to your kind remains during the cold and stormy months of winter.'

"'We do not ask to share your lands,' the red princess sadly replied. 'Not long since, we consented to the same with treasonous wyverns, only to find our trust betrayed and ourselves cast from our own rightful hills. Now we seek new lands, wild and unclaimed, to shelter us before the winter comes.'"

Tek tore a clump of leaf-grass from the ground beside her and shook her head. Jan watched the soft fall of her parti-colored mane against the graceful curve of her throat. Her green eyes caught the moonlight. Jan felt again the flush of warmth suffusing him. Truth, never had a mare lived — not even red Halla — more comely than Tek. As the singer lifted his voice again, Jan wondered if that long-dead princess of whom the other sang had had green eyes.

"'We will go in search of such a place for you,' the blue herons said. 'Our wings are strong and the winds of summer fair. Your people are spent from your long wayfaring. Sojourn here for the season beside our Sea while we seek out a place such as you describe.'"

Teki sang on, finishing the lay with the herons' discovery of the grassy Vale at the heart of the Pan Woods, verdant in foliage, its steep slopes honeycombed with grottoes to lend shelter against wind and rain, the whole valley uninhabited save for witless goats and deer. Exultant, the unicorns had claimed the Vale, securing at last a safe wintering ground: their new home in exile until the foretold coming of Alma's Firebringer would one day lead them to reclaim their ancestral lands.

Listening, Jan found his thoughts straying to the fierce, furtive pans, whose territory he and his band must on the morrow begin to cross in order to reach the Summer Sea. Bafflement and frustration over the worsening gryphon raids crowded his mind as well, mingled with thoughts of the distant wyverns and this fitful, generations-long impasse his people termed a war.

Heavily, Jan shook his head. The moon upon his forehead burned. Somehow, he must find a way to conquer all these enemies and return his people to the Hallow Hills. Legend promised that he could do so only with fire. Yet he possessed no fire and no knowledge of fire, no notion of where the magical, mystical stuff could be found — not even the goddess's word on where to begin.

Alma, speak to me! he cried inwardly.

But the divine voice that had once guided him so clearly held silent still. Despair champed at him. Teki quit the rise, his lay ended. Jan sighed wearily and stretched himself upon the springy turf. Dagg sprawled alongside him, head down, eyes already closed. Before him, Jan saw Tek, too, lay down her head. The moon, directly above, gazed earthward in white radiance. Jan shut his eyes. Others all around, he knew, already slumbered.

He felt himself drift, verge into dreams. Tangled thoughts of his people's adversaries and his own impossible destiny washed away from him. Even memory of Korr's harsh, disapproving stare faded. In dreams, the young prince moved through mysterious dances along a golden-shored green sea. Before him galloped a proud, fearless mare, her name unknown to his dreaming self, though she reminded him of none so strongly as the legendary princess Halla — save that this nameless, living mare had a coat not red, but parti-colored jet and rose, and green, green gryphon's eyes.

Summer

)2(

Tek tossed her mane, wild with the running. Wet golden sand scrunched between the two great toes of each cloven hoof. Alongside her, companions frisked through cool green waves. Summer sea breeze sighed warm and salt in her nostrils, mingling with the distant scent of pines. Ahead of her, the prince loped easily along the strand, his long-shanked, lean frame well-muscled as a stag's. She loved the look of him, all energy and grace. What a stallion he would make when he was grown! Tek laughed for sheer delight.

High grassy downs bordered the shore. Jan led the band toward the maze of tidal canyons known as the Singing Cliffs. Wind fluted through their honeycombs like panpipes, a plaintive, sobbing, strangely beautiful sound. Above their soughing rose the shrieks and ranting of the seabirds which nested there.

Far overhead one speck among the myriad began spiraling earthward. Head up, the pied mare halted alongside Dagg as the prince whistled his band to a standstill. Other specks glided effortlessly down, blue as the sky in which they sailed. Soon they dropped low enough for Tek to distinguish long wings and slender necks, sharp, bent bills and lanky, web-footed legs.

In another moment, they began alighting on the sand. One heron, taller than the rest, her eye roughly level with Jan's shoulder, fanned her feathery head-crest to reveal deep coral coloring under the dusty blue.

"Greetings, Tlat, far-roving windrider," Jan hailed her. "Peace to you and to your flock."

The leader of the herons clapped her bill and studied Jan with one coral-colored eye. Behind and around her, her people bobbled, folding their elongated wings with difficulty.

"So. Jan," she called in her high, raucous voice. "The prince of unicorns returns."

"Yes, I am returned," the dark stallion answered. "Last year found me no mate, so this year I must try again."

"Ah!" the seaheron cried. Bobbing and clattering, her people echoed her.

"How fared your own courting this past spring?" Jan inquired as the herons subsided.

Obviously pleased, Tlat groomed her breast. "Ah!" she piped. "The crested cranes — tried to steal our nesting grounds again this year. Ah! We drove them off."

The prince nodded solemnly. Breathing in the tangy sea breeze and feeling the deep, steady warmth of sun upon her back, Tek bit down a smile. Every year the same report. Though the cliffs held ample nesting sites for all, the ritual clash between herons and cranes continued spring after spring. Tlat gabbled on.

"Now the nests are built, the hatchlings fat and sleek with down. My own brood numbers six! My consorts and I press hard to feed them all."

Behind her, several of the smaller birds, males, began to step in circles, ruffling and fanning their crests. Tek counted half a dozen of them: one consort to father each chick? Jan bowed to them.

"My greetings to your mates, and to your unseen young as well. I trust we will meet when their wing-feathers grow?"

"Yes! Doubtless!" screamed Tlat proudly. "But we cannot stay. Our squabs cry out to us from the cliffs, and we must not let them hunger. Greetings and farewell!"

Tek glimpsed the red chevron on the underside of each pinion as the windriders shook out their wings.

Bowing, Jan replied, "The herons have been our allies for generations. We do not forget the debt we owe. Our courting dances will be the more joyous for your greeting."

"Good!" screeched Tlat. "Beware the stinging sea-jells washed up on shore today. Though they are delicious to our kind, we know you find them unpleasant."

The heron queen stretched her neck and stood on toes.

"Welcome, children-of-the-moon! May your summer here prove fruitful — though how odd that your kind takes but a single mate. Unicorns are strange beasts." Abruptly, the stiff wind caught her, plucking her away almost before the pied mare could blink. Other seaherons followed, rising light as chaff. Tek joined Jan and her fellows in bowing again to the departing herons.

"Good winds and fair weather attend you," the prince called after them. Tek was not sure they could hear him above the thrash of surf and eerie crooning of the Cliffs. The windriders had already dwindled to mere motes overhead. A moment later, she lost sight of them, swallowed by the fierce blue, cloudless sky.

Stinging sea-jells did indeed lie beached downshore as the windriders had warned. Jan kept his people out of the waves until the next tide swept the bladderlike creatures with their trailing tendrils away. Summer passed in a headlong rush. The young prince felt himself growing, bones lengthening, muscles massing. He was ravenous and glad of the freely abundant forage. The sky held mostly warm and fair.

He devoted a good part of his day to chasing the other young half-growns and setting them to races and mock-battles, dances and games. Herons brought news of shifts in the wind so that Jan could whistle his band to shelter in the tangled thickets well before any storm. What time he did not spend tending the band he passed with Dagg, exploring inland at low tide along the Singing Cliffs, stopping now and again for a furious round of fencing.

Tek's admirers, he noted testily, were even thicker this year than last. Yet she seemed to pay them as little heed as ever. Once or twice, he even noted her ordering some overly bold young stallion smartly off. More and more, the young prince observed, the healer's daughter sought him out, teasing him away from the band — even from Dagg — to run with her along the wet, golden beach, dodging through dunes, or up onto the highlands above the cliff-lined shore.

Though he knew she could only be doing so to gain respite from bothersome suitors, Jan found himself increasingly willing to be led away. The pied mare's every word, her every move fascinated him. He loved to brush against her smooth, hard flank in play or simply prick ear to the cadence of her voice.

Long summer days ambled lazily by, the starry evenings fleetingly brief. With each passing moon, the high sun of summer gradually receded toward the southern horizon. Now it shone nearly directly overhead at noon. Nights lengthened: soon they would overtake the days in span. Equinox, marking the summer's end, crept up on the young prince unawares.

He and Tek chased across the high downs above the shore, wind whipping their manes and beards. Overhead, herons soared, diving like dropped stones into the shallows of the Sea, fishing for squid. Tek laughed, plunging to a halt at cliff's edge. Frothed with foam, the surging green waters below shaded into ultramarine at the far horizon. Shouldering beside her, Jan was surprised to find himself now taller than she. Had he truly grown so in these last swift months?

Tek tossed her head. The rose and black strands of her mane stung against his neck. The Gryphon Mountains stood barely within sight across the vast bay, but Jan spared them scarcely a thought. Never had unicorns summering upon the Sea been troubled by raiders. Wingcats attacked unicorns only within the Vale, and only at first spring. Spotting his shoulder-friend on the smooth beach below, in the thick of a group of sparring warriors, Jan felt a sudden chill.

"We should go back," he said. "We've left Dagg."

The healer's daughter shrugged. "He is with companions" — she eyed him coolly — "and seems content."

Jan snorted, champing. "We leave him much alone these days." Even so high above the shore, he still caught the faint click of parrying horns. Wind gusted and sighed. Farther down the strand, another knot of young half-growns frisked, fishing fibrous kelp from the waves and playing tussle-tug. Salt seethed heavy in the wind. Abruptly, Jan turned to Tek.

"You are ever luring me off these days, even from our shoulder-friend. Will not Dagg's company do as well as mine to keep your admirers at bay?"

Tek laughed. "Dagg may be my shoulder-friend as well," she answered, watching him aslant. "But he is not the one I am courting, prince."

Jan felt surprise slip through him like a thorn. He stared at her. She could not have knocked the wind from him more thoroughly if she had kicked him.

"What, what do you mean?" he demanded. "I'm far too callow —"

"Are you?" the healer's daughter asked. "So speaks your sire! But what say *you?*" She sidled, teasing, nipping at him with her words. "Three times before have I come to the courting shore — each time only to depart unpaired. The first two summers, I was newly initiated, just barely half-grown. Last year, it was the one on whom I'd set my eye who was just freshly bearded, unready yet to eye the mares. This year, though, while young yet, he has wit enough to know his own heart — and I count him well grown."

She shouldered him. Jan looked at her, unable to utter a word. A sudden fire consumed him at her touch.

"Hear me, prince," the pied mare said, "for I begin to chafe. Long have I waited for you to catch me up." She shied from him, circling, leading him. The dark unicorn followed as by a gryphon mesmerized. "Surely you do not mean to make me wait forever?"

Trailing after Tek, Jan felt himself growing lost. Her eyes drew him in like the surging Sea. In their jewel-green depths, he saw of a sudden possibilities he had never before dared contemplate: Tek dancing the courting dance with him under the equinox moon, the two of them running the rest of their days side to side, unparted by any other — and in a year or two years' time, fillies, foals. . . .

"I — I must think on this," he stammered, stumbling to a stop, and cursed himself inwardly for sounding like a witless foal. Tek only smiled.

"Think quickly, prince. Equinox falls in only six days' time. Five nights hence, we dance the dance." She snorted, shaking her mane. The scent of her was like rosehips and seafoam. "Remember my words," she said saucily, "come equinox."

She sidled against him, nuzzled him, her teeth light as a moth's wing against his skin. Jan shivered as Tek broke from him, flying away across the downs, skirting the cliff's edge and heading for the steep slope angling down toward shore. Dumbstruck, the prince of the unicorns stared after her. By the time he had gathered both wit and limb, she was already gone.

"So you've decided," the dappled warrior remarked. Jan and he trotted along the narrow strand flanking the Singing Cliffs. Tide was out, affording them passage. The sea breeze hooted and sighed through the twisting canyons.

The young prince halted, unable to mistake his shoulder-friend's meaning. "How did you know?"

Dagg whinnied. "I've known since spring. I wish you both joy."

His mirth had a strangely painful ring. Hearing it, Jan became suddenly aware that Dagg had no young mare like Tek with whom to spend his hours and dream of one day dancing court. Jan shook himself. The thought of making the pledge himself and leaving Dagg behind, unpaired, made his skin taut.

"Hist, nothing's decided until the eve of equinox!" he cried,

shouldering against the younger stallion. "Come, you've time yet
to make a choice — any number of mares would spring to pledge
with you. What of that filly I saw you sparring with the other
day? The slim, long-legged blue . . ."

"What — Gayasa's daughter, Moro?" Dagg laughed again, in
earnest this time. "She's barely got her beard; she was only made
warrior this spring past — far too young." He shook his head.
"And so am I. Another year."

Turning, he broke into a trot. Jan loped after him. "It doesn't
have to be," he said urgently.

Dagg halted, stood gazing off across the green and foaming
waves. "She's not among us," he said at last. "She's not yet here
for me to pledge."

Jan frowned, not following. The dappled warrior turned.

"Do you recall," he asked quietly, "the night of our initiation
two springs past?"

Jan nodded slowly: the night when initiates to the Ring of
Warriors became, for one brief instant, dreamers, to whom Alma
granted glimpses of their destinies.

"Tek says she saw the foretold Firebringer," continued Dagg,
"moon-browed, star-heeled."

The young prince shook the forelock out of his eyes, digging
nervously at the shell-embedded shore with his left hind heel.
Aye, marked as the Firebringer, he thought miserably, *but without
so much as an inkling of where I'm to find my fire!* Dagg glanced at
him.

"You yourself beheld visions of the goddess's Great Dance."

Jan shrugged and sidled. *And only darkness since: not even a
whisper of a dream.*

"What did you see?" he asked his friend suddenly. "You've
never said."

Dagg closed his eyes. "I saw a mare," he said, "small, but
exquisitely made, high-headed, her coat a strange bright hue such
as none I've ever seen. Each Moondance, I've scanned the assembled herd. . . ." He opened his eyes and turned to took at Jan.
"Even though I know my search is hopeless. Her mane stands

upright along her neck. Her tail falls silky as a mane. Her chin is beardless, no horn upon her brow. Each hoof is one great solid, single toe."

The young prince stared at him, dumbstruck. Dagg nodded.

"Aye. She's not of the Ring, Jan," he whispered. "She's a renegade."

Frowning, Jan shook his head. "You and I both know those legends of outlaws losing their horns when banished from the Vale are only old mares' tales."

Dagg stood silent. Again, the young prince shook his head.

"Yet, if not a Plainsdweller," he murmured, "what manner of mare could this dream creature be?"

The dappled warrior snorted, shrugged, his pale eyes full of pain. "I've no notion. I only know she is my destiny — and I'll never find her in the Vale."

They both stood silent then. The breeze through the near Cliffs hummed and shuddered. Cranes wheeled screaming among the herons overhead. Tide came foaming in, wetting the two unicorns' cloven hooves, eating away the beach. The prince's shoulder-friend leaned hard against him.

"Jan, don't wait for me," he said. "Alma alone knows when I'm to find my mate. You've already found yours. Don't hold off. Don't spoil your own happiness — and Tek's — because I can't join you this year in the pledge."

Jan turned to study his friend. Favoring one foreleg, Dagg forced a grin. Half-rearing, he smote at the dark unicorn smartly with his heels. Jan whistled and shied, fencing with him, grateful and relieved. He felt as though he had tossed a hillcat from his shoulders. Wheeling, Dagg sprinted away. Jan sprang to follow, and the two galloped back along the seacliffs to rejoin the band.

On the night before equinox, the firefish were running: small, many-armed creatures that swirled luminous like stars through the great bay's pellucid water. They filled its breadth with a blaze of rose and pale blue light. The herons celebrated the advent of the firefish with noisy whoops, diving from moonlit air into the midst of those swarming near the surface of the waves, tentacles entwined, about their own strange courting rites.

Other windriders skimmed low, their bent bills laden with tangled, suckered arms as they snatched prey from the combers. Their eerie, loonlike cries and staccato splashes sounded through the cool, motionless air. For once, the Singing Cliffs held silent, no wind to wake their ghostly song. Jan and Dagg stood at the edge of a tangled thicket, watching herons and firefish and foaming sea as evening fell.

"Moon's up," Dagg told him.

The huge, mottled disk hung just above the far Gryphon Mountains to the east, dwarfing them, paling the stars. Its light made a long path of brightness across the placid bay. Jan nodded. Dagg fell in beside him as he turned and trotted through the verges of the thicket. Jan's ears pricked. Above the herons' distant plash and cry, the quiet rush of waves along the shore, he heard the sounds of unicorns gathering: snorts and shaking, the dunning of hoofbeats, a restless stamp.

He and Dagg emerged from the trees. Horn-browed faces turned expectantly as the dark prince loped to the center of the dancing glade, a circular, open space at grove's heart, trampled clean of vegetation by generations of unicorns. He halted, chivvying, his own blood running high. His restless followers milled and fidgeted, anxious to declare their choices in the dance. Jan tossed his head.

"This is the night we have all awaited," he told them. "Let those who know their hearts choose mates tonight, pledging faith to one another in the eyes of Alma for all time!"

With a shout, eager half-growns sprang into vigorous, high-stepping cadence, prancing and sidling before their prospective mates. Jan watched the moving river of unicorns, chasing and fleeing their partners in an endless ring. Dagg cantered past twice, three times — but where was Tek? He did not see her. Frowning, the young prince scanned the russets and blues of the others until a flash of pale rose and black revealed the pied mare. She seemed to be deliberately skirting the fringe, ducking behind other warriors to conceal herself from him.

The young prince plunged into the dance. The healer's daughter quickened her pace. With a surge of determination, he sprinted after her. All around him, companions circled, manes streaming, heels drumming. The moon rose higher until the youngest warriors, wearied and unpartnered still, dropped out to stand at the edge of the grove, only watching now. He glimpsed Dagg among them, pulling back, panting, sparing his once-broken foreleg just slightly.

Jan redoubled his pursuit of Tek, dodging through the remaining half-growns. In pairs, some of these had started to slip away, mares leading, stallions following, chasing off into the trees. Jan listened to their whistled laughter, their hoofbeats fading. Deep under cover of darkness, they would dance their own, more privy dances under Alma's eyes alone.

The crowded rush had begun to thin, more than half having slipped off or dropped away, unpaired. Yet still the healer's daughter eluded him. The young prince snorted, wild with frustration. How could she manage it, threading so nimbly among the others, always just a few teasing strides ahead? Once more he started to quicken his gait — then abruptly stopped himself, for all at once, he understood. He must stop trying to catch her, cease striving to run her down like some rival in a race — for this was not a race, he realized suddenly, nor any sort of contest at all. It was a dance.

They moved in a circuit. He could not lose her, and whether it was he who overtook her, or she who circled forward to catch him from behind, what did it matter? Laughing, he let himself fall back into the flowing ring of unicorns, and all at once, she was beside him, the two of them prancing and frisking, chasing and circling one another. Others around them faded from his thoughts. He and Tek formed their own circle at the heart of every larger circle and cycle and dance.

They had left the grove, he realized. The sound of the other celebrants faded behind them as he and Tek loped deeper into the trees. The murmur of sea and shore drew nearer. The shimmer of sealight glistened beyond the shadows, mingled with the pale gleam of moonlight.

Tek moved ahead of him, still beyond his reach, but only trotting now. She glanced over one shoulder, nickering, her green eyes lit by the moon. In another moment, he would catch her and pledge his vows, hear her pledge hers in return. Then they would be conjoined for life, their bond unshakable in Alma's eyes. It was what he had always longed for. He knew that now, and the knowledge warmed him like a fire.

Storm

) 3 (

Jan stirred in the grey light of morning. He lay on dry, sandy soil under knotted, smooth-barked shore trees. The beach lay only a short way off. Sky had grown heavy and overcast, dark slate in color. No longer calm, the grey-green sea frothed, foaming along the strand. *Storm in the wind,* he thought. Even now, at slack tide, the sea was running high.

His head rested upon another's flank, his neck lying along her back. He savored the warmth of the other's side against his own, her breaths even and light. Tek woke and, lifting her head, leaned back against him, caressing his strong-muscled neck with her own. Gently, he nipped her. She laughed, gathered her limbs, and, shaking the sand from her, rose. Jan did the same, nuzzling her.

"My mate," he murmured.

Again the pied mare nickered, shook him off. "Enough, prince! All night we danced, and I am spent. We must rejoin the others and take our leave of the dust-blue herons."

Jan sighed. By custom, the newly paired warriors must be gone from the courting shore by noon of equinox day. He stretched his limbs. Time enough to dance with his mate again when they reached the Vale some three days hence. He smiled, languid still, as Tek started away through the trees.

"What sluggards we have been," she called. "Half the morn is lost!"

Jan laughed, trotted to catch her up. The trees were sparse enough to keep the shore in view. The sea was truly wild this morn. Wind gusted, frothing the waves to spume. The beach had been eaten almost away by the rising tide. Dense clouds thickened the sky. Across the broad bay, great purple thunderheads boiled above the Gryphon Mountains. The air smelled humid, heavy with the coming rain. Abruptly, the dark prince halted. Against the soughing of wind and the crash of sea he heard high, keening screams — too sharp and full-throated to be herons' cries. Tek's ears pricked.

"List," she started. "What . . . ?"

The strident calling intensified. Jan's heart contracted suddenly as he caught the piercing whistles of warriors taken by surprise. Dagg's voice bellowed orders from the beach.

"Gryphons! Haste — rally: make ring! Wingcats are upon us —"

With a shout, Jan charged past Tek, heard the drum of his mate's heels only a half-pace behind. The trees fell away as he burst from the grove to behold his whole terrified band ramping on the wind-whipped shore, sea foaming behind them, while a dozen screaming gryphons circled above. Jan shied, staring, stunned. Never had such a thing been recounted in story or lay, that gryphons should attack unicorns upon the shores of the Summer Sea. Wingcats only raided the Vale — and only at first spring!

Before him, the young warriors scrambled to form a ring. Dagg whinnied orders, hurrying them into rank. Skirling gryphons dived. The flock consisted mostly of lighter, smaller males: the tercels' jewel-green feathers and golden pelts stood out against the storm-dark sky. Only four of the raiders were the larger females — blue-fletched formels with tawny hide. Jan shook his head: these were not mated pairs! Nor, so late in the year, could any hungry hatchlings yet remain in the nest.

Fiercely, the unicorns reared and jabbed at their attackers. Sprinting past her mate, Tek sounded her war cry. Furiously,

Jan trumpeted his own. He dodged a green-and-gold tercel's swoop — then, quick as stormflash, leapt after and felt his horn slash golden hide. The gryphon shrilled. Jan whinnied in defiance. Tek, he saw, had safely reached the ring. He himself was beside Dagg a moment later.

"They fell on us without warning," the dappled warrior panted, rearing and stabbing at a swooping formel. She pulled up before meeting his horn. Dagg smote the ground in frustration. "Just moments before you arrived!"

"No taunts? No challenges?" Jan asked him, then shouted at a young warrior starting after a low-flying tercel to get back into line and not break ring.

"Nothing!" Dagg answered, wheeling to drive off another formel diving from behind toward the center of the ring.

Jan grazed her wing, champed a cluster of feathers in his teeth. He yanked hard, trying to pull her down but, shrieking, she tore free. Dagg gouged her belly, and she slashed at him with one claw.

"It's war, then," Jan said grimly. "Not just hunting."

Across from them, he glimpsed Tek repelling a tercel that dropped toward a mare who had stumbled. Around her, the ring of warriors ramped and jostled, badly crowded by the tight formation. Above them the circling gryphons darted, stooping to slash, then lofting away. The young prince snorted in disgust. A traditional defense was proving useless. Nearly impenetrable to grounded foes, the band's outward-facing ranks availed little against adversaries that darted from the air, attacking the unicorns' unprotected hindquarters at the circle's heart.

"Get to the trees!" he shouted as yet another formel plunged toward the ring's center. "Haste! Break ring! Get into cover of the grove!"

"Jan, what —" cried Dagg, aghast.

"Fly!" ordered the prince. What he urged was unprecedented, he knew — but clearly facing an airborne foe required fresh tactics. "They can't swoop to attack us among the trees!"

Rising wind nearly ripped the words from his teeth. He saw

his mate nipping and hying her fellows, driving them toward the trees. Dagg and too many of the others simply continued to stare. The dark prince whirled and shouldered the young stallion nearest him, striking him across the rump with the flat of his horn to send him off. The half-grown mare beyond bolted as well while the wingcats redoubled their attack.

"Move!" he cried.

The dappled warrior seemed to swallow his consternation at last as the ring, now hopelessly broken, scattered toward refuge in the grove beyond the dunes. For an instant as she fled past him, Tek's puzzled gaze met his. Clearly she did not understand his strategy, even as she carried out his commands. Dagg started after her. Jan himself did not follow, watching as the two of them hung back a bit, forming a rearguard for their escaping fellows. They were the last to disappear into the trees.

"The prince! The unicorn prince!" one of the tercels cried.

Other wingcats took up the chant. The wind off the sea had grown so strong that Jan saw his attackers wobbling precariously as they banked and turned, breaking off their pursuit of the retreating unicorns. The relentless sea surged at his back. As a dozen wingcats beat toward him from above the dunes, he knew he could never hope to win past them to the grove.

"Alma aid me," he whispered. "Stand at my shoulder, O Mother-of-all!"

The Singing Cliffs rose to his left. Their honeycomb of wind tunnels and tidal canyons shrieked in the rising stormwind. Jan noted with relish how the wingcats strained and labored through the air. Whipping gusts tossed and batted at them. Earthbound, he himself was not so hampered.

As the first gryphon to reach him stooped, the dark unicorn dodged, sprinting away down the beach. The angry cries of his pursuers rose behind. The tall Cliffs opened before him. Jan ducked into their twisting maze. The air around him hummed, vibrated. Wind sheered and shuddered through the turning canyons, whistling like warriors, like birdsong, like reed flutes of the woodland pans.

His path looped and folded back upon itself. Powerful air currents buffeted treacherously. Rounding a bend, Jan glimpsed a wingcat formel being dashed by the gale against the cliff's side behind him. She crumpled, falling, and her companions screamed, increasing their speed. Long, keening wails rose on the stormwind as the churning air grew furious, laden with scattered, stinging rain.

Glancing back again, Jan saw more gryphons swept against the cliffs. The tremendous gusts barely reached him in the canyons' depths. Elated, the dark prince sped on while his remaining pursuers struggled to keep aloft despite the pelting rain. Drops fell more heavily, pounding down. Another tercel smashed into a ledge. Blue lightning split the heavens, casting a cold sheen like moonlight across the cliffs.

Tidewater spilled into the canyons suddenly. Jan found himself running through seawater up to his pasterns, flinging sheets of spray with every step. Only three gryphons remained in pursuit, green tercels all. Their shrieks tore at his ears. The cliffs sang, shuddered with stormwind. He heard the hammering of waves just beyond the canyon wall.

More seawater poured into the chasm. Halfway up his shanks, its depth impeded his gallop. Rain pummeled down. The tempest howled. Jan plunged on, limbs straining against the turbulent water's pull. The canyon ran straight now, without a bend. If he did not find a way out of the Cliffs soon, he realized, he might well drown.

The cliffside opened abruptly before him. Jan glimpsed beach and storm-filled sky. Only a single gryphon's voice trailed him now, the others all lost, or dashed to their deaths, or given up. Seawater crashed into the opening, the swell up to his knees, its undertow fierce. Furiously, Jan fought his way through the inrushing tide. The gryphon behind him shrilled in fury, so close the sound sliced the prince's ears.

Suddenly he was free of the cliffs, in a tidal trough deep with running sea. Firm ground lay within sight, a rocky beachhead only a score of paces beyond. Jan plowed toward it through the foaming surf. Again the gryphon's savage cry. The dark unicorn felt talons score his back, a razor beak striking the crest of his neck. He ducked, dodged sharply. Great green wings slapped the waves to either side. The raptor's grip tore into his flesh, fastening upon his shoulder blades.

Screaming with pain, Jan bucked and reared. Lion's claws hooked into his flanks, forcing him down onto all fours again. With a surge of unsought strength, Jan galloped breakneck, thrashing. Broken shells and beach gravel ground beneath his heels. The wingcat's grip slipped, balance faltering. The sea drew back, momentarily shallower — then a huge green wave twice Jan's height broke, overwhelming the young stallion and his attacker both.

Jan felt himself trod down as by a mighty hoof, the breath knocked violently from him. His knees, his ribs grated against the tidal trough's stony bed. He felt the gryphon torn from him by the surge. Struggling against a powerful current, he broke surface, snatched a breath. The black sky above roiled as rain-pebbled waves swept him under again.

Choking and snorting, he flailed madly to keep afloat. He glimpsed the Cliffs — much farther off than he had expected — and strove frantically to swim back to land. But the tow only pulled him farther out to sea. Something green and gold washed onto the distant rocks. The surge dragged it back before flinging it higher. This time it lodged, sodden and unmoving: the body of the gryphon tercel, broken by the waves.

Jan lost sight of shore. Rolling hills of water bobbed all around. Merciless wind whipped, its driving rain blinding him. Again a wavecrest broke over him, forcing him down into churning depths. Again he fought his way up, but more weakly this time. Something drifted against him in the darkness under the waves, brushing his flank. Long tendrils twined about his limbs, pricking him with needles of fire. Sea-jells! Rucked up from deep ocean by the storm.

Panicked, the dark prince floundered, gasping, choking. But

the barbed streamers only entangled him further. Their burning poison began to numb him. Vainly, he searched for land. The sea heaved. Stormwind buffeted. Presently, the sea-jells released him and floated on. Strange drowsiness stole over him. His burning limbs twitched, heavy as stone. Then his eyelids slid shut as he sank beneath the cold and furious sea.

Search

)4(

Tek hunkered down, rump to the driving rain. No gryphons had pursued them into the trees. Dagg hunched close, his nearness shielding her. Tek wished it were Jan flanking her as well — but in the confusion of flight, she had lost track of her mate. The pied mare shuddered. Wind and storm were now so furious she could scarcely see the other warriors huddled among the treeboles of the grove.

At last after what seemed an age, the gale spent itself. Black clouds parted, scudded away across the sky. The clean-washed air seemed dazzling, charged. And cold. The brilliant, midafternoon sunlight held no warmth. The first draft of autumn breathed unmistakably across the shore. The pied mare shook her rain-soaked pelt. Dagg trotted off to round up stragglers. Tek headed the other way, eager to discover Jan — but as she nipped and shouldered her scattered fellows back toward the rest, she felt a beat of fear.

"I don't see him," she called, glancing anxiously through the half-growns following Dagg. The prince's shoulder-friend cavaled.

"I'd hoped he was with you."

Drenched and weary, the battered young warriors milled around them. Tek noted bruises but few gashes, none deep. Most simply seemed badly shaken. Frowning, she lashed her tail. Where was the prince? It should have been he, not she and Dagg, to gather the band.

"Would he have gone scouting?" the dappled half-grown asked.

The pied mare shook her head. Why would Jan search for wingcats on his own when companions would have made the task far safer? The young warriors fidgeted.

"Ho," she called to them. "Which of you sheltered beside the prince?"

Half-growns shifted, glanced at one another. No one spoke. Tek snorted.

"I say regroup on the beach," Dagg offered. "Jan's most likely already there."

Tek whistled the others into line, unease edging into full-blown worry. She doubted her mate would rush to examine a battlesite when all trace of the fray had surely been obliterated by storm and tide. Trotting briskly to the head of the band, she called back, "Dagg, take rearguard."

They picked up a few more stragglers among the trees — but the beach lay deserted, half-eaten by storm. The gale-high tide had only partly receded. The pied mare gazed in dismay at the cast-up sea wrack, the carcasses of dead sealife. She spotted a dark shape lying beached upon the shore and froze, her heart beating hard. Then her terror subsided as she recognized it for what it was: a black whale calf, dead. Roughly the same size as a half-grown unicorn — but not Jan. Not Jan.

Tek champed her teeth, sent the others off to comb the strand. The unicorns fanned out, calling their prince's name. She kept several of the keener-eyed on watch, scanning the sky, not daring to trust the gryphons safely gone. When one of the lookouts whistled, Dagg and the others came galloping back to where she and the sentries stood craning heavenward.

"Wingcats?" he panted.

"Nay," she answered. "Look at the pinions' length: seabirds, not raptors."

"Herons!" cried Dagg. "We can enlist their aid in finding Jan."

As the slender forms of the seabirds dropped within range of her voice, Tek hailed them.

"Succor us, O herons! Your allies have need of your airborne eyes."

Gingerly, awkwardly, the flock alighted, their leader, Tlat, touching down to the damp sand first, followed by her consorts and the rest. Tek noted a number of gangling half-growns among them, uncrested, barely full-fletched. They gazed at the unicorns with round, curious eyes. Beside her, Dagg snorted and sidled impatiently. Tek hissed at him to be still, then whistled the others to keep their hooves firmly planted, lest the flighty windrovers take wing in alarm.

"Ah!" cried the heron queen, bobbing and dancing. "Where is your prince, pied one? Where is the unicorn Jan? First storm of fall has blown, and we have flown our young from the cliffs at last to teach them to forage on their own. Whale meat! Sweet squids! And to show them the unicorns before you must depart. Equinox is past. Fall glides in. You must be off, we know. But where is Jan? I would show him my brood."

Scarcely able to contain her urgency, Tek forced herself to hear Tlat out and to bow her neck respectfully.

"Your many young are beautiful, Queen Tlat, strong-limbed and finely feathered. May their crests grow brilliant. Would that my mate were here to see them. But he is lost to us. We do not know where he is. We were set upon by gryphons just before the storm. Now we cannot find Jan."

"Gryphons!" shrieked Tlat, hopping backwards. "Stormriders, yes."

Her people fluffed and began clapping bills, some dancing in agitation. One young bird started to whoop, and one of Tlat's mates stalked over and pecked it to silence. Tlat preened, fanning her crest, and looked at Tek one-eyed.

"We saw the cat-eagles, yes! Approaching across the bay — we longed to send you warning, but the wind was already too strong.

We dared not leave our cliffs. So they attacked you? War! War! Marauders."

She stabbed at a crab digging itself out of the sand near her toes, cracked its shell, then tossed its contents down. More bill-clattering from the flock. Tek fought for composure in the midst of the cacophony.

"We regret you were unable to bring us warning," she replied, striving to recapture Tlat's attention. The queen of the seaherons stood turning her head from side to side, eyeing the dead crab first with one eye, then the other. "But we ask your aid now. The herons are our fast allies, and we value the deep friendship between our two peoples."

"Friendship," clucked Tlat. "Allies, yes! How may we aid you?"

"Lend us your wings and your eyes," Tek urged her. "Help us to search for my mate, our prince."

"Prince's mate!" the heron queen cried. "Look for your mate — yes. We will! We will help you seek the prince of unicorns!"

With a scream, Tlat unfolded her slim, lengthy wings and fanned the air. The seawind — now no more than a breeze — caught, lifted her. Dipping her long neck to catch up the empty crabshell in her bill, the heron queen rose. Her consorts and children and the rest of her people followed, soaring aloft, shouting, "Find the prince! The prince!"

One of her consorts skimmed near to pluck the crabshell from her bill. It was snatched from his by another bird and passed from beak to beak throughout the flock. Tek stood on the beach, gazing after them, mystified. Another fear had begun to gnaw at her like a biting fly: that Jan perhaps lay wounded among the trees, invisible from the air.

High above, the herons broke and scattered, some skimming up the beach, others down, and many inland, sailing low over the tops of the trees. Shaking herself, Tek whistled her own followers into a similar sweep, desperately hopeful that they would find her young mate soon.

The seaherons spied no trace of Jan that day, nor the next day, nor the next, though they found nearly a dozen gryphons dead in the honeycombs of the Singing Cliffs. Had the remainder carried the prince away? Rising panic held Tek's heart in its teeth at the thought that she might have become the prince's mate but for a night, their wedding dance the last joy of him she would ever know. As heron messengers returned each night, Tek found it harder and harder to stave off despair.

On the third day, Dagg ceased to speak, all optimism dashed. Other members of the band remained painfully silent: angry, grieving, stunned. Tek felt all her wild hopes dying. The day ended in storm, not so violent as that of equinox, but bone chill, beating down the seaoats to rot and whipping the foliage from the trees. When the following cold, grey morning dawned, Tek, herself frozen past any feeling but exhaustion, forced herself to speak.

"He is gone," she told the band. They stood subdued before her, silent. "Surely the gryphons took him. They have killed our prince in open war. We must return to the Vale and bring word of this to the herd."

Dagg bowed his head. None of the others so much as raised a voice in protest. With a start, Tek realized that they had all despaired days ago. Only she had clung to the stubborn dream that Jan might still live. Outrage filled her at her own foolishness.

When the seaherons came again, Tek bade them farewell, thanked them woodenly for their hospitality, and praised again their lank, gawking children. Pledging to return the following summer, she expressed the unicorns' unending gratitude for their allies' diligence in the search. Plumage drooping, crests flattened to the skull, the typically raucous herons only nodded. Tlat even solemnly returned Tek's bow before soaring away with her flock.

Numb, Tek whistled her own followers into line. They straggled after her from the sandy shore, climbed the downs, traversed the coastal plain, and entered once more into the dark Pan

Woods, having failed even to discover and carry back to the Vale their prince's bones to be laid with proper ceremony upon the altar cliffs beneath the sky.

What will I tell his father? What will I tell the king? The refrain repeated itself relentlessly inside the pied mare's skull as she led the band dejectedly homeward. Dagg brought up rearguard. They could not bear to face one another. Tek groaned inwardly, wretched. All the while the image of Korr, dark and brooding, loomed before her.

Fever

☽ 5 ☾

The rhythm of the waves woke him, their gentle wash against and across him soaking his pelt. He felt the cold sting of air briefly, then another wave. The dark unicorn opened his eyes to find himself lying pressed against wet sand. Another swell sluiced over him. Choking, he rolled to his knees, pitched shakily to his feet.

He stood on a low, flat beach, the sand silver-white. No cliffs or downs flanked the shore, only dunes — and beyond them, dense thickets of trees. The dark unicorn blinked in confusion. He did not recognize the grey sea and white sand. He had come from a place of green waves, golden shore. He remembered a storm.

Weakly, the dark unicorn shook himself, staggered. Beach grit abraded his skin. His withers and back were scored by deep wounds, his limbs and belly patterned with raw, raised welts. His mind felt poisoned, numb. The salt air breathed against his wet coat, chilled him to shivering. The waves foaming placidly against his pasterns and shanks felt soothingly warm.

Turning, he gazed cross the calm, grey expanse: no longer storm-tossed, the sky above pearly with a thin overcast of cloud. The wind shouldered against him insistently, full of salt and particles. He faced away from the sea, climbed laboriously higher onto the beach. His hooves sank deep into the soft, dry sand. He set his rump to the wind's relentless, gentle gusts and bowed his head. The sting-welts ached. His shoulders ached. Heat burned in him, guttering against the cold.

"Fever," he muttered.

Feebly, he slapped the draggle of wet mane from his eyes and gazed at the trees beyond the dunes. Trees would shelter him, provide forage. Maybe water. The gummy, salt taste of his own tongue constricted his gorge.

"Water," he told himself dully. "Find water."

Aye, a soft voice answered now. *Get out of the wind and cold. Find shelter. You've drifted a long time.*

The dark unicorn blinked. No speaker met his eye. The windswept beach lay empty, deserted. Strange. The words had seemed to come from within. Feverchills danced along his ribs and limbs. Still muddled, he shook his head.

"Water first," he croaked. "Then . . . find the others."

He remembered companions vaguely: unicorns like himself. What were their names and whence had they come? Somehow he knew the golden, cliff-lined strand he recalled was not their home. Yet neither was this flat expanse of silvery shore.

Find the fire, the inner voice said clearly.

Glimmers of warmth and tremors of cold gusted through him. The dark unicorn shook his head.

"Fire?" he muttered.

He had forgotten his own name. Small grey-and-white seabirds wheeled overhead: dark hooded, with darting pinions. The strange voice commanding him sounded half like the sighing of shore wind and half like their high, piping calls.

Behold.

The dark unicorn started, stared as a brilliant red streak arched burning across the sky in the far, far distance. A dark wisp of vapor or dust blossomed up leagues upon leagues away, beyond horizon's western edge. Long seconds afterwards, a faint concussion reached him: the earth trembled.

Head west, the inner voice instructed him. *Along the shore.*

The dark unicorn staggered, nearly fell. Standing took almost more effort than he could muster. "What is my name?"

West, the voice reiterated. *When you have found my fire, you will once more know yourself.*

The voice faded, faint as a gull's trill on the wind. The dark unicorn blinked dizzily. Shelter, food, and water — he must find them soon, or he would die. Painfully, he dragged his hooves across the low, white dunes, heading westward toward the distant, tangled trees.

Home
) 6 (

The sky spanned clear, the air crisp with the breath of fall.
Tek shook her head. Had they been but three days crossing the Pan Woods, returning from the Summer Sea? It felt
like dozens. Solemn half-grows straggled around her as they
emerged from the trees onto the Vale's grassy lower slopes. Tek
beheld the waiting herd below: mares and stallions, fillies and
foals milling expectantly. Her heart froze as she spotted Korr, the
king; his mate, Ses; and their yearling filly, Lell: princess of the
unicorns now. The pied mare shivered, glad Dagg had come
forward to walk alongside her.

"What has happened?" thundered Korr as they reached the
bottom of the slope. "We awaited your return days since! Why
do you, healer's daughter, head the band instead of Jan? Where
is my son?"

Heartsick, she met Korr's gaze.

"Jan is not among us," she answered. "Gryphons took him. He
is slain."

The dark stallion's eyes widened. Around him, the whole herd
started, shying. Tek heard shrill whinnies of astonishment. Before
her, the king reared, snorting wildly.

"Gryphons?" he demanded. "On the Summer shore?"

Tek nodded and listened, mute, while Dagg recounted the

wingcats' attack, unicorns and herons searching, finding only dead gryphons among the cliffs.

"They've killed our prince," he concluded, voice hard. "It's war. When spring returns, we must strike back."

"Aye, vengeance! War!"

The whole herd took up the cry, whinnying and stamping in a frenzy of mourning. Korr tossed his head, pawing the air and smiting the ground. Ses wept softly. Lell looked frightened, anxious to suckle, but her mother fidgeted, too distracted to stand still. Withdrawn into herself, Tek scarcely heeded the clamor until all at once, Korr spun on her.

"So, healer's daughter," he demanded furiously, "how is it you alone keep silent? All around you mourn and rage against the gryphons' treachery, yet you stand there cold."

The pied mare stared at him.

"I have been three days weeping in the Pan Woods, king — as have all the band — and three days before that searching the Summer shore. I've wept me dry. I've no more tears to spill. My mate is dead! What more would you have of me?"

She found herself shouting by the end of it. She wished that she might shout until she dropped. The king drew himself up short, eyes white-rimmed suddenly.

"Your . . . mate?" he whispered.

Baffled, Tek nodded. "Aye."

"My son?" cried Korr, voice rising. "My son — your mate?"

"Aye!" Tek flung back at him, angry and confused. "We danced the courting dance and pledged —"

Only then did she realize Dagg had begun his recounting on equinox morn, never mentioned who had paired with whom the night before. The king continued to stare at Tek, his breathing hoarse.

"You?" he choked. "You beguiled my son?"

"He chose me," Tek answered. "And I him."

Abruptly, she remembered the preceding spring: Korr's odd but unmistakable disapproval whenever he had glimpsed the two of them in each other's company.

"Seducer!" screamed the king, bolting toward her through the press of unicorns. "Cursed mare. Daughter of a renegade!"

Tek shied, crying out in astonishment. She had to scramble back to avoid Korr's hooves as Dagg and his father, Tas, lunged to turn the huge stallion. Korr shouldered into Dagg, nearly knocking him to the ground. Tas, as tall as Korr, if leaner, threw his full weight against the king's side and forced him to a halt.

Other unicorns crowded forward: her own father, Teki, as well as the king's mate, Ses, and Dagg's young dam, Leerah. The healer's daughter looked on in consternation with the rest of the herd as the king, still shouting, strove to plunge past those who boxed him in.

"Temptress! Betrayer! Because of *you* my son is dead!"

"What are you saying?" Tek gasped. "I loved your son!"

"Liar! Outlaw's get. Four summers unpaired, you lay in wait to destroy him!"

The pied mare shook her head in dismay as the king fought on, struggling to reach her, the look in his dark eyes murderous. Not even Ses could still him.

"Alma will wreak her revenge —"

"Enough! Enough of this, my son."

Startled, the king whirled, and the uproar around him abruptly ceased. Those blocking his path fell back a pace as Sa, the old king's widow, emerged from the crowd.

"What means this frenzy?" Dark grey with a milky mane, she faced him, her expression full of pain and dismay. "You revile your slain heir's widow as if *she* were your foe."

The grey mare's son stood panting. His dam waited.

"Speak," she said. "Why do you fly at one who has done you no injury?"

Panting still, Korr turned on Tek. Clearly he longed to fall on her even yet. Alert, watching him, the pied mare held her ground.

"No injury?" he growled. "You left my son to die upon the shore."

The king gazed with open hatred at the healer's daughter. "You should have stayed with him! Died with him — died *for* him. You were his . . . his mate!"

He choked on the word, as though it tasted filthy in his mouth. Fury sparked in Tek. She felt her eyes sting, her ribs lock tight. She had thought she had no tears left to shed.

"*My son, you shame me.*" Once more she heard the grey mare's fierce rebuke. "You shame yourself and the office you hold. Tek is blameless in Jan's death. Have done, I say."

Swiftly, pointedly, she turned away. The king's jaw dropped. The herd milled in astonished silence. Abruptly, Korr wheeled and bolted across the Vale. Unicorns scattered from his path, then stared after him, stunned. Tas glanced at Ses, but the king's mate shook her head.

"Let him go," she murmured. "Only time can cool him."

Tek shuddered. She felt the pressure of Dagg's shoulder solidly beside hers and leaned against it gratefully.

"Pay him no heed." The dappled warrior spoke gently. "Our news came too suddenly. He's mad for grief."

"Come, child" — the late king's widow turned to her — "my granddaughter now by Law. You are spent from tears and journeying. Rest in my grotto, until the dance."

Trembling, Tek closed her eyes at the thought of Jan's funeral train to be danced at dusk: a great slow procession used only for those of the prince's line. The mourners, all smutched from rolling in the dust and hoarse from wailing, would call out, "He is dead! He is dead! He of the ancient line of Halla, dead!"

"He was my prince," she muttered as she stumbled after Sa through the crowd toward the grey mare's cave. "And faithfully I fulfilled his command — to get the others to the trees." Her father, Teki, nuzzled her. Dagg flanked her other side. Tek swallowed hard. "Now Korr despises me."

"Not so!" Dagg insisted. "How could he?"

They had reached the far slope of the Vale and started to climb. Sa glanced back as though to assure herself that they followed. The crowd behind them had begun to pull apart, the sound of their lamentations floating upward on the still morning air, making the pied mare shiver. The dappled warrior snorted.

"Korr's always favored you highly. Truth, many's the time he's treated you better even than his own son!"

The healer chafed her gently, reassuringly. "The king will relent."

But Tek shook her head, heaved a great sigh, painful against the crushing tightness of her breast. "Nay. Never. I *should* have stayed on the beach with Jan. I wish I had died instead of him."

FireKeepers
☽ 7 ☾

Days blended one into another, sometimes stormy, sometimes fair, but always cold. Fever consumed the dark unicorn. Often, he lay shuddering among the trees, too weak to rise. The mysterious voice spoke clearest to him then, urging him westward along the strand. It almost seemed that he himself were made of fire. More than once he came to awareness amid surroundings he did not recognize, certain that hours or days had passed of which he had no memory. Time wandered by in a dream.

Evening fell. Sun sank in a fiery blaze beyond the western horizon, the sky to the east grown dark as bilberries. Stars burned overhead, thinly veiled by fog. The full moon peering above the waves shone ghostly bright. Frowning, the dark unicorn stumbled to a halt. An amber glow flickered in the distance before him. As he left the strand and headed toward the dusky glimmer across the dunes, he caught a whiff of acrid, pungent scent. The sound of chanting reached his ears.

"Dai'chon!"

One clear voice sounded above the rest, calling urgently, ecstatic, echoed by a chorus of other, deeper voices.

"Dai'chon!"

It was no tongue the dark unicorn recognized. He halted on the rim of a deep pit in the dunes, as though the hoof of some unaccountably vast being had dug a trough in the sand with a single sweep. Perhaps two or three dozen creatures hunched in a circle at the bottom of the pit. Smaller than unicorns, they were shaped like pans, with round heads and flat faces, their upper limbs not fashioned for the bearing of weight.

Their smooth, nearly hairless bodies were swathed in something that was neither plumage nor pelts. The dark unicorn's nostrils flared. It smelled of seedsilk. He stared, fascinated by these two-footed creatures' false skins. All of them knelt around a fire, its bright, reddish flames dancing over blackened driftwood. Grey tendrils of smoke curled upward through the misty air. The dark unicorn shivered.

"Dai'chon! *Dai'chon!*"

Chanting, the two-foots faced a stone embedded in the deepest part of the pit. The sand there was scorched, fused into glass. Deeply pocked and charred, the stone resembled a small, dark moon. The black unicorn recognized readily enough what it must be: a sky cinder. Such heavenly gifts were formed of a substance both harder and heavier than true stone, a substance that resounded with a clang when struck or stamped upon.

Before the sky cinder, a tiny figure stood, pale crescent marking the breast of its dark falseskin. Grasped in one black forelimb rose a long, sharp stake. From the other hung a vine, its end frayed into a flail. The figure's limbs and torso resembled a two-foot's, but its neck was thicker, longer, a brushlike mane cresting the ridge. The muzzle of its face was long and slim, like a hornless unicorn's, with white teeth bared and red-flecked nostrils savagely flared.

Smoke rose from those nostrils. Astonished, the dark unicorn snorted, his own breath congealing in the cold, damp air. Strangely rigid, the little figure never moved. It smelled of fire and skystuff, not living flesh. Some object created by the two-foots? It must be hollow, he realized, its belly filled with burning spice.

Before it, the foremost of the two-foots rose and bowed. Green falseskins draped her. A crescent of silvery skystuff glinted upon her breast. The four kneeling nearest her were also females, the dark unicorn perceived by their scent, the remainder all hairy-faced males. Puzzled, the young stallion frowned. Why so many males, so few females? And where were their elders, their young? The eldest male, though grizzled, did not look much past the middle of his age.

"Dai'chon!" the green-clad female chanted, and the other two-foots echoed her, "*Dai'chon!*"

Forelimbs upraised, she beckoned her four companions, who rose. One by one, the males approached them, bearing seedpods and spicewood, dried foliage, and much else the dark unicorn could not identify. These the females laid carefully, as though in offering, at the feet of the little figure smoking before the sky cinder. What could the purpose of such a strange object be? the dark unicorn wondered.

The eldest of the males stepped forward with a great bunch of ripe, fragrant rueberries. The dark unicorn's belly clenched at the sight and scent of food. He leaned after it longingly. Reaching to receive the gift, the moon-breasted female glanced up. Suddenly her eyes widened, and she gasped. The dark unicorn froze. Drawn by the delicious heat of the two-foots' camp, he realized with a start, he had emerged unawares from the mist and shadows into the light of the fire.

The other females lifted their eyes. The males forming the circle before them turned. Abruptly, their chanting ceased. For five wild heartbeats, two-foots and unicorn stared at one another. Then the male crouching nearest the dark unicorn sprang up and bolted with a cry. Screaming, the leader's four companions dropped their offerings and fled. With shouts of fear, the remaining males scrambled after them, dashed desperately up the steep sides of the sandpit and vanished into the fog.

The dark unicorn stood dumbstruck, dismayed. The camp below lay in disarray. Only the green-clad female remained, transfixed. The young stallion shifted nervously, nearly staggering from hunger and fatigue. Tossing the forelock back from his eyes, he switched his long, slim tail once against his flank, uncertain what best to do or say. Below him, the other's gaze darted from his mooncrested brow to his steaming breath to his fly-whisk tail. Catching the firelight, the dark skewer of his horn glinted.

Behind her, the black figurine with its hornless unicorn's head stood wreathed in smoke, its chest emblazoned with a silver crescent, the hornlike skewer clasped in one forepaw, the frayed vine dangling from the other. The two-foot leader's words came in a rush.

"Dai'chon," she whispered, crumpling to the ground. "Dai'chon!"

She pressed her forehead to the sand. Confused, the dark unicorn gazed at her. Had she collapsed from fear? Unsteadily, he descended the pit's sandy, glassy slope and nosed her gently. The black hair on her head smelled clean and very fine, like a new colt's mane. Trembling, she raised her head. Carefully, he tried to repeat her words.

"Taichan," he managed, but his mouth found the strangely inflected syllables almost impossible to frame. He tried again: "Daijan."

"Tai-shan?" the other said suddenly.

She touched the moon image upon her breast and gazed at the pale crescent underscoring the horn on his brow.

"Tai-zhan," he tried, finding that a bit easier. "Tai-shan."

The creature before him listened, rapt. The dark unicorn snorted, not pleased with his awkwardness. The two-foot language was full of odd chirps and grunts.

"Forgive me," he told her, reverting to his own tongue. "I mean you no harm."

The crackling blaze of the fire drew him. He stepped nearer, trembling with cold. The two-foot made no move to halt him, only gazed at him as though spellbound. Dried fruit, fragrant seedgrass, and other offerings lay strewn about the sand. Hungrily, the dark unicorn eyed the tempting stuff.

"May I share your forage?" he asked. "I've found little but bitter bark and shoreoats for . . . for many days."

His thoughts remained tangled, his memory confused. He could recall nothing from before his emergence from the sea. Still kneeling before him, the other made no reply. Unable to resist, the dark unicorn bent his head to a branch of thornfruits at his feet. Tough and leathery, they nonetheless smacked more succulent to him than the tenderest spring grass. He found himself tearing into the prickly rounds, unable to stop. He scarcely noticed when the green-clad two-foot softly rose and drew nearer.

"Tai-shan," she said gently, as if caressing the word. "Tai-shan."

She held something out to him in one graceful, smooth-skinned paw. The thing smelled like nutmeats, but sweeter, and resembled a large brown seedpod. He had never seen such a thing before. Curious, he bent to take the flattened oblong and ground it between his teeth. Honey. It tasted of honey — all sugary and waxless and free of angry, swarming bees. It also tasted of the crisp kernels of hazel trees, but without the fibrous shells. Deliciously warm, the thing was crusted on the outside, softer within.

She held out another of the honey nutpods, offering it, too. Eagerly he accepted, and the next she fed him, and the next. Picking among the scattered leavings of her followers, the two-foot leader brought him grasses, fruits, herbs, followed by a long drink of clear water from a vessel hollowed out of wood. Ravenous, the dark unicorn ate of the firekeepers' strange, rich provender until he thought he would founder. His first full belly in weeks and the delicious heat of the dancing blaze made him suddenly, unutterably drowsy. He could not have kept his eyes open a moment more or taken another step if he had wanted to.

His knees gave. He stretched himself out on the warm dry sand. The two-foot seated herself beside him. He felt her gentle touch along his neck and laid his head upon her flanks. She stroked his cheek and chin, combing the long, nimble digits of her forepaws through his matted mane. The dark unicorn closed his eyes. Beside him, the bright flames crackled and hissed. Weeks ago, the mysterious voice had bade him seek out fire, and he had done so. Perhaps now, presently, he would also discover his name.

"Tai-shan," the gentle two-foot crooned, stroking him.
"Tai-shan."

Tai-shan awoke to find the fog had lifted. Morning light streamed
around him. The leader of the firekeepers sat beside him still. Her
followers had returned during the night, he realized with a start.
Still clearly in awe of him, they moved about their campsite fur-
tively, keeping beyond the fire. Garlands of withered flowers and
grass festooned him. He nosed them, puzzled. Those offerings
that had formerly rested before the sky cinder now lay about him.
The two-foot leader beckoned to one of her female companions.

"Daïcha," the other murmured, bowing, and hastily withdrew.

She had placed something resembling a great bird's nest on the
sand before him. Tai-shan rolled to his knees and shook himself.
The nest-thing was filled with nutpods, fruit, seaoats and dune
grass, dried kelp and tender twigs. Once again he ate ravenously.
The eldest male spoke respectfully to the two-foot leader. She
answered, shaking her head. The dark unicorn listened carefully,
but the only phrase he recognized was the one the other female
had used: daïcha. He concluded that such must be his rescuer's
title or name.

His own name, so it seemed, was to be Tai-shan, the name the
daïcha had given him the night before. He felt stronger now, his
fever diminished. His head was clearer, though he still remembered nothing of who or what he had been before emerging from
the sea. The dark unicorn rose. Beyond the fire, two-foots froze
in alarm, but their leader called to them in a calm, steady voice,
and none bolted.

Tai-shan turned and climbed to the top of the dunes bordering
the pit. He gazed seaward, trying to gain his bearings. A great
whale lay beached upon the strand, the largest he had ever seen.
Some of the two-foot males milled about it. Abruptly, the dark
unicorn realized what lay below was not a whale at all. Whale-

shaped, aye — long and streamlined with a ribbed belly — but it smelled of waterlogged wood, not stinking whale.

Curiosity roused, Tai-shan trotted toward it. The male two-foots on the strand cautiously drew back as he sniffed the thing's wet, barnacle-encrusted underside. Other two-foots stood on the flat, canted back of the thing. One of them disappeared through a square hole into its depths, and the dark unicorn understood with a shock that the place was hollow, like a shell.

This great wooden thing was a shelter, a kind of cave. Tai-shan marveled at the firekeepers' ingenuity: wood crafted into shelter, seed fibers matted to make false skins, logs hollowed into water traps, strips of treebark laced into nestlike containers, delicious foods hoarded like the troves of treefoxes — and fire! Truly a strange and inventive people.

He smelled rain presently. Glancing back toward the dunes, the dark unicorn caught sight of clouds blowing in. The breeze had picked up. Anxiously, he lashed his tail. Must he take to the woods again, trusting their thin cover to keep the worst of the wet off him? He shivered, still very weak. Away from the two-foots' fire, he had already begun to feel chill.

Topping the dune, he saw the two-foots in the pit below also gazing at the sky. The *daïcha* clapped the undersides of her fore-paws together and spoke to her female companions. The eldest male barked orders at the rest. They began hastily to gather up all their strange belongings. Reverently, the *daïcha* carried the small, black figure up the crater's slope, followed by her folk.

The salt breeze stiffened, heavy with the scent of rain. Cresting the slope, the two-foots hurried past him, down toward the cave-shell on the beach. The breeze began to whip, carrying spatters of moisture. The fire sizzled, crackling. Worried, Tai-shan watched its flames beaten down, growing smaller and smaller beneath the falling drops. Rainwater killed fire, he realized suddenly, and without fire, he could never hope to survive the coming winter on this barren, forbidding shore.

On the beach below, the *daïcha*'s companions clambered up

onto their caveshell's back. Their goods, he saw, had already been loaded and carried below. Most of the males remained milling on the beach. The wet wind gusted, dampening them all. Behind him in the deserted pit, the dancing flames sizzled and died.

Before him on the beach, the *daïcha* carefully handed the little figurine up to two of her companions on the caveshell, then boarded herself, assisted by the grizzled male. Tai-shan blinked suddenly, realizing. Though the fire in the cinder pit was clearly doomed, that within the smoking figurine, now being carried away in the reverent grasp of the *daïcha*'s companions, still burned. This fire was to be kept sheltered in the caveshell, safe from the killing damp. It was this fire he must follow, then.

The dark unicorn loped to the foot of the dune. The males gave ground as he crossed the beach to stand before the caveshell. The *daïcha* called down to him, beckoning with her forelimbs. Tai-shan hesitated, gauging the distance between them. The wind whipped harder, rain beginning to fall in earnest now. The *daïcha* called again. The young stallion sidled, measuring his strength. At last, bunching his hindquarters, he sprang onto the flat, tilted back of the caveshell.

The slick wooden surface boomed beneath his hooves. For a moment, the caveshell rocked precariously. He had to scramble for his footing until it steadied. The remaining two of the *daïcha*'s female companions screamed and scattered while the males on the shore cried out in consternation. But the *daïcha* laughed in delight, stroking the dark unicorn's neck and leading him toward the rear of the caveshell. A low barrier edged the shell's perimeter. Tai-shan had little fear of sliding off. Still, the cant of the wooden surface disconcerted him. He moved unsteadily, unused to the feel of slanted deck underhoof.

At the caveshell's tail end, the *daïcha* disappeared through a narrow ingress. Following, Tai-shan found himself in a small wooden chamber. Scattered about the floor lay soft falseskin pads stuffed with rushes, upon which the other females huddled. The chamber was warm, the air heavy with the savor of spicewood and smoke. Before the opposite wall, the black figurine stood, breathing fire. Bowing before it, the *daïcha* murmured, "Dai'chon."

Tai-shan lay down against the near wall. The *daïcha* knelt beside him, chafing him with a soft, dry falseskin, smoothing the damp from his coat like a mare licking her foal. The sensation was delightful. Sighing, he closed his eyes. Presently he heard her companions moving cautiously about the chamber. He scarcely marked their activity, any more than he heeded the grunting and shouting of the males on the beach beyond.

Sleep had nearly claimed him. His surroundings seemed vague and distant now. Stormwind gusted. Rain drummed against the chamber's walls. Beneath him, the floor shuddered. Much splashing and clambering and shouting from without. He heard a low grating like distant thunder. None of the two-foots in the room gave any sign of concern. Only half-waking, he ignored it all.

The tilted floor seemed to right itself momentarily, becoming more level. Then it began rocking gently, very gently, smoothly tossing and rolling like treetops in a summer breeze. Such an odd dream to be having, the dark unicorn mused. It felt like drifting in the sea. He let his thoughts dissolve into the hypnotic swaying of wooden planking beneath him, the soothing rush of wind outside, the plash of nearby sea, and the gentle creaking of rain-soaked wood. He slept.

Tai-shan awoke with a start. The deck beneath him was swaying in earnest: pitching and tipping. It was no dream. Alarmed, he lifted his head. The *daïcha* was not within the wooden chamber. Two of her companions dozed on falseskin pads across the narrow space from him. The dark unicorn struggled to gather his legs under him as the caveshell's floor shifted and tilted. He no longer detected the quiet patter of rain. Time to return to the beach, he realized.

Maintaining his balance with difficulty on the slowly tossing, gently rolling surface, he passed through the chamber's egress and emerged onto the open expanse of the caveshell's back. The sky had indeed cleared. Only stray puffs of cloud now flocked the heavens. It was midafternoon. To his astonishment, he beheld a great tree growing from the caveshell's back, webbed with vines. Male two-foots swarmed the webbing. Others standing below hauled on the dangling ends.

Tai-shan stared, fascinated. The caveshell lurched and heaved. He spotted the *daïcha* on the far side of the tree, conferring with the eldest male. Cautiously, the dark unicorn started toward her, then pitched to a halt with a horrified cry. The beach had vanished. The caveshell was bobbing in the middle of the sea!

Whinnying, he reared. Male two-foots dropped their vines and scattered, shouting. The wooden surface beneath the dark unicorn's hooves bucked violently. He nearly fell. Panicked, he sprang to one edge of the caveshell's back. Open sea lay beyond, deep and blue-grey. The caveshell pitched the other way, sending him skidding toward the opposite side — sea there as well. Nothing but grey waves moved all around, empty and calm.

With a scream of consternation, Tai-shan wheeled. The caveshell tilted precipitously, hurling him against the near rail. He kicked at it. One hind leg tangled in a tarry coil of vine. Frantically, the dark unicorn pivoted, twisting and plunging. He lost his footing and went down. He heard the eldest male barking orders, but his ears were too full of his own terrified whinnies to heed.

"Tai-shan! Tai-shan!"

The *daïcha*'s frantic cries penetrated his frenzy only dimly. Twisting and bucking, the dark unicorn glimpsed her struggling toward him. The eldest male had hold of her forelimb, seeking to keep her back, but she shook him off angrily and came toward Tai-shan slowly, speaking gently now in her lilting, unintelligible language.

"Tash, 'omat. Bikthitet nau. Apnor, 'pnor. . . ."

None of the other two-foots moved. Panting, heart racing still, the dark unicorn stood shuddering. The *daïcha* leaned against him, stroking his neck and chest. Her touch trailed lightly along his flank, then down his haunch. He tensed as he felt her grasp the vine that so painfully encircled his pastern. Then he realized she was worrying it, using her nimble, long-fingered paw much as a unicorn might use her teeth to loosen the vine and pull it free.

"Tai-shan," the two-foot lady crooned. "Tai-shan."

Still stroking him, she gestured beyond the rail, beyond even the blue-grey curve of sea. With a shock of wild relief, the dark unicorn spotted what he had missed before: land — just at horizon's edge, a narrow ribbon of shoreline stretched. He felt the jaws biting down upon his heart ease. The caveshell was not simply adrift, hopelessly lost. The shore remained — barely — in sight.

Tai-shan's balance swayed. Fever burned in him still. Wearily, he sank down. Later perhaps, when his strength returned, he could spring over the rail and swim for the strand. Doubt chilled him suddenly. Did he dare desert the caveshell — leaving the fire behind? Exhausted, his mind fogged, he shook his head. Time enough to ponder that later. For now, resting his chin along the top of the low rail, he lay quiet. The sun felt warm along his back. The *daïcha* called to her companions, who approached with food. She sat beside him as he ate.

It occurred to him then for the first time that her people did not seem the least disconcerted at their caveshell's now resting in the sea. Strange. Baffling. Perhaps they *wanted* it to be in the sea — but why? Presently, at the eldest male's direction, his two-foot minions unfurled a great falseskin from the tree. It belled out like the huge, round belly of a pregnant mare.

The image emblazoning it resembled the strange, fire-breathing figure before which the *daïcha* and the other two-foots had bowed: dark-limbed, its body like a two-foot's, a crescent moon upon the breast, a skewer in one forepaw and in the other, a trailing vine, yet its head that of a hornless, beardless unicorn with blood-rimmed nostrils and glaring eyes.

By late afternoon, Tai-shan had come to realize that the cave-shell was moving, the distant shoreline changing. The great falseskin caught the sea breeze like a gryphon's wing and pulled the caveshell along parallel to the strand. Gradually it dawned on him that his hosts and their entire shelter were sliding westward without themselves taking a step. The dark unicorn lay amazed.

Later, the wind fell. The grizzled male gave orders, and most of the younger males descended into the caveshell's belly. Moments later, Tai-shan spied long, slender limbs emerging from the vessel's side. A hollow booming began, like the beating of a mighty heart. The slim, straight limbs dipped, shoved backward, rose, and dipped into the sea again. The caveshell was using its many legs to crawl like a centipede across the waves.

At dusk, the wind returned, and the caveshell's limbs withdrew. The steady booming ceased, and the males emerged from below to unfurl their windwing again. As the air darkened and chilled, the *daïcha* rose. Tai-shan followed her carefully back to her wooden chamber.

Inside, basking in its fire-warmed air, he listened to the great tree creaking and straining outside, its taut vines rubbing against each other as the windwing heaved and burgeoned. The gentle lifting and falling of the caveshell seemed almost restful now, much as he imagined the rocking motion of a mother's walk must feel to her unborn foal. No panic troubled him, now that he realized the firekeepers were traveling, taking him with them. He wondered what their destination might be.

Snowfall

) 8 (

Tek had always known fall as a time of feasting in the Vale: a season for fattening on sweet berries, ripening grain, tallowy seeds and nuts. This year, however, the healer's daughter felt no joy. The air's pervasive chill cut her to the bone. Much vegetation had been nipped by early frost, and storms blew in every other day, roaring across the Pan Woods to rot what little provender remained and force the unicorns to spend full as much time huddling underhill as they did foraging for food.

The pied mare shivered, watching the swirl of grey clouds overhead. All the herd seemed to share her gloom. Somehow, many muttered, the children-of-the-moon had displeased Alma. Now the Mother-of-all was making her displeasure known. Tek snorted at so much witless talk. Yet as regent, Korr did nothing. Still wrapped in grief, the king barely uttered a word even to Ses. Jan's young sister Lell, the new princess, was a mere nursling: many seasons must pass before she might lead the herd in anything but name.

The pied mare sighed, keenly aware of the loss of her mate. Jan would never have tolerated his people's superstitious champing. Instead, he would have set them all to gleaning every scrap of available forage before first snow. Angrily, Tek shook her head.

Her breath steamed like a firedrake's in the wet, chilly air. Another storm approached.

Korr's silence and Lell's youth left the late king's widow, Sa, as the sole voice of authority among the unicorns. Tirelessly, the grey mare ventured abroad, recounting what had been done in seasons past when winter came early and hard, what foodstuff helped best to deepen the pelt, thicken the blood, and form a rich layer of fat. She urged her fellows to be out and about early each morn, despite the cold, to forage all they might on whatever they might, and spent long hours combing the hillsides of the Vale for browse.

Standing in the entry to the grey mare's cave, Tek cavaled, lifting and setting down her heels in the same spot to get the stiffness out of her legs. It was such a foraging expedition that the late king's widow headed now, reconnoitering the Vale's far slopes with a band of young warriors not half her age, searching for berry thickets and honey trees. The healer's daughter hoped to see them safely back before the storm broke.

Hoofbeats above drew her half out of the grotto, craning upward, expecting Sa — but it was Dagg. The dappled half-grown slid down the last of the steep slope and crowded past into the dim grotto's shelter. Dagg shivered, shouldering against her and stamping for warmth.

"So," she asked, "how was graze on the high south slopes?" She knew that Dagg had, at the grey mare's urging, set out early that morning to scout that particular ridge. She herself had roved the lower south slopes with a third band the afternoon before.

"Lean," Dagg answered dejectedly. "We found little but bramble."

The pied mare murmured in sympathy. Dagg twitched, lashing his tail.

"We've got to find more forage!" he burst out. "We've enough to feed the herd for now, just barely. But none among us is putting on any flesh — none, that is, but you."

He glanced at her with open envy. The healer's daughter shifted, unsettled by his gaze. Her belly had indeed begun to swell ever so slightly — but it was not fat, as would surely grow plain to see as soon as the weather grew colder, forage scarcer, and her ribs began to show. She wondered anxiously if it could be gut worms or colic — but she did not feel ill. And though none of what slender fodder she found seemed to be going to fat, still her girth, day by day, infinitesimally increased.

She had not wanted to trouble her father, Teki, as yet. The usual round of minor complaints among the herd consumed his time: bites and scrapes, strained tendons, thorns. Soon enough, she speculated with a shudder, more major ills would claim his attention, brought on by cold and lack of feed. Moreover, the healer had his teeth full simply gathering the many herbs required for the coming winter, most of which were proving even scarcer than the forage this year. Some days, she knew, he searched from daybreak to dusk, and still returned with only a few poor sprigs.

Shouldering against Dagg, the pied mare sighed. She wished her mother, Jah-lila, were here to advise her. The Red Mare was a loner, a midwife and magicker who lived apart from the herd. Some called her the child of renegades, yet she herself was no renegade — despite Korr's wild charge — for since coming among the herd before Tek's birth, Jah-lila had never been banished. Rather, the Red Mare now lived in the southeastern hills beyond the Vales by her own unfathomable choice.

Calling Teki her mate, she had left her weanling daughter in his care years ago, that Tek might be raised within the Vale. At long intervals, Jah-lila still ghosted through, never announced, as often as not to consult with the pied healer but briefly and be gone within the hour. Sometimes the young Tek had not even glimpsed her, merely caught scent of her dam in Teki's grotto upon returning home at day's end. The pied mare shook herself. No use wishing.

"It's only that I don't run myself ragged, as you do," she told Dagg, dragging her mind back with an effort to the dappled warrior beside her.

Her words were true enough. She could not seem to run as nimbly as she had before: her burgeoning belly got in the way.

Again Tek shook herself — and dismissed her own mysterious condition with a shrug.

"With luck, Sa and her band will have found something in the Pan Woods," she added, hoping. She worried less for herself and Dagg than for the herd's fillies and foals. It was they who would suffer heaviest from the coming winter's lack. And after the young, it would be the elder ones, the mares and stallions Sa's age.

Dagg nodded vigorously, facing about now in the limestone grotto, the cave the old king's mare had long inhabited with her mate. Since the death of Korr's father, the grey mare had had no one to help her warm the empty space until now. Since returning from the Sea, the healer's daughter had sheltered with Sa. During Tek's absence, Teki had accepted a number of acolytes: young fillies and foals not yet initiated. The pied stallion was busily teaching them his craft — and though she felt more than welcome, the prince's mate sensed ruefully that lodging in her sire's now-crowded grotto would only have put her under heel.

"When do you expect Sa to return?" Dagg asked her, coming to stand beside her at the cave's narrow entryway.

A flutter of white feathers drifted from the sky. The pied mare snorted, her breath curling and smoking like cloud. "Soon, I hope."

"First snowfall," Dagg muttered. "Birds' down."

More lacy flakes gusted past, whirling and dancing. Tek watched the rapidly thickening flurries with dread, thinking of the cover it would provide, concealing what remained of the Vale's dwindling supply of foodstuffs, making the unicorns' foraging even harder than before. Would Korr respond? she wondered. Would the advent of winter at last bestir the king?

Hoofbeats roused her, a dozen sets, coming not from the hillside above this time, but from across the flat below. Dagg whickered, and Tek peered ahead through the ashen turbulence. Dying day grew greyer by the moment. In another few heartbeats, she spotted Sa, the rest of the band scattering, each to his or her respective grotto. The grey mare trotting up the brief, steep slope toward Tek and Dagg whinnied in greeting. Healer's daughter and dappled warrior fell back from the cave's entrance to allow her passage. Once within, the grey mare stamped, shaking the snow from her back and mane.

"What news, kingmother?" Dagg asked. "Did you discover forage?"

The grey mare chuckled.

"Did we indeed! A thicket of tuckfruit ripe as you please — neither birds nor pans have found it yet. We ate till I thought we would burst! Tomorrow I'll lead the rest of you to it."

Tek whooped, half shying as Sa reached playfully to nip her neck. The grey mare frisked like a filly, and the healer's daughter whickered, amazed how suddenly her mood lifted at the prospect of a full belly of sweet, greenish tuckfruit. Come the morrow, they would feast for the first time in days! She ramped, scarcely able to restrain her exuberance. Dagg chafed and chivvied her, laughing himself now. With the certainty of at least a day's ample forage ahead, all thought of both the herd's troubles and her own slipped unmissed from her thoughts.

Landfall

)9(

The firekeepers' settlement sprawled along one bend of a broad, cliffed bay, rank upon rank of their timber dwellings crowding the slopes above. Tai-shan stood gazing in astonishment as the caveshell angled toward land. A crisp, clean breeze slapped at the billowing windwing. Other caveshells glided by, their own windwings whitely belled.

The *daïcha* stood alongside him, her green falseskins fluttering, the silvery crescent upon her breast flashing in the late afternoon sun. A throng of two-foots milled upon the nearing beachhead. As the caveshell ground ashore, they surged and shouted. Laughing, the *daïcha* lifted one graceful, hairless forelimb and gestured in greeting.

Tai-shan heard gasps, cries of wonder and alarm as he leapt to join the *daïcha* on the strand. Half the spectators seemed ready to flee at the sight of him — the rest shouldering forward for a better view. A company of two-foots pressed back the jostling crowd, using long, straight staves tipped with glinting skystuff. Each such male wore a burnished head-covering, also of skystuff, topped with a purple plume. Beyond them, the throng waved and cheered.

"Greetings!" the dark unicorn called to them in his own tongue. "Greetings to you, noble two-foots!"

The *daïcha* cried out a long phrase ending in "Tai-shan." The crowd took up the word, chanting his name as the *daïcha* led him up a stony path between the tall wooden dwellings. Green-plumed two-foots armed with skewers, not staves, escorted their green-clad leader and her companions along the rising path. The dark unicorn walked alongside. Solid ground felt strange beneath his hooves after so many days at sea. More two-foots — held back by the purple-plumes — crowded the narrow way.

"Tai-shan! Tai-shan!" roared the crowd.

The tumult grew deafening. Two-foots leaning from openings high in their timber dwellings' walls flung brilliant seedpods, withered flowers, and shavings of aromatic spicewood onto hard, flat cobbles of the path. Through the shower of offerings, the dark unicorn gazed in amazement at the vast settlement. Fire burned everywhere, glowing in blackened hollows of skystuff, crackling upon treelimbs set in niches, and dancing in hanging boxes of semitransparent shell.

The sun sank lower, edging toward dusk. The petal-strewn path, he saw, climbed toward a magnificent dwelling that crested the slope. A barrier of timber surrounded the place. As they neared, green-plumes rushed forward to shove at a pair of heavy wooden panels mounted in the timber wall. These pivoted inward, creating an entryway. Sun slipped below horizon's edge. The air grew dark and chill. As the *daïcha* led him through the entryway, the dark unicorn glanced back at her people's immense settlement spilling the shadowed hillside below, the whole slope ablaze with little flickers of captured fire.

The commotion of the crowd abruptly muted as the huge wooden panels boomed shut. Tai-shan found himself in an open, cobbled space lit by burning brands. Around him, the *daïcha*'s train milled expectantly until an ornate panel in the nearest dwelling swung open and a male two-foot strode out, accompanied by more of the purple-plumes. He appeared young and vigorous, darkly bearded and attired in falseskins of deep violet and gold. A circlet of skystuff gleamed among the black curls crowning his head.

"Emwe! Emwe, im chon," the *daïcha* cried gladly.

She and her fellows dropped to the ground. Startled, the dark unicorn cavaled — then stilled his hooves as he remembered that the two-foots used this crumpled posture to show homage. This purple-clad male — the *chon* — must be the settlement's ruler, he concluded in surprise. Who, then, must the *daïcha* be — his sister? His mate? Facing the two-foot ruler, Tai-shan dipped his long neck in a bow.

The *chon* clapped the undersides of his forepaws together, and the crouching two-foots raised their heads. Baring his teeth, he beckoned to the *daïcha*, who hurried to him. He enfolded her in his forelimbs for a long moment. When he released her, she turned, talking to him excitedly and gesturing toward Tai-shan. The other's eyes widened as he took note of the dark unicorn for the first time. Tai-shan tossed the forelock out of his eyes, and the other exclaimed in astonishment at the sight of his moon-marked brow.

"Dai'chon!" he whispered.

Gently, the *daïcha* corrected him: "Tai-shan."

The *chon* called out a sharp command. Purple-plumes hurried to snatch firebrands from wall niches and hold them near. Tai-shan stood in a ring of fire. The *chon* strode forward and circled the dark unicorn, peering at him in obvious fascination. He exchanged animated comments with the *daïcha*, who stood back, watching anxiously. Disconcerted, Tai-shan pivoted to remain facing his host.

Emwe. Emwe, im chon. He struggled to repeat the *daïcha*'s greeting, but as before, the unpronounceable words came out whistled, garbled: "Am-wa. Umuwa m'shan. . . ."

The two-foot ignored his words, staring pointedly at the dark unicorn's cloven hooves. Tai-shan cavaled uneasily. Without warning, the *chon* stepped forward to lay one forepaw against his chest. The other he ran swiftly along the dark unicorn's back to the croup. Tai-shan jerked away with a startled snort. The other's peremptory manner astonished him. Only the *daïcha* had dared to touch him before — and he realized now it was her touch alone that he welcomed. His skin twitched.

Clucking, the other made to approach him again, but the dark unicorn dodged, shaking his head vigorously. The *chon* halted, eyes keenly narrowed suddenly, lips pressed tight. Then with a barking sound that might have been laughter, he stepped back from the ring of fire to rejoin the *daïcha*. She seemed relieved. Once again, he embraced her, speaking warmly to her. She smiled and nodded. Abruptly, he turned to quit the yard, and his purple-plumes, still bearing their torches, accompanied him through the great shelter's paneled entryway.

The *daïcha* beckoned her female companions and her green-plumes to her as she led Tai-shan across the darkened yard to another, smaller building. The lighted interior felt luxuriously warm, the tang of fire pervading the air, and the musty, sweetish scent of vast quantities of dried forage. The young stallion sneezed, unused to such a savor of abundance so late in the season. His nostrils flared suddenly. He halted dead.

"Unicorns!" he exclaimed. The musk, spicy scent of his own kind hung all around. "Unicorns!"

Only silence answered. Not so much as a slap of mane or a stamp replied. Nevertheless, a rush of euphoria filled the young stallion's breast. Surely these must be the lost companions he had sought so long.

"Where are you? Show yourselves!"

Once again, only silence. The *daïcha* was urging him onward. Eagerly, he followed, hoping she might lead him to his fellows, though his memory of them and of his former life remained dim. They proceeded down an aisle between two rows of wooden compartments — all empty, though the scent of unicorns remained strong. Oddly, he scented mostly mares — here and there, a whiff of filly or foal — but no mature males, none even old enough to be called half-grown.

The *daïcha* halted before the last compartment, one far roomier than the rest. A two-foot in green falseskins had just finished raking out the old, yellow grass thickly carpeting the floor. A companion stood throwing down heaps of fresh. The dark unicorn breathed deep, finding at last the scent he had missed.

Though this space, too, stood unoccupied, it had lately housed a stallion, young and vigorous and in full prime.

The *daïcha* swung open the compartment's front panel, and the dark unicorn entered. Forage and water were brought to him. Tai-shan ate greedily: berries and fodder, nutmeats broken from the shell, all crushed, blended together somehow, and steaming. Afterwards, the *daïcha* drew a bristly clump of spines through his coat. They felt like a thousand tiny birds' claws scrabbling, scratching away the grit and seasalt and old, sloughed skin.

The dark unicorn sighed deeply, sank down at last and closed his eyes. Softly bedded and sumptuously feasted, solicitously groomed and well sheltered against the cold, he let his thoughts drift back to his last glimpse of the firekeepers' dark dwellings spilling the slopes below, illuminated by spots of flame like a hillside strewn with burning stars. He had never known such luxury. On the morrow, he would seek out the other unicorns that abode here and learn from them of this strange and marvelous haven to which he had come.

Companions

☽ 10 ☾

Snow fell in gusts, bitterly cold. Tek stood on the valley floor while around her jostled most of the unicorns from the southwest quarter of the Vale. The pied mare shivered, even in her thick winter coat, dense now as a marten's pelt. They had come upon no more windfalls like the tuckfruit — days ago, and like her fellows, she had no layer of fat to keep out the cold. Sa brushed against her. Dagg appeared out of the press and halted along her other side.

"What do you think the king intends?" he asked her softly.

The healer's daughter shook her head. It was the first assembly Korr had called since the courting band had returned from the Sea, weeks past. Around them, the herd milled expectantly, huddled for warmth. Tek caught snatches of conversation, speculation. She spotted runners standing ready to carry the king's word to the far reaches of the Vale. Seasoned warriors all, she noted, especially chosen by the king. Beside her, the pied mare heard Dagg snort.

"Were Jan among us still," he muttered, "those runners would include half-growns as well."

She nodded. "True." *Jan might even have traveled to the far reaches of the Vale himself to spread the news,* she mused.

Faintly, the healer's daughter smiled, remembering. Her young mate, the prince, had been fearless of change: ever one to break with precedent when precedent failed to serve. The newer warriors had all adored him — though old traditionalists, she knew, had greeted Jan's innovations with consternation. And none so markedly as Korr. Bitterly, she sighed. How different the king was from his son!

A sudden stirring swept the crowd as, through the diffuse grey of falling snow, Korr's massy, storm-dark form appeared. His mate and Dagg's father, Tas, flanked the king. Her own sire, Teki, brought up the rear. The crowd parted as the procession neared, and with a shock, Tek spotted Lell pressed close to her mother's flank.

The flame-colored mare moved slowly, shielding her filly with tender care. Alongside walked Leerah, Tas's mate, lending her shoulder, too, against the biting wind. The amber filly stumbled, racked with cold. The king never so much as glanced behind. Tek gazed at Korr, angry and aghast — for his daughter's presence could only be by king's command. Ses would never willingly expose her tiny nursling to such weather. The brow of the king's mate was furrowed, her jaw set.

The pied mare sidled uneasily. Abruptly, she realized she should have melted back into the crowd at the king's approach: too late now to do so unseen. She stood her ground, and Korr passed directly before her, spoke not a word, merely leveled at her his ferocious stare. Tek's heart clenched. Grimly, she lifted her chin, refused to flinch beneath the dark stallion's gaze. In a bound, he mounted the council rise and turned, looming above them like a thunderhead.

"Unicorns!" he called. "Children-of-the-moon! Since I learned the harsh news of my son's death, you have seen me but little. I was deep in grief, struggling to fathom why Alma should claim my son, your prince, bereaving us all."

Korr's fine, deep voice penetrated even the muffle of wind and snow. Glancing about her, Tek glimpsed a thin young mare shushing a companion, an old stallion pricking his ears. Long starved for the sight of their king, the unicorns quieted, listened attentively.

"My son was a fine warleader, was he not?" continued Korr. "A bit rash and hotheaded, to be sure — but quick in wit and great in heart, a courageous warrior! You loved him well."

A cry of agreement went up. The healer's daughter watched a cluster of spindly half-growns a few paces off, snorting and stamping in assent. Beyond them, a gaunt pair of elders nodded. A rush of gratification welled up in her. They *had* loved Jan — even the older warriors whom the young prince's reformations had so often confounded. The king raised his head.

"Aye, you loved him. As did I. But what of Alma?" The great stallion's tone abruptly darkened. "How must Alma have felt to see my son's wildness, all his princely verve and quickness of mind — though never ill-meant — used but to bend her Law and flout her will and tempt us, her best beloved, along untried paths, kicking aside her time-honored practice as though it were worthless nothing?"

Tek felt a frown furrow her brow. What was this talk of Alma and the Law in the selfsame breath? "Alma does not make the Law," she murmured. "The Council of Elders makes the Law and always has —"

"Could such have been the will of Alma," the king inquired, still facing the herd from the rocky rise, "to see her anointed prince, my son, flagrantly leading her children astray?"

Tek snorted, baffled. Was the prince of a sudden to be deemed the anointed of Alma?

"Only the prophets are anointed of Alma —" Dagg started beneath his breath, but the king's words cut him off.

"No!" Korr thundered, his voice rebounding from the far hillside. "Such blasphemy could *not* have been the goddess's will. And so she swept away my son — as she will sweep away all who fail her trust."

The dark stallion wheeled, stamping, tossing his head, full of fury now. The healer's daughter watched him, astonished. She heard Sa beside her champ her teeth. Beyond Dagg, a young warrior mare — ribs showing — was standing stock-still despite the cold. Beside her, a couple of half-starved colts poised motionless, as though caught by a wyvern's glare. Her own limbs felt stiff. Hastily, Tek shook herself. All around her the herd stood frozen as if mesmerized. "First Alma sent her gryphons," ranted the king, "but we paid no heed. Then she seized our prince, my son. Now she has sent this harsh winter to chastise us!" The pied mare listened dumbstruck, appalled.

"Jan was a brave prince, my own get, and I loved him," the dark stallion cried, "but he was wrong! In his pride, he defied Alma. In destroying him, the goddess speaks clear warning: we must turn back! We must return to the old ways and the true worship of Alma. Only if we once more devote ourselves unswervingly to her will can spring return and again bestow upon us her blessings."

Beside her, she felt Dagg snorting in disgust, glimpsed the troubled look on Sa's face deepen into dismay.

"Old ways — which ones?" she heard the grey mare breathe. "And true worship — what on earth can my son mean? Is now even the weather to be ascribed to Alma?"

Nearby, an old mare, clearly exhausted and perilously thin, swayed as though any moment her limbs might give way. Tek lashed her tail furiously, scarcely able to contain herself.

"Uppermost in our minds ought to be not who among us worships most fervently," she hissed, "but how many fillies and foals will see this killing winter through!"

Yet save for a few stamps and uncertain glances among the crowd, most still remained attentive to the king. She caught sight of one haggard stallion murmuring accord. The shivering mare beside him nodded. About the foot of the rise, the seasoned warriors who were to act as the king's runners cavaled restlessly, snorting and tossing their heads in agreement.

The pied mare half shied. Truly alarmed now, she searched the faces of those flanking Korr upon the rise. With relief, she noted again the fierce, if unvoiced, disapproval of Ses, and her heart went out to Lell, cold and miserable, shuddering against her

mother's side. Behind them, Tek saw her own father, Teki, standing silent, his expression profoundly saddened. Tas, however,
stood nodding calmly, as did his mate. Tek felt another surge of
indignation. Were the pair of them so blind in their loyalty to
the king that they actually supported this folly?

"In following my son," Korr proclaimed, "we have all become
Ringbreakers and renegades. But no more! Thus I say to you in
the name of my daughter, the princess Lell, that from this day
forward, any who breach Alma's sacred Law shall be banned."

A ripple passed through the crowd. Tek saw warriors, half-
growns starting as though abruptly awakened.

"Banned?" Sa beside her gasped.

"But banishment in winter means death!" Dagg exclaimed.

The king's dam shook her head, one cloven forehoof striking
at the frozen ground, her tone quietly outraged. "The herd has
never imposed exile, regardless of the crime, between first snowfall
and spring. What 'old tradition' is this?"

At the foot of the rise, the king's warriors circled. Tek suddenly
froze. Korr no longer surveyed the entire assembly. His stare now
fixed squarely on her.

"Be it known," he thundered, "Alma tolerates not even the
slightest infraction. Tread with caution, I charge you all — or be
cast from the herd!"

Tek felt Sa's astonished start, Dagg's indrawn breath, and held
herself rigid, refusing to quail. Though he had spoken no word
directly to her, had not even called her by name, Korr's meaning
could not but be evident to all: let the healer's daughter stumble
in even the tiniest regard, and he would find a way — any excuse,
or no excuse — to banish her. The crowd shifted, murmuring.

Tek felt her fury spark. Did the dark stallion truly believe fanatical devotion to Alma had power to alter weather, grow forage
beneath the snow, and avert gryphon raids in spring? How neat
it all was! Korr had but to declare himself the mouthpiece of
Alma, and displeasing him became defiance of the goddess herself. Now he would have them all believe that the Law — indeed,
even custom — was fixed immutably by the goddess's behest.

And was "tradition" to be anything the king now said it was, even if he had just this moment invented it? Angrily, she eyed the band of seasoned warriors who, at the king's nod, had begun to ascend the rise.

"Behold my newly appointed Companions," he cried to the herd. "They are Alma's eyes and ears among you now!"

Gazing about, Tek noted alarm on the spare, hungry faces of many. One older mare looked badly shaken, the lean young half-grown beside her merely puzzled. The pied mare shivered. Yet one stallion she had noticed nodding earlier still evidenced rapt attention. A convert, she realized uneasily. A bitter taste came into her mouth. On the rise, the king's warriors arranged themselves in a double phalanx. Sa snorted indignantly.

" 'Companions,' indeed!" she mused beneath her breath. "More nearly a personal guard. What does my son intend them to protect him from — the truth?"

Tek shook her head. No king or queen in all the history of the unicorns had ever appointed — or needed — a personal guard. As by prearrangement, the king's Companions started to stamp and cheer. Still none among the herd spoke out. Colts shrank against their mothers. Half-growns found their mates. Dawning throughout the crowd Tek glimpsed expression of anger, betrayal, and fear. Flanking the king, his guards whinnied and shouted enthusiastically, but few others joined them. How many, she wondered, while unwilling to risk voicing questions or protests aloud, nevertheless harbored grave doubts? How many had begun to share her own suspicions? The pied mare shivered uncontrollably.

"The king," she whispered, so soft she herself scarcely heard, "is well and truly mad."

"You have heard my will," the dark stallion cried, "which is Alma's. Remember it!"

Tek watched him vault from the rocky rise. The herd shrank back from him. Korr seemed imbued by a cold and desperate energy. His train followed more cautiously, picking their way down the icy, slippery stones. Trotting briskly, the king headed back through the ever-thickening snowfall toward his grotto across the Vale. His Companions remained behind on the council rise, necks arched, chests thrown forward, legs stiff. Slowly, as though stunned, the assembled unicorns began to disperse.

"He hasn't any food to give us," she heard Sa beside her murmur, "so he has fed us lies! Some of us have even swallowed them, and now feel full and well-fed, though in truth we are famished still." She eyed the king's guard upon the rise with open contempt. "When no food can be found to fill an aching belly, a scrap or two of arrogance contents some very well."

Fidgeting, Dagg stood gazing after the king's retreating train. "I can't believe my sire and dam approve this," he burst out. "I can't believe anyone could!"

One of the Companions on the rise turned to gaze at Dagg. Tek hurriedly shushed him, but fuming still, the dappled half-grown ignored her.

"And your father, Tek!" he cried. "The healer raised not a word of protest, though plainly he did not agree."

A second Companion had joined the first, their heads together, now conferring.

"Has our king lost all reason —?"

"Peace; hold your tongue, you young foal!" Sa ordered suddenly, sharply.

Tek turned, startled. Beside her, Dagg fell silent, stared in confusion at the grey mare. She had spoken far louder than necessary. Above them, the two warriors watched. Abruptly, the grey mare wheeled.

"Come with me," she commanded crisply, "both of you. I've a word to say regarding how fitly to comport yourselves in your loyalty to our king."

Astonished, Tek followed as the king's dam trotted away from the rise through the throng of dispersing unicorns. Dagg fell into step at her side, his expression baffled. As soon as they were out of earshot of the king's Companions, Sa halted, turned.

"Pray forgive my shortness, Dagg," she told him gently. "That was for show, to save my son's pack-wolves the pleasure of correcting you. Take heed, for the wind has changed, and if you cannot scent it yet, you will."

Dagg champed his teeth. "Aye, the wind *has* changed," he managed gruffly. "It stinks."

"Hist, lower your voice!" the grey mare cautioned, dropping her own to the merest whisper. "We dare not speak freely anymore — for some, no doubt, will seek favors from my son by reporting dissent."

"Since when was dissent a crime among the unicorns?" Dagg hissed angrily, though taking care now that his voice did not carry. "Since when was speaking one's mind to be feared?"

"Since *now*," Tek spat. The vehemence in her words plainly surprised him. "It's one of Korr's new 'old traditions.' '*Alma's will*'!"

She snorted, shaking her head. Her breath steamed, rising like dragons' breath. She shifted, wincing, for her swollen belly pained her. She heard Dagg's beside her growl. Shuddering, she longed for the wind-sheltered warmth of the grotto she shared with Sa — but she knew they had all best use what scant daylight remained to forage, else they would shiver the cold night through, unable to sleep for hunger. The grey mare nodded.

"I fear you are right, Dagg," she said softly. "Grief seems to have stolen my son's reason." All around, the dispersing unicorns drifted, pale haunts through the ashen snowfall. Sa looked at them. "Clearly, we have much to do."

Dagg glanced around him, frowned. "To do?"

The healer's daughter snuffed. "We must scout out the rest of the herd, of course," she answered, "and uncover our allies."

Dagg shook his head, still lost. "Allies?" he asked, then abruptly blinked, voice dropping to a whisper, truly hushed now for the first time. "Defy Korr, you mean? Disobey the king?"

Tek shrugged. "Who knows?" she murmured. "We cannot know what is possible until we count who and how many his opposition are."

"Young warrior," Sa said tartly, "you seem to forget: my son is not the ruler of the unicorns. Lell is our princess now, though not even she can make or unmake the Law. That is the Council's prerogative." The old mare smiled grimly. "If enough of the herd so demand, the elders — of whom I am one — might choose another regent."

The dappled half-grown let out his breath. Clearly, he had never even considered such a thing. Yet that of which the king's dam had just reminded them was true: it was the Council who — quietly, unobtrusively, year after year — made the Law, declared the succession, and invested warleader or regent with power. If they chose, the elders could rescind that power. Tek's own heart thumped. The Council could depose the king.

"It's settled, then," she said after a moment. "Dagg and I will scout the herd. But —" she added, glancing a warning in his direction and lifting her chin slightly toward the king's distant Companions.

The dappled warrior nodded. "We must proceed with the greatest caution, aye."

"That we must," Sa agreed. "But not you, Tek. You must avoid entanglement in this above all."

Tek started, stared. "How so?"

The grey mare shook her head. "Dear one," she said, "did you not mark the way my son looked at you?"

Bitterly, the healer's daughter laughed. "All the herd marked it."

Sa nodded. "Aye, he has singled you out to his wolfish 'Companions' and all the rest. They and others will be watching you close, and what could be more disastrous for you than to be accused of subversion?"

"No more dangerous for me than for you," Tek answered hotly.

Dagg snorted beside her. The snow was falling thick as mare's milk now. Their breath steamed around them like wafts of burning cloud. "Nay, Tek. Far more dangerous for you," Sa was saying. "I am the king's dam after all. Do you truly think that even grief-maddened as he is, my own scion would turn me out into the snow? And Dagg was your mate's shoulder-companion from earliest colthood. I doubt Korr would do him serious harm for anything short of open rebellion."

Again she shook her head.

"But you, my child. Though once Korr appeared to esteem you, at times even above his own son, his feelings towards you have greatly changed."

Stubbornly, the pied mare ducked her head. "I'll not be warned away," she said. "I'll not let the pair of you charge boldly into wolves' teeth without me alongside."

Dagg shouldered her gently. She leaned against him, grateful for his support. The grey mare sighed ruefully.

"Very well, child, I cannot stop you. But have a care! In your present state, I fear the king's ire can only increase as the winter months go by."

Tek shook her head, puzzled yet again by Sa's words. She sensed the same reaction from Dagg.

Once more she said, "How so?"

The king's dam snorted, eyeing the young mare's gently swollen belly.

"My dear, have you not yet realized?" she answered dryly. "You are in foal."

Moonbrow

☽ 11 ☾

Tai-shan savored his new life in the fire-warmed enclosure, well pleased with the layer of winter fat at last beginning to sheathe his ribs. Whenever the weather held fair, the green-clad *daïcha* accompanied the dark unicorn to the open yard that he might frisk, leaping and galloping fiercely. Yet — maddeningly — he caught not so much as a glimpse of others of his kind. Gradually their scent within the enclosure's vacant compartments grew old.

The chill, dark afternoon was growing late, the *daïcha* just leading him back toward shelter. The weather had turned much colder than the morn. Ice slicked the squared cobblestones where formerly puddles had lain. His breath steamed like a dragon's in the bone-dry air. All at once, Tai-shan pricked his ears. Abruptly, he halted. The muffled sound of hooves and far-off whistles reached him.

With an astonished whinny, the dark unicorn wheeled and bolted across the yard toward the sound. He scarcely heard the dismayed exclamations of the *daïcha* behind him. His own heels rang sharply on the icy stones. The low, calling whickers grew louder as he ducked down a narrow passage between two buildings. Emerging, he beheld another, far more spacious yard, unpaved, and surrounded by a barrier of wooden poles. Beyond milled a group of unicorns. Tai-shan's heart leapt like a stag.

"Friends," he cried. "I have found you at last!"

The others turned in surprise. They were all mares, he noted, save for a couple of well-grown fillies, and all quite small. Their coloring was disconcerting, dull shades of brown mostly, not at all the hot sunset reds and skywater blues of the fellows he only dimly remembered. Among these strangers' subdued, earthy hues, one mare alone stood out. Slender, clean-moving, her coat a vivid copper that was full of fire.

"A stallion!" he heard her whisper.

A companion nodded, murmuring, "Aye, a stallion — here! And mark the color of him."

"So dark — near black."

"He *is* black . . ."

Tai-shan trotted toward them. "I am a stranger here," he called. "Can you tell me what place this is?"

None of the mares replied, though one of the fillies exclaimed, "Look! Upon his brow —"

The coppery mare shushed her. The dark unicorn halted, puzzled. Beyond the wooden poles, the mares shifted nervously, eyeing him with mingled curiosity and alarm. Several seemed on the verge of bolting. At last, cautiously, the tall coppery mare started forward. Her companions cavaled and whickered, calling her back, but she shook them off.

"Who — what art thou?" she demanded of him, seemingly poised between boldness and terror. "Whence comest thou?"

The dark unicorn blinked. The other's odd manner of speech was new to him, softly lilting. He found himself able to understand it only haphazardly.

"I am . . . I am called Tai-shan," he began, aware all at once that he still could recall no name other than the one the *daïcha* had given him. "I come from . . . from far away —"

"Moonbrow?" the young mare interrupted. "Thou art the one our lady hath named Moonbrow?"

Tai-shan frowned. Was such the meaning of his name? "You speak the two-foots' tongue?" he asked.

"Two-foots!" the other exclaimed. All at once, she burst out nickering.

"Why do you laugh?" the dark unicorn asked her.

"Thou calledst our keepers 'two-foots'!"

"Keepers," the dark unicorn murmured. Short for *firekeepers*, doubtless. "You speak their tongue?"

The coppery mare tossed her head. "Nay. No *da* can manage that. But I reck it some."

By *reck*, he guessed she must mean *understand*.

"*Da*," he said. "What is . . . ?"

He choked to a halt suddenly, noticing for the first time what he had missed before: the mare across the wooden barrier from him was hornless. No proud spiral skewer — not even a nursling's hornbud — graced her brow. He half-reared, exclaiming in surprise, and saw that her fellows behind her were just the same: foreheads perfectly flat. Their manes stood upright along their necks like the manes of newborn foals. Like fillies', their chins were beardless. Stranger still, their tails were not tufted only at the end, but were instead completely covered by long, silky hair. Beneath smooth, unfringed fetlocks, each hoof was a single, solid toe.

"You are no unicorns!" he cried.

"Unicorns?" The coppery mare cocked her head, pronouncing the word as though it were new to her.

Tai-shan stumbled back from her, staring. "What manner of beasts are you?"

"*Daya*," the other said. "I and my sisters are the sacred *daya* of Dai'chon."

He heard footfalls behind him and glimpsed the *daïcha* hastening toward him. At the same moment, a commotion among the mares caused him to turn again. Beyond them, another of their kind was just entering the enclosed yard through a pivoting panel in the barricade of wooden poles. This was a stallion, as hornless as the mares. His coat was reddish umber, shanks black below the knee. He wore an odd kind of adornment about his head, made of fitted links of shining skystuff. A silver crescent resembling the *daïcha*'s spanned his brow. The pair of two-foots accompanying him each grasped a long strap attached to the muzzle of the thing.

"Our lord cometh!" one of the fillies cried.

"Hist, away!" her elder sister urged the coppery mare.

Behind him, Tai-shan heard the *daïcha* draw her breath in sharply. Catching sight of him, the umber stallion pitched to a stop. His two-foot companions halted in seeming confusion. The *daïcha* hastened forward, calling out to them and waving one forelimb as though urging them to depart. Eyes wide, the two-foots began tugging at the long straps, but the hornless stallion planted his round hooves, stiff-legged, refusing to budge. Head up, he stared at Tai-shan. Abruptly, the umber stallion let loose a peal of rage.

"What meaneth this? Who dareth to approach my consorts?"

The dark unicorn snorted, confused as much by the other's hot and angry tone as by his strange way of speaking. Before him, the mares screamed and scattered, thundering away toward the opposite end of the barricaded yard, all save the coppery mare, who cried out to him hastily.

"Peace, my lord. Naught unseemly hath occurred. This is Moonbrow, that our lady hath . . ."

"Moonbrow?" the other snarled. "The outlander that hath usurped my stall?"

Tai-shan frowned. The meanings of several of the other's words he had to guess at. *Outlander* must mean one from outside the two-foots' settlement. Perhaps *stall* referred to the wooden enclosure in which he now sheltered. Ignoring his escorts, the umber stallion stamped and sidled.

"Wouldst claim my harem as well?"

Tai-shan shook his head. He had no idea what a *harem* might be.

"I seek nothing that is not my due," he called across the barricade. "I long only to learn what place this is —"

"A place where thou'lt find no welcome, upstart!" the stallion spat, eyes narrowed, his small, untasseled ears laid back. "Stand off, harlot," he shouted at the coppery mare. "Thou'rt pledged to me!"

Trembling, the coppery mare began to back away. Once more, the *daïcha* called sharply to her fellows. They tugged with determination at the straps of the stallion's headgear, but he shook them furiously off.

"Trespasser!" he flung at the dark unicorn. "Thief!"

Tai-shan ramped and sidled for sheer bafflement. "What is my trespass?" he cried. "I assure you, I am no thief. . . ."

"Dost challenge me?" the other shrilled, rearing. "I'll brook no such outrage!"

With shouts of surprise, his two-foot companions lost their grip on the straps as all at once, the stallion charged. Confounded, Tai-shan sprang back.

"Peace, friend," he exclaimed. "I seek no quarrel. . . ."

"No quarrel!" the other roared. "Our keepers should have cut thee, not made thee welcome, freak! *I* am First Stallion here!"

His words made no sense to Tai-shan. Across the yard, the two-foot escorts cried out in alarm as the umber stallion thundered toward the dark unicorn. Tai-shan tensed: the wooden barrier between them was only shoulder high, an easy leap — then abruptly he realized it was the coppery mare, not he, who stood directly in the other's path. With a startled cry, she scrambled aside — too slowly. The umber stallion champed and struck at her savagely.

"Hie thee back to thy sisters, strumpet!" he snarled. Then to Tai-shan, "Be grateful a fence standeth between us, colt, else it would be to thee I'd give this drubbing."

Cornered against the barrier, the coppery mare cried out, unable to dodge. Tai-shan saw blood on her neck where her assailant's teeth had found her. She stood on three limbs, favoring one bleeding foreleg. With a shout, the dark unicorn leapt the barrier and sprang between them, shouldering the umber stallion away from the coppery mare.

"Leave off!" he shouted. "She has done you no hurt."

Behind him, he heard cries of amazement. The place seemed full of two-foots suddenly, running and calling. The *daïcha*'s voice rose commandingly above the rest. At the far end of the yard, the panicked mares galloped in circles. Green-clad two-foots ran to contain them. The umber stallion fell back from Tai-shan at first with an astonished look, then seemed to recover himself. Viciously, he lashed and flailed at Tai-shan, who braced and struck back, striving to hold his ground lest he himself be driven back and trapped against the barrier.

"Nay, do not defend me, Moonbrow," the coppery mare gasped, limping painfully out of the umber stallion's reach.

The *chon* burst into the yard suddenly. Tai-shan heard him shouting above the tumult, the clatter of footfalls as his purple-plumes rushed forward with their long, pointed staves. Screaming, the flatbrowed stallion lunged and champed Tai-shan on the shoulder, drawing blood. The dark unicorn struck him away with the flat of his horn.

"Moonbrow, have done!" the coppery mare called to him urgently. "Thou darest do him no injury. He is sacred to Dai'chon!"

Tai-shan glimpsed the *daïcha* dashing forward to intercept the charging purple-plumes. She waved her forelimbs, crying out frantically to the *chon*. Taking note of her, apparently for the first time, he barked an order and threw up one of his own forelimbs. Lowering their staves, the purple-plumes strayed uncertainly to a stop.

Eyes red and wild, the umber stallion wheeled and plunged once more at the dark unicorn. Tai-shan reared and threw himself against the other's side, catching him just as he pivoted. The flatbrow's hindquarters strained, forehooves pawing the air. The dark unicorn lunged, shifting his whole weight forward hard until, hind hooves skidding, his opponent crashed to the icy ground.

"Hold," the dark unicorn cried, springing to press the tip of his horn to the other's throat. "Enough, I say!"

Eyes wide, the fallen stallion stared up at him. The other's red-rimmed nostrils flared. His breaths came in panting gasps.

He made as if to scramble away, but Tai-shan pressed his horntip harder.

"*Peace*," he insisted. "I sought no quarrel with you, nor did this mare."

Across the yard, the other mares had quieted. They stood silent, astonished. The two-foots as well. Eyes still on the umber stallion, Tai-shan stepped back, horn at the ready.

"Be off," the dark unicorn snorted. "And do not think to trouble this mare again while I stand ready in her defense."

With a groan, the defeated stallion pitched to his heels and limped away. His two-foot companions came forward cautiously to catch hold of his headgear's trailing straps. Other two-foots hied the mares from the enclosed yard through the pivoting panel. They disappeared down a passage between two buildings. The crestfallen stallion allowed his escorts to lead him after the mares without further protest. Tai-shan turned back to the coppery mare.

"Are you hale?" he asked her. "Did he do you much harm?"

The other gazed on him in seeming wonder. "Naught but a bruise and a gash, my lord Moonbrow," she murmured. "No more than that."

Warily, another two-foot edged toward them along the wooden barrier. The young mare snorted.

"Sooth, lord," she exclaimed, "ye must be winged, to have sprung such a height with such ease — and from a standing start!"

The dark unicorn shook his head, amazed. These hornless *daya* must be puny jumpers indeed if they found such low barriers any impediment.

"Tell me," he asked her, "why did you suffer that other to use you so? No warrior of my race would have stood for such —"

"Warrior!" the young mare whickered. "Lord, I am no warrior, only the least of the First Stallion's consorts — so new he hath not even claimed me yet. Only the First Stallion is warrior here, and he hath reigned four years running, defeating all comers at the autumn sacrifice — yet ye overcame him in a trice. . . ."

Drawing near, the two-foot clucked. The mare turned meekly, as from long habit, and started to go to him.

"Wait!" Tai-shan exclaimed. "Will I see you — you and your sisters — again?"

The coppery mare hung back, seemingly torn between the desire to stay and an obligation to accompany the two-foot. He clucked again. The coppery mare shrugged.

"If our keepers so will."

The overcast hung very low and grey. Feathery flakes of snow, the season's first, had begun to float down through the darkening air. Reluctantly, the coppery mare turned to follow her two-foot escort.

"Hold, I beg you!" the dark unicorn cried. "Tell me your name."

For a moment, glancing back over her shoulder, the other's chestnut eyes met his. She nickered suddenly, despite the obvious pain of her injured leg.

"Ryhenna, my lord Moonbrow," she called back to him, "that meaneth *fire*."

She limped slowly, three-legged, beside her escort toward the opening in the wooden barrier across the yard. Tai-shan turned to find the *daïcha* deep in debate with the *chon*. She stood directly before him, forepaws resting on his upper limbs, which encircled her middle. Purple-plumes surrounded them. The ruler listened, frowning, seemingly reluctant to accede to whatever it was the *daïcha* was insisting upon. The dark unicorn saw him twice shake his head.

In a bound, Tai-shan sprang over the wooden barrier again and was surprised once more to hear exclamations of astonishment from the two-foots. The *chon* and the *daïcha* both turned, startled. Tai-shan whickered to the lady and made to approach. The ruler's clasp about her tightened protectively. His purple-plumes tensed. At his sharp command, they raised their pointed staves and hurried to block the dark unicorn's path.

Tai-shan halted with a puzzled snort. Turning in the *chon*'s grasp, the *daïcha* protested. Reaching out one forelimb to the dark unicorn, she continued talking to the *chon*. The two-foot ruler eyed the young stallion suspiciously, but at a cautious nod from him, his purple-plumes fell back, staves still at the ready. Tai-shan went forward to nuzzle the *daïcha*. She crooned to him and stroked his nose.

Releasing her, the *chon* laid one forepaw briefly upon her shoulder, then turned and strode away across the yard in the direction the mares and the stallion had taken. His purple-plumes marched after him. Dusk had fallen. The snowfall was coming down more thickly now. The *daïcha*'s female companions arrived, carrying firebrands. Tai-shan held himself still as, by their flickering light, the lady ran her slender forepaws gently over his nicks and bruises. She dabbed them with a pungent salve from a hollow vessel that was the color of soft river clay but rigid as stone.

The *chon* returned, striding across the yard once more with his purple-plumes. He bore in one forepaw the same silvery adornment the umber stallion had lately worn. The long, trailing straps had been removed. Its dipping, crescent browpiece gleamed, flashing in the darting firelight.

The *chon* handed his prize to the *daïcha*, who accepted it with a delighted laugh. Curious, the dark unicorn bent forward to examine the thing more closely. It smelled of skystuff and bitter oil. Holding it up in one forepaw, the *daïcha* caressed his muzzle and cheek. Tai-shan had no notion what the purpose of such an odd device might be, yet he felt not the slightest misgiving as, moments later, the lady of the firekeepers fastened it securely about his head.

Winterkill

) 12 (

The first weeks of winter had proven arduous. Sa shivered hard, frigid wind gusting her flank. She moved painfully, limbs aching. Sharp little crystals of ice seemed to have formed in her joints, making them ache. In all her many years she could not remember a winter so cold.

The weather worsened by the day. Forage grew steadily scarcer and ever more difficult to uncover beneath the hard-frozen snow. King's scouts no longer reported newfound forage to the herd at large. Korr alone decided who should learn of such. Those who gained his favor were led to the spots: those who earned his displeasure were left to fend for themselves.

The grey mare clenched her jaw. The shame of it: her son playing favorites when a mouthful of withered grass might mean the difference between starvation and survival this winter! Unicorns were dying now, herdmembers frozen or starved to death — nurslings and weanlings first, followed by the oldest stallions and mares.

Sa shook her head grimly as she picked her way over the rocky trail, eyes alert for any patch of green among the constant grey. Next it would be the older, uninitiated fillies and foals. Then the half-growns. Finally the warriors in their prime. The weather

remained too harsh even to permit the proper funeral dances for
the dead.

The grey mare's innards rumbled hollowly. She had not eaten
since the afternoon before. Hunger had driven her high up the
slopes, far from the constant wailing in the valley below: mothers
discovering their young dead in the night, warriors stumbling
across aged sires and dams too weak to rise. The Council of
Elders had been devastated: three of its members already dead,
five others gravely ill.

Korr ordered the herd assembled daily now, holding them for
hours, captive to his rantings. He spun wild tales of the will of
Alma, who mercifully punished her beloved followers for their
transgressions. It was all absurd. Exposed to the elements, unable
to move about for warmth, the herd listened to their mad king's
tirades under the vigilant eye of his chosen Companions —
"wolves," as many now called them when out of range of their
ever-pricked ears.

Yet others, weak and weary, starving and cold, swallowed
down the king's words as though they were sweet graze. The
grey mare snorted, shaking her head. To be sure — standing
dumbly rapt took far less energy than plowing through the cold,
pawing hard-packed snow in search of forage, or breaking the
hoof-thick ice of streams to snatch a sip of freezing water, Sa
mused bitterly.

Her vitals growled again. Thinking not of her own ills, but of
Tek's, Sa felt her brow furrow. As the pied mare's belly continued
to swell, she kept more and more to herself these days, foraging
far from others' eyes, wary lest they deduce her condition and
bring the news to Korr. His eye, Sa noted when it fell upon the
healer's daughter, remained dark and full of fury still. At Korr's
rallies, Sa insisted that Tek stand between her and Dagg, in hopes
of disguising the younger mare's burgeoning belly from the king's
watchful gaze. Did he know? Did he guess? She could not tell.

The grey mare's only consolation was in noting that her granddaughter Lell was no longer forced to attend: Ses's influence,
surely. Silently, Sa thanked the flame-colored mare for standing

up to her mate. Korr had stopped referring to the nursling princess almost entirely, no longer calling upon his daughter's title as the source of his authority. It was all Alma now: often it proved impossible to discern if the will he spoke of was the goddess's or his own.

Fortunately, she, Dagg, and Tek had managed to scout out a few others of rebellious mind. Approaches had to be cautious, much discussion slipped into brief spaces, since the king's wolves maintained close tally on who associated with whom. To her surprise, many of the old traditionalists who had so resisted her grandson's innovations now spoke with longing of the "fair old days" of Jan's brief reign.

And yet — infuriatingly — most of the herd continued meekly to submit to Korr's tyranny. They followed as in a daze, too weak or ill or spiritless to turn away. Disgusted, the grey mare snorted and pawed the frozen earth. Did these poor fools not realize that every waking moment must be devoted to forage if any were to survive to see the spring? With or without Council approval — and despite the king's fanatical personal guard — steps must be taken and *soon* to quell her son's worsening madness, or he would starve them all.

A flash of green caught her eye suddenly. Sa halted along the rocky trail. The cliffside fell away sheer to one side of her, more than a dozen stridelengths to the slope below. Not far beneath the dropoff, clinging to the cliff, rose a tiny spruce, its slender trunk leaning out over open space, its spindly branches tipped with dark, succulent needles, half a dozen mouthfuls at least. The grey mare gazed at the tempting forage, all thought of Korr's madness and the Vale's dire plight slipping from her mind as her empty gorge cramped in an agony of hunger.

Cautiously, she moved to the edge of the precipice and leaned out, nostrils flaring to catch the delicious, resinous savor of the greenery. Her long neck reached scarcely halfway to the little fir's tender tips. No wonder no unicorn had yet managed to claim this prize! Carefully, she inched nearer, straining. The pungent scent of pinesap made her dizzy for a moment. Her hooves skidded. She jerked back from the icy dropoff, tossing her head hard for balance, and managed to catch herself.

Think! She must think. How to get at that marvelous food, the first she had encountered since wolfing down a few old, dried thornberries and the bitter thorn they had hung upon the day before. Not until after she had finished had she stopped to consider — and realized she ought to have taken half back for Tek.

She had returned to the grotto that evening to find her grandson's mate huddled shivering — having turned up nothing that day. Now, standing at the edge of the precipice, gazing out at the little spruce, the older mare steadied her resolve. She would pluck the fir, but she would eat none of it. Not one twig! Her belly growled again in protest, but she champed her teeth against the grinding pain. Tek's unborn needed this nourishment far more than she.

Wind gusted harder, nearly overbalancing her on the treacherous ice. Her bones ached. She cavaled awkwardly to regain her equilibrium. She would need to use the greatest care — but she *must* get the branch. A mere scrap in summer, its foliage made a rare feast in these lean times. Sa champed her teeth again, against the aching stiffness in her joints this time. Once more she approached the cliffside's edge and leaned out.

She reached once, missed, reached again — striving to grasp the branch where it grew slender enough to break. The thin bough wavered in the wind, almost within range of her teeth. She braced her hooves and tried again. The wind whistled, numbingly chill. The icy stones of the cliffside clicked, cracking with the cold. The branch bobbed so near she felt it brush the whiskers of her nose. She snapped and missed.

The wind soughed, tugging, shoving at her. The little branch nodded and danced. She had it! All at once, she had it in teeth. The grey mare felt a rush of triumph as she strained the final infinitesimal distance to capture the elusive twig. Moisture rushed to her mouth. Scabrous, aromatic bark abraded her tongue.

Then without warning, the icy surface beneath her gave way.

She jerked in surprise, hooves skidding. The treacherous wind whipped her mane stinging into her eyes. The limber branch tore free of her grasp and sprang away. She tried to rear back, scrambling wildly, but could find no purchase on the crumbling stone. Then she was hurtling headlong through empty space. The hillside below rushed up to meet her.

Ryhenna

☽ 13 ☾

Winter deepened. Snow fell almost daily, piling in great drifts beside the two-foots' wooden dwellings and along the high timber wall. Now when the *daïcha* led him from the warm enclosure, Tai-shan trotted at once through the cobbled passage into the wide, unpaved yard where the coppery mare and her flatbrowed sisters waited. Rather than springing over the barrier of poles as he had done before, he schooled himself to wait until the *daïcha* had swung wide the wooden panel to let him pass.

"Ryhenna!" he had cried out joyfully, trotting forward toward her on the day following their first meeting. A long strip of white falseskin wrapped the young mare's injured foreshank.

"Emwe, im chon Tai-shan," she answered boldly. "Greetings, my lord Moonbrow."

Whickering, the dark unicorn shook his head. The silvery adornment felt odd about his muzzle still, but he was fast growing accustomed to it. It jingled softly when he moved. "Speak, I beg you," he bade Ryhenna. "Tell me of this place."

Their conversation proceeded in fits and starts. Every other sentence, it seemed, he had to ask her to explain some unfamiliar word or phrase. The two-foots' vast settlement, he learned, was called a city, this walled complex housing the *chon* and his retinue, a palace. The *daya* themselves dwelled in a shelter known as a stable. By the time daylight waned and the *daïcha* beckoned him to return with her to his quarters, the dark unicorn's head was spinning.

As the days passed, he asked Ryhenna to teach him as much as she knew of the two-foots' odd, guttural tongue. Gradually, over the passage of weeks, he began to pick up other phrases on his own: *tash* for "no"; *homat* for "stop"; *apnor*, "enough"; *himay*, "stay" or "stand still." To his rue, the *daïcha* remained as oblivious as before to his clumsy attempts at speech — but failure only sharpened his resolve to persevere. Eventually, he vowed, he would make himself understood. Chafing, Tai-shan practiced and bided his time.

Among the flatbrows in the yard, it was mostly the coppery mare to whom he spoke. Her sisters remained unaccountably shy, casting their gazes aside deferently when he spoke. Yet all seemed eager to gambol and frisk. Though most were full-grown mares, not one had any more skill at arms than a nursling filly — but they gladly learned the dances and hoof-sparring games he managed to recall from the haze of his past, and they taught him their own versions of nip and chase.

Theirs seemed an utterly carefree existence, their every need met by willing two-foots, who appeared to ask nothing in return. Meanwhile the *daya*, he noted, followed their keepers' lead in everything, coming promptly when called, going docilely where directed. Indeed, he did not recall ever glimpsing any of the *daya* moving about the palace grounds without a two-foot escort. Truly an odd arrangement.

While nervous of speaking directly to him, Tai-shan noticed, the *da* mares spoke much of him among themselves. One morning he overheard two mares and a filly discussing him when they thought his attention elsewhere. Unobtrusively, the dark unicorn listened.

"Our new lord seemeth a far sunnier consort than our last."

"Indeed! So even-tempered, so gentle and mannerly."

"A great one for sport."

"Ah, child, but how long ere he tireth of these gambols and seeketh better sport?"

Light, nervous laughter.

"Soon, I hope!"

"To be sure, child. Give it but a whit more time —"

"Aye, though wonderfully well-grown, he *is* a very young stallion."

"And hath lately languished ill."

"Sooth, his jumping beareth witness that he recovereth apace!"

More nickering.

"That it doth."

"Patience, sisters. By my reck, we shall all stand broody to his stud by spring."

Tai-shan had not the slightest idea what they could mean. So many of their odd words were unfamiliar to him still. Yet he hesitated to ask for an explanation and in so doing reveal his eavesdropping: more often than not when he singled one out, she merely fidgeted like a filly, exclaiming, "Sooth, lord! Ye honor me too much."

Only Ryhenna seemed to possess a bolder spark, addressing him frequently as "thou," a term he surmised to be for use between equals and friends, rather than the more formal "ye" her sisters used. His questions often sent her into peals of mirth. Exasperated, the dark unicorn gave up trying to scowl, for the other's laughter was infectious and before long, he, too, was nickering. Ryhenna told him all she knew of the marvelous city beyond the palace gate.

"Our gentle keepers are mighty sorcerers," she said, punching through the knee-high snow blanketing the yard. The strip of white falseskin wrapping her foreshank had been removed only that morn, though she had long since ceased to limp. "The keepers' mastery of heavenly fire hath enabled them to build all thou seest that sheltereth both themselves and us, their *daya*."

Tai-shan trotted beside her. Their white breath wafted and steamed.

"But where do the *daya* go in spring, after the snow melts?"

he asked her. Surely once the weather warmed, her kind must leave this cramped and barren place — perhaps they roamed the grassy slopes beyond the city until the return of winter snows? Ryhenna turned to him, puzzled.

"Go? My lord Moonbrow, the *daya* do not go. We remain here under our keepers' care."

Tai-shan blinked, surprised. "Always — even in summer?"

The coppery mare nodded. "In sooth," she answered proudly. "Our lives here are enviable: fed, groomed, sheltered, and exercised by the *daïcha*'s minions. Why should we wish to leave?"

Dumbstruck, the dark unicorn snorted. His breath swirled in the curling mist between them. Across the yard, Ryhenna's sisters whickered and chased. Tai-shan gazed about him at the walled grounds of the *chon*'s palace. A pleasant enough idyll for a season, he supposed — and far preferable to winter's privations and killing cold — but after the thaw at equinox? To be shut up atop this high, rocky cliff while all around the open hills greened and fragrant meadows beckoned to be raced across and rolled in?

The coppery mare shook her head.

"Dwelling within the *chon*'s palace is our privilege as bluebloods, sacred to Dai'chon."

Dai'chon. That word again: the one the *daïcha* and her minions had chanted upon the beach before the sky cinder. The same word both she and the *chon* had exclaimed at first sight of him. Tai-shan frowned. He had heard it upon the lips of *daya* as well as two-foots since and never yet asked Ryhenna what it meant. He was just drawing breath to do so when a look of sadness passed over the coppery mare's features.

"Others, of course, are not so blessed as my sisters and I," she murmured.

"Others?" Tai-shan forgot all about his intention to ask Ryhenna for the meaning of the word *dai'chon*. "There are other *daya* besides you and your kith — do they dwell in the city beyond?"

During the long uphill procession from the bay to the palace crowning the cliffs, the dark unicorn had caught not so much as a glimpse or a whiff of any four-footed creature besides him-

self — but then, the crush of two-foots and the confusion of new
surroundings had been so great he had been aware of little beyond the tumult and the shower of dried petals and shavings of
aromatic wood. The coppery mare shrugged.

"They are only commoners, of course. Of no consequence."

"Commoners?" Tai-shan pressed, moving nearer. "What are
they?"

Again the coppery mare shrugged, moving off. "Merely common *daya* — those not sacred to Dai'chon."

Before he could question her further, the *daïcha* called out to
him from the wooden barrier's gate. Across the yard, other two-
foots clucked to the *da* mares. Ryhenna trotted obediently toward
them. The dark unicorn stood gazing after her as she joined her
sisters and followed the two-foot escorts from the yard. Behind
him, the *daïcha* called again.

That evening, alone in his warm, straw-bedded stall after the
daïcha had feasted and groomed him, Tai-shan reflected on the
coppery mare's words. Who were these "common" *daya*? Were
their lives different from the pampered comforts enjoyed by himself and the sacred bluebloods? In truth, despite its luxuries, now
that he had regained his vigor, the unending sameness of life
within the confines of the palace grounds had begun to wear on
him.

Almost all he knew of the city beyond, he realized, came to
him through Ryhenna — yet today she had hinted that she herself
had never even ventured beyond the palace gate. Had any of her
sisters? Surely some of them must — yet all save Ryhenna remained too shy to converse with him. The dark unicorn snorted.
His only direct knowledge of the settlement below was little more
than a confused and fading memory. Desire seized him suddenly
to explore the two-foots' city of fire and behold with his own
eyes whatever mysteries it might hold.

Wych's Child

☽ 14 ☾

Tek waded through the drifting snow, her rump to the biting wind. Sa had not yet returned to the grotto, and with the early dusk not far away, the pied mare grew anxious for her. Tek shivered hungrily as she picked her way across the slope. Late afternoon was very dark. Stumbling across the grey mare's body at the foot of a sharp drop took her by surprise. Sa lay smashed on the icy stones, one foreleg splayed, her head and neck twisted at an impossible angle. Tek halted, staring in horror. High up the cliff, she spotted the place where the other must have lost her footing. A little fir tree, hardly more than a sprig, grew out of the rock.

Grief overwhelmed Tek. The sky above her seemed to spin. She sank down, nuzzled the grey mare's body, already stiff with cold. Wind gusted, heavy with snow. It dragged against the cliffside, moaning. Surely a snowstorm was in the wind. She knew that she must rise, must return soon to the shelter of the caves. Dusk was fast approaching, and if she were caught by storm, she might never find her way back. Slowly, with effort, she gathered her cold-numbed limbs and rose. Someone must bear news of Sa's death to the king, she realized with a groan. The thought chilled her even more than the wind.

Motion behind her made her start and wheel. Downslope two

of the king's Companions came into view. They halted in surprise. Stallions both, one was dark, midnight blue with a pale,
silvery mane. He looked to be of the same generation as Korr.
The other, perhaps a year or two older than Tek, was middle blue
and spattered all over with eye-sized blots of black.

"It's Tek," he muttered to his fellow, "the Red Mare's — the
wych's child —"

The older Companion cut him short. "Alma's beard," he exclaimed. "Look — the king's dam, Sa!"

Still numb with grief, Tek fell back as the two stallions climbed
hastily to stand over the grey mare.

"Dead!" the younger one exclaimed.

The heads of both Companions snapped up. Their glances
flicked to her from the carcass at their feet. The dark, midnight
blue leveled an accusing gaze at Tek.

"What do you know of this?" he demanded.

Tek's mouth felt thick and dry. "I . . . she must have fallen."

"Did you see it happen?" the younger, spotted one snapped,
advancing uphill.

Tek shook her head. "Nay, I —"

The older stallion, too, came forward. "Why did you let her
climb that dangerous cliff?"

"I wasn't with her —"

The younger stallion snorted.

"Why not?" the older, the dark blue, interrupted. "These slopes
are steep."

"And forbidden to any but king's Companions," his comrade
added.

The pied mare blinked. No such proscription had been announced. She backed another step as the pair continued to advance. She could barely make them out now for the snow and
the gathering dark. Heads together, the two began conferring in
low voices, never taking their eyes off Tek.

"If she wasn't with her, she *should* have been. Sa was an old
mare."

"It's a crime not to protect the king's dam."

"Crime?" Tek's jaw dropped. What new laws were these? The two stallions ignored her.

"Aye, but if she's lying?" the spattered younger one asked. "What if she *was* with the mare?"

"What are you saying?" Tek demanded sharply. The snowy wind moaned. The air was grey and dark.

"Everyone knows you're a wych's child," the midnight blue said. "Your dam was born beyond the Vale."

"Korr banished her for magicking."

"My mother lives in the southeast hills by her own choice," Tek exclaimed. "She was never banished!"

"She enchanted Jan the prince when he was no more than a weanling," the younger stallion insisted.

"To protect him from wyvern sorcery," Tek snapped, outraged. Her mother, the Red Mare, had ever used her mysterious arts for the good of the herd.

"You're no better than your wych mother," the older stallion growled. "You seduced our good prince from the path of Alma."

"Liar!" Tek burst out, astonished, stung. How dared the king's lackey spit such filth at her?

"Traitor," the other stallion continued. "You ran away when the prince was assailed by gryphons, leaving him to his death."

"Untrue!" shouted Tek, half choked with wrath.

Her words echoed off the cliff. The king's Companions tossed their heads, champing. The two of them continued toward her across the slippery, rocky ground. Tek could do little but retreat upslope. The narrowed eyes of the spotted Companion glinted at her from their mask.

"Ringbreaker — you ran. Everyone knows it! It's common knowledge."

"'Common knowledge' to those who were not there!" She wanted to fly at him and skewer him. She wanted to trample him underhoof.

"You befriended our king's dam," cut in the other, older unicorn, "that you might share her cave and eat her forage when your own sire cast you out. Her kind heart was her own undoing."

"What do you mean?" cried Tek.

The other bared his teeth. "That you lured Sa here, to dangerous cliffs, on the pretext of finding forage. That you were with her at her death and failed to inform the king."

"Perhaps you caused her death," the younger guard pressed.

"Never!" gasped Tek. "I had only just come upon —"

They gave her no time to finish.

"A cunning tale. The mare is cold. She's been dead hours."

"I wasn't with her!"

"The king will decide."

"Come with us," his younger companion said. "Come willing, or we'll compel you."

Panic gripped Tek. If she went with these two now, she realized, she was as good as dead. They had the king's ear, and their groundless accusations would carry far more weight with him than any truth. Then the king might do whatever he wished. Banish her, even attack her. Who was to stop him now? Under the watchful eye of the king's wolves, the whole herd would stand silent, cowed.

The two stallions stood waiting. The spotted one's eyes gleamed, gloating. Tek wondered what forage he expected in exchange for giving her life to the king. The dark blue stallion motioned impatiently with his head.

"Come," he told her. "It grows dark, and the sooner this is dealt with, the better."

"The sooner you will feed, you mean," grated Tek.

A cold rage such as she had never known seized her, displacing fear: it would not be simply her own life lost, she realized in a rush, but that unborn within her as well.

"You lying wolves!" she cried. Through the gathering darkness, the rising wind and snow, they were little more than blurs to her. "Those of you who still have your wits, yet willingly follow him are worse than Korr! I carry the late prince's get in my womb. Therefore harm me at your peril!"

Eyes wide, both stallions studied her midsection uncertainly.

"Her belly's swollen," the older blue murmured.

His companion tossed his head as if to dodge a meddlesome fly. "Great with hunger — just as ours," he snorted. "All the mares that conceived this fall past have miscarried, the weather's been so foul and the forage so slight — *her* doing. Wych," he snarled. Then, louder, "Wych!"

He started forward, but the older blue nipped his shoulder to stay him. "List! What if what she says is true, that she carries the late prince's heir? That would make *her* more fitting regent than Korr. . . ."

Hearing him, the pied mare started, appalled suddenly at how hunger and grief had dulled her wits. She had never once since discovering her pregnancy considered that as the late prince's mate and mother of his unborn heir, she herself held a better claim to the regency than Korr. The king therefore could only view her burgeoning belly as a threat, invalidating as it did his young daughter's claim and making him, as Lell's regent, into a usurper. For an instant, surprise blinded her.

To what lengths, Tek wondered starkly, would his chosen Companions go to protect both their leader's — and their own — unfounded authority? All at once, in wild alarm, she realized how rashly she had spoken. Her words, intended to keep these two at bay, were having the opposite effect. Their eyes — particularly those of the younger Companion — had grown even more hostile, and though she was a trained warrior, young and strong, one of the finest, she knew that, big-bellied now and half-starved, she had not the slimmest hope of matching two such strapping opponents. The pair glanced at one another.

"She lies. She's a wych," spat the younger, his spots shifting and shuddering as his skin twitched with cold. "If she carries a foal, it can't be that of our late prince! Yet she'll claim so to the herd — if we let her. She'll sway them with her lies and turn them against the king."

The other appeared dubious, but also alarmed. Despite the dimming light and thickening snow, Tek spotted the thin rim of white circling his eye.

"What are you saying?" he whispered.

The younger Companion set his teeth. "That we settle the matter without troubling the king. She's clearly guilty of the grey mare's murder. And she abandoned the late prince to his death by gryphons — that's as good as murder."

His eyes upon the pied mare narrowed. He dropped his voice yet lower still.

"We'll say she resisted, tried to flee when we made to stay her."

Fury filled Tek. She felt reckless, bold.

"Would you kill me?" she spat, coming forward. She snorted, teeth set, anger throttling her. "Alone on this hillside without witnesses to thwart or even question you? Who would be murderers then?"

The older blue fell back a pace. The spotted Companion champed impatiently, ignoring her.

"Nonsense! None would dare dispute us. We're the king's chosen Companions, empowered to act in his name."

"Then the worst you may do me is banishment," growled Tek. "You have heard that sentence from the mouth of Korr himself!"

Halted now, the older Companion shifted from hoof to hoof, tail switching one flank, clearly in a quandary. His eyes flicked from his fellow to Tek. Angrily, the younger stallion champed him.

"Coward! Are you afraid of a mare?"

"A wych," he whispered. "A wych, you said."

"The prince's mate," cried Tek. "Mother of his heir."

"Are you not starving?" the spotted Companion demanded of his comrade. "Tell me how much forage we found today — scarcely a mouthful! Think of the feast we'll be shown if we do this for the king. . . ."

"Renegade! Lawbreaker," shouted Tek. "All the herd will know."

The older stallion sidled, still undecided.

His younger companion hissed, "Korr alone need know the truth of it. He'll thank us for serving his interests and sparing him need of dealing publicly with the seducer and betrayer of his son. Are you with me? Then hie!"

Nipping his companion hard on the neck, he lunged toward the pied mare, his horn lowered. With a cry, Tek reared to fend him off. She had the advantage of slightly higher ground but knew her belly would make her slow. With a deft twist of the head, she caught and deflected the black skewer aimed squarely at her breast. Hard blows from both forehooves dashed its owner away. He stumbled upon the slippery, icy rock, skidding downhill.

His comrade, the dark blue, still cavaled uncertainly. Tek gauged him with a glance and decided he would not charge. Below, the younger stallion regained his footing and was lumbering upslope toward her again. She lunged, head down, forcing him to dodge — clumsily, because of the slope. Their horns clashed and grated. She grazed him along the neck and leaned into the thrust. Blood spattered. Ferociously, Tek parried his stabs, jabbing and slicing.

How long can I sustain such a pace? she wondered wildly. *Summer last, sleek and well-fed, unburdened by pregnancy, I could have sparred all day and never lost my wind.*

Already her breaths came painfully short, steaming white clouds on the air. Her assailant grunted and heaved, hard-pressed to hold his footing on the steep hillside, unable to fight his way upslope past her. Twice more her forehooves drove him back. Abruptly, he backed off, eyes blazing. Tek dared not follow, afraid to put his comrade behind her lest, despite his earlier hesitation, he move to attack at last. Panting, the pied mare held her ground.

All at once, the spotted stallion charged again and tried to bull his way past her. Head ducked, shouldering at her, he strove to knock her off her feet. Tek lunged, her forelegs bent, knees pressed against his heavy shoulder. Hind legs locked, he leaned uphill, fighting to keep from overbalancing. Desperately, the pied mare braced her own hocks and shoved with all her might.

She felt him topple. With a scream, he crashed onto his side, rolling and tumbling away down the ice-slicked slope. He managed to right himself — yet still he plunged, limbs folded, unable to slow his hurtling descent. At last, at the distant treeline, he slammed to a halt. Tek watched, full of wrath still, gasping for breath. She hoped all his limbs were broken. She hoped he never rose.

A snort and movement to one side of her made her whirl. The other's comrade was coming forward. Hastily she scrambled back, readied herself for another clash — then realized he had no wish to engage her, only to peer over the steep slope's edge to where his fellow now lay, struggling weakly. The older stallion stared a long moment at the writhing form far below before returning his gaze to Tek, his eyes glassy.

"Wych," he whispered. "You truly are a wych! No mare in foal could overcome a stallion in full prime. . . ."

She stood panting hoarsely, desperate for breath. Had she allowed him even a moment to consider, he surely would have seen how close to spent she was. She doubted herself capable of another such frenzied effort as had allowed her to overcome her first, rashly foolish assailant.

"Would you be the next?" she demanded. The blue stallion flinched. Her voice seemed thunderous. "Make but one move to harm the life I carry, and I'll pitch you over the side as easily as I did your comrade."

A faint whinny came from far down the slope, weak and strangled with pain. The blue glanced toward his injured companion, then warily back at Tek. The snowfall had become smotheringly heavy, the wind rising even higher and more fierce. Was it dusk yet? The pied mare shook her head, dizzy with panting. The afternoon had grown so dark she could not tell the hour. The dark blue unicorn glared at her, then with a champ of helpless fury, turned and started picking his way cautiously down the steep, slippery hillside toward the younger stallion below.

"Flee while you may, wych," he spat at her. "I must see to my comrade. But be warned, the king will send my fellows to hunt you down."

Grey snow whipped between them in the dusky air, and for a moment Tek half expected him to change his mind, come charging back up the slope. She let no trace of fear show in her eye, making herself breathe slow and deep. The other's injured fellow whinnied again. Angrily, he turned from her and continued gingerly down. Weak with relief, Tek wheeled in the opposite direction and fled.

City of Fire
☾ 15 ☾

Tai-shan shook himself full awake with a start. The warm enclosure was very still. Shadows slanted steep around him. All the lamps had been doused hours ago. Since resolving the evening before to explore the two-foots' city of fire, he had little more than dozed the long, slow night through. He leaned to tug with his teeth at the peg fastening the gate of his stall, swung it open with a nudge.

He trotted down the aisle between empty stalls. The wide wooden closure of the shelter's egress stood ajar. A thin mewl of protest sang from its hinges as the dark unicorn shouldered through. The courtyard outside lay deserted in the predawn darkness. A near-full moon hung low in the sky, barely topping the timber wall.

Tai-shan galloped hard, hooves ringing hollow on the frozen cobbles. He sprang and cleared the wall, clipped one hind heel painfully on the rough upper edge. Too long he had been lazing, feeding over-well in the palace of the *chon*. Time to be done with that! Coming down on the other side of the wall, he shook himself, full of energy. His breath steamed, curling in the frosty air. The layer of fat beneath his pelt kept out the cold. The stone-paved path sloping away from him lay empty and snow-covered, ghostly white. He trotted toward a distant glimmer of firelight.

Through a small, square opening in the wall of one of the wooden dwellings lining the cobbled way, he glimpsed a firelit room. The heat of the place was fierce. Two-foots bustled about, their falseskins folded back to reveal forelimbs coated in a fine, white dust. The stoutest punched at a substance resembling pale mud while her assistants plopped pawfuls of the stuff onto dust-covered flats. They pressed berries and nuts into each gooey pat before thrusting the flats into small stone chambers that were full of fire.

A savor of honey, oil, and grain pervaded the air. Tai-shan watched, fascinated, as the soft blobs sighed and expanded, then dried, hardened, and began to turn brown. The dark unicorn's jaw dropped. What lay forming in the heated vaults were honey nutpods! As the two-foots retrieved the flats from the firechambers, Tai-shan shied away from the hole in the wall, his senses reeling. These two-foots created their own provender by means of fire! He would never have guessed such a thing to be possible.

Once more, he trotted down the cobbled path. Lamplight bled through a crack between wooden panels covering one of the square wall-openings in another shelter he passed. Halting, the dark unicorn nosed at the shutter, eased it back and peered cautiously through. A pair of two-foots knelt in the chamber within. The elder, a bearded male, kneaded a pale, doughy substance resembling the grain paste, but grey instead of white. It smelled like river silt.

Carefully, the elder male smoothed the silt into the shape of a hollow vessel. The dark unicorn had seen the two-foots' stone jars used to store unguents, oil, and drink — but what possible use, he wondered, could exist for a jar made of mud, too soft to hold even its own shape for long?

Beside the bearded male, his assistant, a smooth-cheeked half-grown, stood bundling himself into a thick falseskin. Carefully, his elder handed him the wet mud jar, and the half-grown ducked with it through an egress to the outside. Tai-shan let the wooden shutter swing softly shut. He trotted to the edge of the building and peered around.

The young half-grown stood in a small yard before a conical structure of stone. Heat rippled the air above. Another firechamber, the dark unicorn guessed. The young two-foot opened a port in the chamber's side, placed the soft vessel of mud within and slammed the port. More vessels stood alongside the chamber, Tai-shan noticed. Stamping his feet against the cold, the half-grown bent to catch up a pair, then turned and hastened back toward shelter. The jars clinked solidly against one another as he did so, the sound sharply musical.

Once again the dark unicorn's mind raced. Had these hard vessels already been in the chamber of fire? Had flame somehow transformed the yielding clay as it had the grain paste? Were the firechambers themselves — indeed, the very streets of the two-foots' city — made of stone at all, or of blocks of heat-hardened clay? Tai-shan shook his head, marveling at the vast and complicated city around him. Had fire been the tool to create it all?

The sky above him was lightening, the moon nearly down. Strange tracks in the snow beside him caught the dark unicorn's eye. One set was clearly that of a *da*, the other, that of a two-foot. But two deep, narrow ruts scored the snow alongside, one on either side of the paired tracks. Tai-shan cocked his head. Frowning, he studied the parallel grooves, unable to make out what could have made them.

Dawn came swiftly. The stars above paled and began to fade. The dark unicorn followed the strange tracks as they turned off the main thoroughfare onto a narrow, winding side-path. His ears pricked to the sound of foot-traffic somewhere nearby. Rounding a curve, he found himself in a great open space, crowded with stalls. Stacks of painted tile and heaps of sweet hay, bolts of brilliant falseskin and fat brown sacks of grain, rows of fire-clay vessels and strings of pungent, edible bulbs filled the air with richly varied scents. Tai-shan's nostrils flared. Before him, two-foots milled, the odd tracks he had been following obliterated beneath their trampling heels.

Intent upon their own tasks, the two-foots spared scarcely a glance for the dark unicorn. Wandering speechless between the stalls, he beheld a two-foot male, flushed and sweating over a red-hot rod of skystuff. With a heavy implement, the two-foot pounded the rod, reshaping it into a flattened skewer. The dark unicorn beheld other wonders, all engendered by fire: fresh herbs withered and preserved by parching on heated stones, brittle honeycomb softened and fashioned into burning tapers, muddied falseskins stirred clean in steaming cauldrons, and stinking, bubbling vats in which pale hanks of seed fibers steeped to vivid shades of vermilion, golden, bronze-green, and midnight blue.

The sun broke over the hills. More and more two-foots crowded into the square, surveying the contents of the stalls and conversing with their overseers. Goods and little disks of silvery skystuff changed hands. An oddly familiar scent reached the dark unicorn. Smoky and sweet, it clung to his nostrils. Turning, hunting it, he nearly stumbled over a very old two-foot who crouched upon a patterned falseskin spread upon the paving stones. Baskets of spicewood shavings and dried flower petals surrounded her, and figurines of blackened skystuff.

Tai-shan recognized their form: the body of a two-foot with the incongruous, flatbrowed head of a *da*. Fragrant smoke rose from the red-rimmed nostrils. A crescent moon blazoned the breast of each figure, most of which stood fiercely poised, brandishing in one forepaw a long, flattened skewer and in the other a tuft-ended vine. Tai-shan noticed, however, that a few of the figures were different. The skewer had become a horn upon the *da* head's brow, the vine a unicorn's tail sprouting from the base of the two-foot torso's back. The crescent moon-shape appeared not upon the chests of these different figurines, but upon their brows.

Selecting a curl of spicewood from one of the baskets, the elderly two-foot cupped it in one forepaw and struck a sliver of skystuff against a stone. Sparks flew up, bright as fireflies. The dark unicorn stared, incredulous, as the spicewood curl began to burn, sending up a fragrant, smoky plume. The two-foot unfastened a hinge in the belly of the unicorn-headed figure before her and thrust the crackling curl inside. Smoke rose through the figure's nostrils.

Tai-shan stood dumbstruck, staring. The two-foots could *make* fire! For all his hosts' mastery of the sorcerous stuff, it had never once occurred to him that they held the secret of its creation. Fire was the greatest mystery his people knew: it glanced through storm-tossed heavens; its substance formed the sacred sun and stars. Generations of unicorns lived and died without ever glimpsing an earthly flame. Yet these two-foots could summon such at will. Tai-shan stood trembling — for it was a power he knew his kind could never share. Lacking nimble forepaws, no hoofed creature such as himself could even hope to manipulate skystuff and flint into striking a spark. No unicorn could ever kindle fire.

"Dai'chon!" The exclamation brought Tai-shan back to the wintry square. The two-foot firesmith had caught sight of him. Her eyes widened. She started up. "Dai'chon!"

"Emwe," Tai-shan replied haltingly, pronouncing the difficult inflections with the greatest care. He bowed courteously. "Emwe ki Tai-shan."

Greetings from Moonbrow — with Ryhenna's help, he had deciphered enough of the two-foots' tongue to attempt a simple phrase. Fervently, he hoped he had spoken clearly. A rush of triumph overtook him as he saw comprehension light the other's eyes. Dropping her flint and the sliver of skystuff, she sank to her knees, pressing her forehead to the patterned falseskin. Tai-shan frowned, puzzled by her response. Muffled sounds came from the elderly two-foot, like moans.

"Pella! Pell'!" *Look, behold.* He heard gasps all around him suddenly, shouts of dismay and cries of what sounded at first to be his name. Yet when he pricked his ears, he discovered that many of the two-foots were calling out "Dai'chon" instead of "Tai-shan."

That baffled him. He had no idea still what the word could mean.

"Emwe!" he cried out boldly as two-foots began to cluster around him. "Tai-shan nau shopucha!" *Moonbrow greets you.* To his consternation, many fell back at the sound of his voice and, like the old female, crumpled to the ground. Were they so surprised to hear him speak? Others, by contrast, pressed forward eagerly, forelimbs extended as to caress him. The dark unicorn sidled.

"Tash," he cried out quickly. "Homat!" *No, stop.*

Mercifully, they seemed to understand. Others were sinking to their knees now. An onlooker tossed one of the tiny disks of silvery skystuff at him. It clattered onto the cobbles near his hooves. Tai-shan danced away, half shying in surprise. More disks of skystuff followed, along with bits of spicewood, dried flower petals, berries, and nuts.

"Homat!" the dark unicorn cried again: *stop.* "Apnor!" *Enough.*

Instantly, the shower of offerings ceased. The dark unicorn cavaled. Before him, two-foots melted back, allowing him passage. Almost all had fallen to their knees by this time. The rest stood gaping. Tai-shan bowed his long neck to them all and hurried on. None followed. Relieved, Tai-shan slipped through the crowd. The possibility of admirers swarming after him, pelting him with gifts, made his skin twitch.

Dodging around a stall, he nearly collided with a *da* standing before a massive wooden bin heaped with tubers. They smelled musty of starch and earth. A webbing of vines lashed the *da* to the bin, which creaked and swayed atop a pair of great wooden disks caked with muddy snow. The dark unicorn stared. Dragging such a strange contraption, Tai-shan wondered, could this *da* — or another similarly burdened — have cut the odd ruts which had first led him to the square?

"Dai'chon!" the *da* exclaimed, falling back with a start. "Great lord, ye walk among us. So it *is* true. At last. At last!"

Dull brown like other *daya*, this *da* looked much thinner and shabbier than the bluebloods he had met in the palace of the *chon*. Odd marks crisscrossed the deeply swayed back, and one skinny flank bore a crescent-shaped scar. The *da*'s posture, formerly weary and slumped, changed to joyous cavaling as the scrawny neck bowed reverently.

"Nay, friend," the dark unicorn answered. "You mistake me. I am called Tai-shan."

Still bowed, the other exclaimed, "Ah, lord, by whatever name ye choose, your faithful know you at a glance."

As Tai-shan shook his head, the *daïcha*'s adornment rattled loosely about his face. The *da* before him wore a similar device, the dark unicorn noted, one fashioned of brown strips of hide, not links of burnished skystuff.

"I am a stranger to this place," Tai-shan told the other. "Tell me, what is this great burden you drag?"

The other whickered. "Truth, it is nothing, lord. I haul it gladly, in your name."

"What is it that you haul?" Tai-shan asked, scarcely following the other's reply.

The *da* shrugged humbly. "Whatever my keepers put in the cart: firewood, grain sacks, jars of oil. Bolts of fabric. Foodstuff. Dung."

"Why is that?" the dark unicorn persisted. The point of such labor escaped him.

"Our keepers have need of such goods," the other told him. "We *daya* cart for them."

Tai-shan frowned, eyeing the chafed spots on the other's raw bones where the vines had rubbed. The cart looked heavy. Amid the myriad clashing odors of goods and two-foots all about, he caught scent of the *da* before him at last, a warm, musty aroma close to that of unicorns. Yet though clearly older than half-grown and not past prime, the flatbrow had the air of neither stallion nor mare: genderless as a beardless newborn or the very, very old.

"Of course, my lord," the other was murmuring, "the burdens of gelded commoners need not concern you, dwelling so far above us as ye do, First Stallion to your own sacred brood mares in the stable of the *chon*. . . ."

Tai-shan's frown deepened. Many of the other's phrases were new to him.

"Gelded?" he asked. The word had an ugly ring.

The flatbrow's head cocked, as though the explanation were self-evident. "Fillies and foals are born in equal numbers, my lord, as ye know — but only the finest colts become breeding stallions." He sighed. "As for the rest, we are made geldings."

Once more the dark unicorn shook his head, still not following. "These . . . these geldings," he said. "You get no young?"

The other glanced sadly away. "Nay. We lose all interest in the mares after the priests cut us."

Tai-shan fell back a step, staring. "Cut you?" he stammered. "Cut you?"

The one before him nodded. "Aye, underneath. Back between the legs. Then they mark us upon the flank with fire. Thus we are gelded and given the brand. Then our servitude begins."

The dark unicorn snorted, gagging. His nostrils filled with the imagined screams of mutilated foals. His senses reeled. Could such a shameful thing be true?

"But why?" he demanded hoarsely. "Your claim makes no sense — why maim innocent colts?"

The gelding *da* stared back at him, plainly alarmed and baffled by the dark unicorn's response. "Such is the geldings' lot, my lord, just as mares are for brood and stallions for stud — by your own decree! It is the will of Dai'chon."

Appalled, Tai-shan backed away from the gelded *da*. What was this infernal *dai'chon* with which *daya* and two-foots alike seemed to have associated him? No, he would not believe a word the other said — it went against his every impression of the gentle *daïcha* and her folk. The flatbrow's words could be no other than a cruel jest, a haunt's tale to play upon a stranger's ignorance — and yet before him loomed the heavily loaded cart, the crescent scar upon the stranger's flank, that odd, blank odor of gender-lessness.

Shouts from behind distracted his attention. The dark unicorn whirled. The crowd of two-foots he had fled only moments before had followed after all. Tai-shan sprang away into the hustling, jostling press. He wanted only to find his way out of the crowded square and be gone from this place. He had gotten no more than a dozen paces before eager followers closed around him from all sides, most falling to their knees as before.

"Tai-shan!" some of them called out, and others echoed, "Dai'chon!"

The two words, so similar in sound, slurred and blended together. The dark unicorn ramped and sidled. Surrounded by kneeling two-foots, Tai-shan could find no opening through which to flee. All at once, screams and shouts of alarm arose from the back of the throng. Violet-plumed two-foots shouldered through the crowd, shoving their kneeling fellows roughly aside with long, sharp-tipped staves.

Scrambling to their feet, many fled, but others only fell back a few paces, staring sullenly, as the purple-plumes cleared a path from the edge of the square. Beyond, a broad thoroughfare climbed toward the *chon*'s palace, visible on the hillcrest above. Down this avenue, a glittering raft approached, mounted on poles and borne upon the shoulders of eight brawny two-foots. Atop the platform sat the *chon*, resplendent in falseskins of purple and gold. He glared at the crowd.

A heavy cart stood stalled directly in his path. Laden with blocks of fire-baked clay, it canted to one side, one of its wooden disks caught between two paving stones. The *chon* gestured impatiently, and purple-plumes wielding flails sprang forward, striking both at the pair of *daya* hitched to the cart and at their two-foot escort as well. The crowd cried out in protest. Many surged forward, but purple-plumes with staves held them back. Eyes rolling, the gelded *daya* strained mightily, but were unable to heave the trapped cart free.

"Homat! Homat!" *Stop,* Tai-shan cried — but his words were lost in the hubbub of the crowd. Leaping past the armed purple-plumes, he lent his own strength to that of the frightened *daya* as, shouldering the cart from behind, he felt it lurch free and roll ponderously out of the *chon*'s path. The crowd surged and began to cheer.

"Tai-shan! Dai'chon!"

At a sharp order from the *chon*, the purple-plumes with flails turned them on the crowd. Others, still clearing the *chon*'s path, shoved and struck their fellows with such violence that some at the front of the press were knocked to the ground. The dark unicorn fell back in consternation as the purple-plumes created sufficient space for the *chon*'s conveyance to be set upon the ground.

"Asolet!" roared the purple-plumes. "Asolet!" *Silence*.

The crowd quieted as the *chon* rose and stepped from the raft. Brow furrowed, forelimbs folded across his chest, he stared at Tai-shan. The dark unicorn sensed the other wished to approach, for he shifted from foot to foot, his bearded chin thrust forward, mouth set. Murmuring, the crowd watched. Tai-shan bowed his neck to the two-foot ruler.

"Forgive me, *chon* of the two-foots," he began in his own tongue. His store of words from his hosts' odd, clicking language was still far too slender for him to attempt it now. "I see my absence from the palace has troubled you. . . ."

Still the other hesitated, eyeing him warily and without comprehension — indeed almost, the dark unicorn thought uneasily, as though he had not spoken at all. The two-foot ruler approached him cautiously. He made loud clucking sounds. His manner seemed both determined and afraid.

"Bim," he growled, slowly and clearly, as though addressing a wordless nursling or a half-wit. "Bim, Tai-shan!"

Frowning, Tai-shan held his ground. What was the other saying to him? Though the two-foot made no move to touch the dark unicorn, clearly he wanted Tai-shan to do something. *Come*, perhaps? Return to the palace, most likely. The young stallion took a few steps in that direction. Both the *chon* and his purple-plumes holding back the shifting crowd sighed in obvious relief.

"I beg you to pardon the commotion my presence here has caused," Tai-shan offered. "I had no notion. . . ."

The *chon* ignored him, already climbing back onto his conveyance. The brawny bearers crouched to lift it, when shouts halted them. Tai-shan turned to see several purple-plumes striding from the crowd into the open space before the *chon*. One dragged an elderly female roughly by one forelimb. Another two carried a heavy bundle between them. This they tossed with a clash onto the cobbles. Figurines of blackened skystuff spilled from the patterned falseskin. The dark unicorn recognized the old firemaker suddenly, along with her wares.

One of the purple-plumes knelt before the *chon,* speaking urgently. The ruler's frown deepened as his eyes turned briefly to Tai-shan before coming to rest on the tangled heap of figurines. He barked an order, and a kneeling two-foot snatched one of the figures from the pile, held it up before his ruler's gaze. This was one such as the dark unicorn had seen in the past: a hornless *da*'s head atop a two-foot's frame, skewer and frayed vine grasped in the forepaws, crescent moonshape upon the breast.

Next, the kneeling purple-plume lifted one of the newer kind, the sort of figurine Tai-shan had not seen before today, with its unicorn's head and tail, moon blaze upon the brow. The *chon*'s eyes widened. He snatched the new figurine from the kneeling purple-plumes and stared first at it, then at Tai-shan. With a cough of rage, the *chon* hurled the unicorn-headed figure onto the cobbles. Shoving his kneeling minion aside, he pulled other, similar figures from the heap. These, too, after a brief inspection, he cast down in disgust.

Murmurs ran through the crowd. The *chon* growled another order, and the elderly female was dragged before him. Uttering horrified cries, she collapsed at his feet, hiding her face with her forepaws. Brandishing one of the unicorn-headed figures, the *chon* stood over her, shouting. Tai-shan stared in astonishment, unable to follow the other's tirade.

Onlookers shifted, rumbling, trying to push past the purple-plumes' pointed staves as the *chon* grasped the old female's falseskin and dragged her upright. She wailed and cowered. Impatiently, he shook her, as though demanding some reply. At her timid shriek, he flung her to the pavement once more. Outrage flared in the dark unicorn's breast. Did these two-foots bear no respect for their elders? Was their leader allowed to abuse his people so?

"Tash! Apnor!" *No, enough,* he cried. "Homat!" *Stop.*

But the *chon* did not so much as turn his head. Once more, Tai-shan knew, the tumult of the milling, agitated throng had drowned out his voice. Desperately, he clattered across the cobbles to stand between the angry *chon* and the cowering firesmith. Another cheer rose from the crowd.

"Desist, I beg you," the dark unicorn exclaimed. "How has this old one offended you?"

Eyes wide, the two-foot ruler fell back before Tai-shan — and the dark unicorn realized he had spoken in his own tongue, not the *chon*'s. Clearly, the other could not understand his words. Behind Tai-shan, the aged female wailed and wrung her forepaws. Gently, the dark unicorn bent to touch the old firesmith, hoping to reassure her — but with a shriek, she shrank away, lurched to her feet and, ducking under a purple-plume's staff, disappeared into the crowd. More cheering. The astonished look upon the face of the *chon* changed rapidly to one of fury. His purple-plumes leaned against the surging, cheering throng, which had begun to chant alternately "Tai-shan!" and "Dai'chon!"

The *chon* roared orders, and purple-plumes dashed forward to surround the dark unicorn, their pointed staves braced and ready. Tai-shan wheeled to stare at them as shrieks of alarm and angry shouts rose from the crowd.

"Tash! 'Omat!" the dark unicorn shouted at the *chon* through the deafening noise. "Call off your minions. I mean you no harm. . . ."

Tai-shan's skin twitched as something brushed his near flank. A similar sensation slithered about his throat. Vines! At the *chon*'s command, the purple-plumes were casting vines to ensnare him. With a whinny of disbelief, the dark unicorn reared. He kicked desperately at the two-foot holding the vine that encircled his hind heel. The kick knocked the other to the ground. The vine slackened. Tai-shan danced, and the cruel pressure against his pastern eased.

All at once, his head was jerked violently around. Three purple-plumes gripped the free end of the vine about his neck,

using their combined weight to anchor him while another pair
flung a second vine about his throat. It tightened suddenly, throttling him. Choking, unable to breathe, the dark unicorn lunged
at the three purple-plumes nearest him. Two dropped their vine
and managed to dodge, but the third, slower than his fellows,
suffered a slash across the ribs. With a yell, he sprinted away,
clutching his bleeding side.

Tai-shan shook his head vigorously, trying to slacken the remaining vine. He needed air! The purple-plumed pair held on,
hauling on the vine to keep it taut. The dark unicorn ducked and
lunged at them. They dodged. Others darted near and tossed
another noose. Tai-shan reared, flailing, to keep them back. His
limbs were growing numb. Coming down on all fours again, he
staggered.

The crowd heaved, thundering wildly. The dark unicorn saw,
but could not hear, the *chon* bellowing orders to his minions.
One of the purple-plumes strode toward Tai-shan with forelimb
cocked, his sharp-tipped staff held level with his ear. Shouts and
shrill cries from the crowd all around. The dark unicorn realized
dimly that the *chon*'s advancing minion meant to hurl the pointed
staff at him. Black spots wandered across his vision. Weakly, he
shied as the purple-plume's forelimb tensed.

A shout from across the square halted the two-foot in his
tracks. Whirling, he lowered his staff. The *chon* and the others
also turned. The crowd began to stamp and cheer. Tai-shan spun
unsteadily to behold the *daïcha* hastening down the cleared path,
flanked by her own, smaller company of green-plumes. Though
they bore no staves, slung from the middle of each dangled a
flattened skewer.

For a sickening moment, the dark unicorn thought the two
armed groups would clash — but then the *daïcha* signaled her
own followers to a halt while she hastened on alone, her expression one of outrage and fear. Straining for breath, Tai-shan stumbled toward her drunkenly. The throng was ranting, screaming
now, the *chon* continued to roar. The dark unicorn felt his limbs

buckle, his knees strike the paving stones as the *daïcha* wrenched the still-taut vine from the purple-plumes' grasp.

As from a great distance, Tai-shan heard her frantic cries, felt her nimble digits clawing at the vines cutting into his throat. He tried to speak, but could get no air. The world had grown very still and dark. All around him, the frenzied noise of the crowd diminished to a whisper. "Dai'chon! Tai-shan!" were the last sounds he heard.

Swift-Running
☽ 16 ☾

Dusk had fallen by the time she reached the Vale. The deep
snow and heavy cloud-cover, which had seemed so dark by
day, now faintly glowed in a shadowy half-light that was brighter
than true night: enough to find her way by, barely. Wind and
snow continued to blow. Heaving, half-frozen, Tek stumbled
into her father's cave, nearly trampling a grey roan filly lounging
just within the narrow entryway. The healer himself lay at the
back of the crowded little cave, surrounded by his other acolytes,
half a dozen fillies and foals well past weaning but too young yet
to be called half-grown. The young ones looked up in surprise as
the black-and-white stallion broke off the lay he had been reciting.
Tek recognized it from even such a brief snatch: "The Mare of
the World."

"Daughter," he exclaimed. "Is someone ill? Wind outside will
be a blizzard soon."

The pied mare shook her head. The sudden warmth of the
grotto's small, close space unbalanced her. She swayed where she
stood.

"Sa is dead," she panted. "Fell . . . on the slopes. I found her.
Two of the king's Companions say I murdered her."

Teki pitched to his hooves. His acolytes scattered. The pied
mare sidled in agitation.

"They know I am in foal."

The healer's eyes widened. "Hist," he said over his shoulder to one of the fillies, "keep watch and let me know at once if you see king's Companions or any other."

Tek's eyes sought his, searching his face as he came forward to stand breast to breast with her. His nearness warmed and steadied her.

"Now tell me, daughter," he continued, "did any see you come into the cave?"

The pied mare shook her head.

"Good. Snowdrift will soon cover your tracks."

Champing, the healer ducked his head, deep in thought. Expressions curious and alert, five of his acolytes stood huddled to one side: three reds and two blues, the grey once more posted at the entryway.

"Mark you," he instructed them all. "What now befalls must remain our secret. Breathe no word of it, not to your sires and dams, not to anyone. We never saw Tek this night. She did not come here. You understand?"

Solemnly, the acolytes nodded. Standing so near him, Tek noted all at once how small the healer was. More slight than most unicorns, Teki's value to the herd had always lain in his knowledge of herbcraft and lore rather than prowess in battle. What the pied mare had not fully realized before now was that she stood taller at the shoulder than he. Being longer both of rib and shank, her robust, lank-limbed frame was of altogether a different sort than his.

How odd, she mused, her thoughts careening wildly. Unicorn colts almost always resembled their sires more than their dams, not only in the color of their coats, but in size and build as well. Yet, though pied like the healer, her colors did not precisely match his, being rose and black, not white and black. And though they had always gotten on famously from the day her dam had left her in the healer's care, their temperaments, too, were dissimilar: Tek's passionate and bold, Teki's contemplative. Indeed, it struck her now that were a stranger to view them at this moment, side to side, surely that one would never guess them to be scion and sire.

Strange, she mulled. *I never noticed this before.*

"You must flee, daughter," Teki was saying, glancing up. "No-where in the Vale is safe for you now. And this is the first place the king's wolves will come sniffing when they find Sa's grotto empty."

The pied mare felt her skin grow cold. Teki called a name, and the grey filly at the entryway pricked her ears.

"Go at once to the cave of Leerah and Tas. Fetch their son here as quick as may be. But mark you!" he called as the filly wheeled. "Do not say why I need him. Be certain Leerah and Tas know nothing of Tek's presence here. Though Dagg is our ally, his sire and dam remain loyal to the king. Do you heed?"

Hastily, the filly nodded and dashed off. A blue foal stepped to take her place at the entryway. Gravely, the healer shook his head.

"Flee?" Tek pressed him. "Father, where am I to go? The king's wolves will hunt me down even on the far side of the Vale. If I hide on the shelterless outer slopes, I will freeze. The Pan Woods beyond are full of vicious, hungry goatlings, and the Great Grass Plain too distant to even hope for. . . ."

Her breath ran out, her agitation rising. The Vale was her home, the children-of-the-moon her people. She could never live content in the solitude beyond the Vale as her mother did — beyond the reach of the Ring of Law as the Plainsdwellers did. If she fled now, she would be declared a renegade and barred forever from return. Jan's heir could never inherit.

"Come, daughter." The healer turned and herded his acolyte away from the rear of the cave. "Eat of this herb. It will fortify you against exertion and the cold."

Tek stared at the little clump of withered leaves drying on the low ledge bordering the grotto's wall, each three-lobed leaf nipped to a spiky point. The musky, bitter scent wrinkled her nose. Her skin grew taut, for she recognized the grey-green clump: an herb so perilous that even her father — for all his healer's skill — had always eschewed it. Though it temporarily masked hunger and numbed one to cold, its aftereffects were ravenousness and utter exhaustion.

Sometimes those who ate of it fell into such deep slumber they could not be roused. Others, tasting repeatedly of the herb, grew stark-eyed and wild, spooked by every bird and leaf, their ribs standing out like the bones of dream-haunts. Soon, even if they wished to renounce the herb, an irresistible craving compelled them to seek it out and devour it again and yet again. Eyeing the shriveled leaves, the pied mare shuddered.

"Would you poison both me and my unborn?" she whispered.

"List, daughter," the healer returned. "No more than two mouthfuls, and only that small sup because we are desperate."

He snorted unhappily, and the chill in Tek's breast eased to realize that he regarded her sampling the herb with as little relish as did she.

"Your dam, Jah-lila, brought these sprigs to me," he continued softly, "summer last while you were courting at the Sea. She would not tell me what purpose for them she planned, only that I should know their use when the hour befell. I suspect now that her seer's gift must have foretold your need to her."

His tone grew urgent.

"Great risk attends, to yourself as well as to your young — but even greater risk if you refuse it and remain here, or if you flee and have not strength enough to outrun your pursuers. I pray you, make haste and eat!"

Full of trepidation, Tek reached to nibble first one mouthful, then another of the shriveled wort, desperate enough to undertake even this to protect her unborn. The herb's bitter taste made her mouth draw, puckering her lips tight against her teeth. Her eyes watered. Her nose stung. Teki stood watching her. Presently she felt a tingling invade her limbs, moving in waves along her ribs. Her shoulders twitched. The grotto felt uncomfortably warm. She cavaled, lashing her tail, a sensation like summer flies swarming her flanks. What lay in her womb seemed to quicken and shift. The grey filly stumbled through the cave's entryway, and Tek jumped like a deer. Dagg followed, shaking heavy snow from his winter shag. He stared at the pied mare in surprise.

"What's amiss?" he asked. "Tek, I see white rimming your eyes."

Tek fidgeted, her heart racing. The herb kept it hammering against her ribs. She champed, trying to wash the unsavory taste from her mouth, but her tongue had turned to sand, her lips too numb to let her speak. Her throat closed up as she tried to swallow. Dagg's puzzled look changed to one of alarm.

"What's happened?" he demanded.

Quickly, Teki sketched the events of the previous hour. Dagg's eyes grew wide.

"How fierce is the storm?" the healer asked.

Dagg shook his head. "A true blizzard. The drifts will be deep before the night is done."

"Good." At a startled look from the dappled warrior, the healer added, "Tracks will be obscured and pursuit much hampered. You must be off, daughter, for I see the herb has begun its work."

Tek shook herself, sweating, unable to stand still. The heat in the cave oppressed her. She longed to be out in the battering wind, to cool herself by rolling in snow. The unborn young within her stirred and struggled. Her eyes felt glassy. Her mind seemed unable to hold any single thought for more than an instant before it buzzed away like a gnat.

"What ails her?" said Dagg.

Both he and her father seemed to be moving with maddening slowness. Still standing within the cave, she felt as though she were hurtling at a headlong run. Teki gave a reluctant sigh.

"I have given her swift-running."

"Ghostleaf!" Dagg exclaimed, giving the herb its more common name. The dappled warrior stared at Tek in dismay. The pied mare glared back at him. She felt skittish and resentful without real cause. The eyes of Teki and his acolytes distracted her. She wanted only to run, to lose herself in endless, heatless flight.

"But where is she to go?" asked Dagg.

"To her dam, Jah-lila," Teki replied. "Tek must seek out the Red Mare in the southeast hills beyond the Vale. Not even I know exactly where she dwells. . . ."

Tek scarcely listened, scarcely able. Already, in her mind, she bounded effortlessly through wind and drifts in the semidarkness of snow-lit night toward the far southeast tip of the Vale and the wild hills beyond. She had spent all her nursling days there at the Red Mare's side until, weaned, she had followed Jah-lila on the long trek to the Vale. Why had her mother done it? Why cast her away into the healer's care?

Reared within the great valley's sheltering slopes, Tek had never returned to the southeast hills since that distant time: herd-members were forbidden to traverse the Vale's boundaries on their own. Now she eyed the cave's egress impatiently, chafing to be gone, eager to once more run breakneck over the southeastern hills, free of kings and Rings of Law.

"Then how will she ever find the Red Mare?" Dagg was asking the healer.

Teki shook his head, his movements troubled, stiff. His acolytes milled nervously. Again, the healer sighed. "She may not. In such storm, anything may befall." Dagg stood speechless. The pied stallion glanced at Tek. "But she must try. You, Dagg, I would ask to accompany her — though I will give you none of the running herb. I doubt you will be able to pace her far, but I beg you to stay with her as long as you can."

"Of course!" snorted Dagg, wheeling. "Come, Tek. We must lose no time."

The healer leaned to nuzzle the young mare he had reared long years with brusque, awkward affection. She fidgeted away: the herb made her chary of any touch. Sadly, Teki gazed after her with ghostly, black-encircled eyes.

"All rests now upon the shoulders of the goddess."

"Hist!" cried the foal standing lookout. "I see figures, but whether the king's or others, I cannot tell."

"Off with you!" Teki exclaimed. "At once! If the Companion

who attacked Tek survives, I will doubtless be summoned to attend him. Out into the storm quickly, daughter — Dagg. Go now, and you will not be seen."

Tek bolted through the cave's entryway into the cool, stormy night. Snow lay deep; the wind gusted fiercely — yet neither seemed to impede her. She sprang up the Vale's icy hillside easily. Glimpsed only dimly through the falling snow, figures converged on Teki's cave below. Dagg had already fallen behind, panting with the exertion of the climb. How slow he was! Tek bit back a wild laugh. Giddy pleasure at her own miraculous strength surged through her. Let the king's wolves think the pied wych vanished without trace in a storm of her own conjuring.

Suddenly she was among the trees, the lower slopes of the valley lost from view. Her breath steamed; her heart sprinted. She wondered how long before the effect of the herb wore off. Morning, Teki had said. Was she to run all night, then, without tiring? Without feeling the cold? The prospect thrilled her. So must mighty Alma have felt prancing across heaven, tossing her mane and digging immortal hooves into the turf of the world, casting up mountains with every step.

Tek sped on through the snowy scrub and trees, skimming the hillcrest rimming the Vale, heading south and east. She heard Dagg crashing through the underbrush in back of her, plowing gamely through knee-deep snow to catch her up. She wondered how long she must endure his floundering escort, poor mortal, as he battled wind and slope, snow and the cold to exhaust himself in her wake.

I am the Mare of the World, she thought: *she who ran dusk to dawn, besting the sun in his race for horizon's edge, to become the moon that rules the night and wards all unicorns. . . .*

Laughing, the pied mare galloped on through the frigid, stormy night, lost in godlike velocity, dream motion, preternatural speed.

Nightmare

☽ 17 ☾

The dark unicorn twitched, shuddered in sleep, the dream unfolding before him as real as real. He beheld a pied mare bounding through wind-whipped snow, her pace hurtling, effortless. Breath spurted from her nostrils in jets of white cloud. A dappled companion plunged determinedly along her snow-filled tracks, his own gait staggering with exhaustion, ribs heaving in ragged gasps. He ran with a limp in one foreleg, as though the pain of some old injury, long healed, now recurred to plague him. He fell farther behind the pied mare at every step.

The dreaming stallion shifted, striving to move closer to the scene before him. He recognized this pair somehow, despite the distance and the dark, though whence he knew them or who they were — friends, foes — he could not say. Above them, a narrow gorge loomed, threading a path through the high, icy slopes of the great valley through which they fled. A howling pursued them, though whether of wolves or the gale the dreamer failed to discern.

Abruptly, the dappled runner lost his footing, struggled to rise, and went down again. He vanished from view in the whirling, blinding snow. Wild-eyed, the pied mare climbed on, sparing not a backward glance. The slender canyon before her was already so deep in drifts as to be nearly impassable: another hour would see it snowed under till spring. The pied mare pulled farther ahead now, where the dreaming stallion could not follow. Stormy darkness swallowed her as she disappeared into the pass.

Tai-shan woke with a start. He lay deep in soft hay. The wooden walls of his stall within the *chon*'s stable surrounded him. Firelight flickered, casting shadows. It must be evening, he realized groggily. His throat throbbed, burning. The muscles felt bruised. He swallowed painfully, remembering the strangling vines with which the purple-plumed minions of the *chon* had trapped him that morning in the square. Gasping, he struggled to roll to his knees, get his legs under him.

"Tai-shan!"

The *daïcha*'s soft voice brought him full awake. She knelt beside him in the hay, caressing his cheek and neck.

"Tash. Homat. Bithitet nau." *No. Stop. Calm yourself.* He was amazed by how much of what she said he was now able to understand. "Himay." *Stay still.*

She murmured on, other phrases he could not follow. With a square of white falseskin dipped in herb-scented liquid, she gently sponged the raw, oozing chafe marks encircling his neck. As the cool, pungent scent filled his nostrils, the dark unicorn felt the tightness in his throat begin to ease. Gratefully, he breathed deep. Still crooning, the lady dabbed the crusting scabs with tingling oil.

Wild longing filled Tai-shan to be able to respond to the *daïcha*'s words in kind. Just that morning, he recalled, before the arrival of the *chon*, he had managed to make himself understood to the aged firesmith and other two-foots in the square. But as he drew breath now to speak, his injured throat contracted hard. His neck felt wrenched. Half-stifled, he tossed his head, striving for air. A bitter disappointment filled him. The painful swelling would have to subside, he realized, before he could once more hope to replicate the *daïcha*'s gargled, clicking tongue.

Champing in frustration, he rose. The *daïcha* withdrew, slip-

ping through the stall's gate to rejoin her green-garbed assistants
who clustered there. Restlessly, Tai-shan circled the little enclosure, his breathing labored. *Why?* The outraged question burned
in him, unaskable. Why had the *chon* ordered his minions to
attack when he, Tai-shan, plainly had offered their leader no
harm, only sought to stand between him and the frail old female?

A stirring among the *daïcha*'s retinue made the dark unicorn
turn. A male two-foot approached, bearing a steaming wooden
hollow. His falseskin bore a decoration of purple and gold. With
a brief bow to the *daïcha* and her followers, the purple-badged
male began emptying the hollow's contents into the stall's feeding
trough.

Moisture came to Tai-shan's mouth as the savor of steamed
grain, chopped fodder, and dark, sweet canesap reached him. His
belly rumbled painfully. It had been nearly a day since he had
eaten last. The *daïcha* stood looking on with a puzzled frown. All
at once, her nose wrinkled. Hastily, she caught the forelimb of
the purple-badged male. With one forepaw, she brought a dollop
of the mash to her lips. Her eyes widened. She spoke sharply to
the purple-clad two-foot.

He bowed his head respectfully but stood firm, refusing to be
ordered off. Tai-shan heard the word *chon* pass his lips several
times. The dark unicorn eyed the provender in his feeding trough
suspiciously. Obviously it came from the two-foot ruler — yet
no *chon*'s minion had ever brought his feed before. Did the *chon*
intend this gift as a peace offering? If so, what could the *daïcha*'s
objection be — that the ruler had not come himself to deliver it?

At last, the lady broke off. Angrily, she wrested the wooden
hollow from the male and emptied the remainder of its contents
into the trough, then thrust the hollow back into the other's grasp
before striding purposefully off, gesturing her companions to remain behind when they made to follow. Tai-shan heard her utter
the word *chon* herself a number of times before she reached the
shelter's egress — as though she meant to seek him out that very
moment.

Gingerly, the dark unicorn sampled the fare before him, grinding the water-swelled grain between his teeth, crushing the tart, chewy berries and crunching the nuts. They had used honey, he decided, as well as cane. The mash was delicious. Eagerly, he bent his head to the trough. Swallowing proved painful still, but he was almost too hungry to care. The barest hint of bitterness undershadowed the sweet.

"My lord Moonbrow!"

The unexpected voice of Ryhenna snapped the dark unicorn's head around. A green-garbed two-foot proceeded down the aisle between stalls, leading the coppery mare on a tether.

"Ryhenna," the dark unicorn whistled in surprise, able to manage his own, fluting language well enough, though his throat still felt raw. Never before had he seen her — or any *da* — within this shelter, though obviously it had housed more than a few before his arrival. "What brings you here?"

The young mare tossed her head, crowding up against the gate of the stall. Before her, the two-foots fell back.

"I and my sisters are to be housed with thee now, by the *daïcha*'s command," she told him. Behind her, Tai-shan glimpsed her fellows being led into adjacent stalls. "O my lord," Ryhenna murmured, eyeing the bruises and abrasions about his neck, "tell me what hath befallen thee. The rumors have been wild! Such rushing about among our keepers this morn — stablehands beaten, stalls searched. When thou camest not among us in the yard at noon, I knew not what to think."

The dark unicorn shook his head and sighed. He had had no inkling what an uproar his absence from the palace would cause.

"I ventured into the city . . . ," he began.

"Into the city?" Ryhenna exclaimed. "Alone, before dawn? But the gate is barred, my lord."

Tai-shan cocked his head. "I went over the wall, of course. How else?"

Was such not the way *daya* departed the palace grounds when no two-foots were about to unbar the gate? The coppery mare simply stared at him.

"Over the wall?" she whispered. "My lord, thou'rt divine —

no mortal *da* might ever hope to clear a wall so high! And to wander alone through the City of Fire. . . ." Her tone mingled admiration and dismay. "How fearless thou art! What wonders thou must have beheld —"

Frowning, the dark unicorn snorted. "Ryhenna," he asked her, "have *none* of the *daya* here ever ventured forth into the city?"

"Never, lord!" the coppery mare exclaimed. "The city is forbidden to the sacred *daya*."

Tai-shan gazed at her in astonishment. Beyond her, more of the mares with whom he sported daily in the yard were being led into stalls. They glanced at him shyly, gladly, but said nothing. The *daïcha*'s followers, even the one holding Ryhenna's tether, stood off to one side now, murmuring quietly among themselves and watching him. The dark unicorn shook himself. The fire-warmed enclosure felt suddenly very close and still.

"Aye, I saw many wonders in the city," he told the coppery mare. The tightness in his throat was growing painful once more. "I met a peculiar kind of *da*, Ryhenna. One that called itself a gelding. It told me two-foots maimed it as a foal. I saw a firescar upon its flank and welts from blows across its back. I saw other *daya* cursed and beaten, encumbered to heavy loads by webbings of vine."

The coppery mare nodded, shrugged. "To haul and carry for our keepers — such is the gelded commoners' lot. Ours is a lighter service: sacred mares for brood and stallions for stud."

The dark unicorn blinked. "Brood?" he echoed. "Stud?" He had heard the odd words somewhere before.

Ryhenna nickered. "The taking of mates and getting of young," she laughed, "according to our keepers' pleasure."

Tai-shan stared at her, open-mouthed. "Are you saying the two-foots choose your mates for you?"

"Of course," the coppery mare replied. "Did we choose one another? Nay, for what mare hath wisdom enough to choose her stud, nor any stallion his mares? Our keepers choose."

"How do they dare?" the dark unicorn burst out hoarsely. "What gives them the right?"

Ryhenna drew back from him, surprised. "They have every right, my lord," she replied. "Our lives belong to them. The keepers *own* us, Moonbrow."

The dark unicorn shook his head, unable to believe his ears. His limbs had begun to feel strangely heavy and numb. An unpleasant warmth stole through him. The cloying taste of sweetmeal clung sticky to his mouth. He shook himself. The coppery mare fidgeted.

"What are you saying?" Tai-shan demanded of her. "Are the *daya* prisoners here? Do the two-foots hold you against your will?"

"Our will?" Ryhenna exclaimed. "Lord, we have no will. All *daya* must bow to the will of Dai'chon."

"What is this . . . Dai'chon?" the dark unicorn began. He felt flushed suddenly, and very thirsty. The coppery mare seemed not to have heard him. Her voice grew distant.

"Dai'chon directeth us to serve our masters. Thus hath it been for time out of mind. We know no life other than this."

Tai-shan turned toward the hollow of water that always hung filled and fresh beside the feeding trough in one corner of his stall. The scent of sweetmeal lingered in his nostrils, sickeningly sweet. The water in the hollow looked cool and inviting. Moving toward it, he stumbled. His own clumsiness amazed him.

"The keepers provide for our every need," Ryhenna was saying. "They feed, house, and protect us. . . ."

"Choose your mates for you," the dark unicorn muttered. "Trap you with walls, bind you to carts. Beat, brand, and geld you . . ."

"Nay! Not *us,* Moonbrow," Ryhenna protested. "Only commoners suffer so, and what do they matter? We sacred *daya* never haul or carry."

With an effort, Tai-shan turned to study her. She seemed perfectly in earnest, her amber eyes upon him clear and troubled. Behind her, her fellows milled whickering in their stalls, ears pricked. The dark unicorn staggered. The *daïcha*'s followers eyed him keenly.

"How then, Ryhenna, if you do no work," Tai-shan mumbled, his lips sluggish, tongue unaccountably thick, "do the sacred *daya* . . . serve their masters?" He had trouble completing the thought. "What do you . . . give the two-foots, in return for your keep?"

He grew dizzy. His vision blurred. Ryhenna seemed no more than a chestnut shadow. His legs collapsed under him, settling him heavily to the soft straw bedding of his stall. The depth of his abrupt fatigue astonished him. The bittersweet mash lay in his belly, weighty as a stone. The *daïcha*'s followers murmured gloomily. Soft, puzzled cries came from Ryhenna's sisters. The coppery mare leaned toward him over the gate of his stall.

"We give up our lives for our keepers, Moonbrow." Her words were the last he heard before darkness muffled all. "We die for them."

Magicker

) 18 (

Morning was half gone, bitterly cold, the sky above grey overcast. Not a breath of wind stirred. Not a feather of snow fell. The blizzard had blown itself out hours ago. Tek floundered through chest-high drifts. Wild, rolling hills beyond the Vale surrounded her. She had lost track of Dagg sometime the night before. Her limbs, no longer weightless, swung woodenly. The unborn in her belly lay motionless, still as the frozen air.

Keep going! she told herself, half rearing to shoulder through the next great swell of snow.

She must find her mother, Jah-lila, the Red Mare, soon, or she was lost. Wolves had been trailing her since daybreak. At first, the ghostleaf singing in her blood, she had easily outrun them. Now, the herb long spent, she staggered, hooves dense as meteorstone, near the end of her strength. Her pursuers' cries floated eerily above the rolling meadow: eager yips interspersed with long, trailing notes. They were nearer now, much nearer than before. Trees marked a canyon many paces ahead of her. The pied mare struggled toward it.

Casting over one shoulder, Tek glimpsed the first of the pack. A second and then a third burst from the scrub into open meadow behind. They bounded through the deep snow, joyous harks rising into wails. Frantically, Tek hurled herself against the drifts, fighting toward the forested cliffside, but her strength was gone. She stumbled, dragged herself up, collapsed again. She realized she would never reach the trees.

A figure burst from the canyon ahead of her: a deep cherry color as brilliant as mallow-flower against the trackless snow. Too large for a wolf, the red figure plunged toward her, black mane flying, traversing the meadow with a will. Dazed, staring, the pied mare strayed to a stop.

"Keep coming!" the other cried.

Tek plowed on toward the tree-sheltered canyon. The other unicorn charged past her, straight at the wolves. Tek swung around, astonished.

"Go!" the other ordered.

The pied mare plunged on. The wolves behind were howling, in full cry now. Did the Red Mare mean to meet them all? Pausing as she reached the shelter of the cliffs, Tek saw her dam pitch to a halt beside a pile of drifted snow. Twin branches rose from it, stark and leafless against the whiteness of the field. Half a dozen similar mounds clustered nearby. Tek herself had wandered through the midst of them only moments before. Furiously, the Red Mare began to dig.

Tek stared, baffled. The coming wolves bayed. Every few moments, the Red Mare lifted her gaze to gauge the distance between herself and the closing pack. All at once, Tek realized that what the other excavated was not a snowdrift at all but the carcass of a great deer, twin antlers rising like leafless branches from the snow. Others of his kind lay all around — a whole herd stranded, frozen. They could not have lain winterkilled long. The last flurries of the dying blizzard had barely covered them.

The Red Mare scraped and pawed at the snowbound stag. The wolves were very near. Jah-lila leapt away just as the leading three reached her. Snapping and snarling, two fell upon the carcass. Only the foremost bothered to pursue the dark red unicorn even a few strides. Jah-lila pivoted and lunged, horn aimed. The wolf dodged, turning, loped back to the carcass as the last of her packmates arrived. They fell ravenously upon it, tearing the half-frozen flesh to pieces, which they fought over.

Thus would they have done to me, given the chance, the pied mare thought, heart beating like a bird inside her ribs. *Or the king's wolves.*

Her dam plunged toward her across the meadow. Drawing even with Tek at the canyon's mouth, she tossed her head, motioning the younger mare to follow.

"Ho, daughter! Well met," she cried. "Come. My grotto lies not far above. Sooth, what a canny filly I bore, to recall the way home after all these years!"

Limbs tottering, Tek fell in behind Jah-lila, already climbing the steep hillside through the dark and barren trees.

The cave was deliciously warm. The narrow entryway turned back upon itself, kept out the wind and snow. Sunlight, too, faltered — but the grotto was not dark, for the upper walls and ceiling of the interior were covered with tier upon tier of fan-shaped lichens and mushrooms. They glowed in luminous blues and reds, soft yellows, pale mauves — here and there a faint, brassy green. They emitted warmth as well as light. Shivering, Tek stared. She had forgotten the ghostlight of her mother's grotto.

A huge heap of fragrant, dried grass occupied half the cave. The pied mare blinked, dumbstruck. How had such a vast store found its way here? The most any unicorn might carry was a mouthful at a time. Surely the grotto contained enough fodder for a dozen unicorns to feast the winter through without ever needing to venture outside for forage. How had Jah-lila acquired it all?

Exhausted, Tek shook her head. More than a day and a night had passed since she had last known food or sleep. She heard Jah-lila stamping in the entryway, shaking the snow from her pelt. A moment later, the Red Mare rounded the turn. In smaller alcoves adjoining the grotto's grass-filled main chamber other provender lay: bark and berries, spruce boughs, roots, seedpods, and nuts. Their tang made the pied mare's knotted stomach burn.

"Lie down, my child," her dam bade her.

Tek's legs buckled like shafts of old, dead wood. Her cold-locked muscles ached in the musty warmth of the cave. She had forgotten to shake off in the entryway, felt the snow on her beginning to melt. Lying down beside her, her dam passed a warm, rough tongue over Tek's shaggy coat, stroking her dry.

The pied mare closed her eyes. Her mother had changed little in the years since Tek had last seen her — coat still a brilliant mallow red such as no other unicorn possessed. Much about her mother set her apart, the healer's daughter mused. Jah-lila's black mane stood upright along her neck instead of falling silky to one side. Long, silken strands sprouted the whole length of her tail, not just at the end. Hers were a beardless chin, untasseled ears, and fetlocks unfringed with feathery down.

But most of all, Jah-lila's black hooves set her apart. They were oddly round: solid and uncloven, not like Tek's own split hooves — not like the divided hooves of other unicorns. It was those hooves Tek remembered best from her fillyhood. She had never realized how unique they were until she had followed her mother to the Vale and first seen the cloven heels and bearded chins, tasseled ears, fly-whisk tails, and fringed fetlocks of others of the herd.

Tek stirred, uneasy. Why had the Red Mare done so? Why abandoned her weanling to Teki's care and returned to the solitude beyond the Vale? Tek tensed, remembering how as a tiny filly little older than Lell, she had overheard the vicious whispers of her Vale-dwelling fellows, hissing that Jah-lila was not and could never be a *true* unicorn, since she had not been born among the herd, but in some far, unimaginable place. Red Mare. Renegade. Magicker. Tek's eyes came open with a start.

"Eat," Jah-lila instructed, nudging a heap of sweet-smelling fodder toward her.

Eagerly, Tek champed at the withered grass. Unpalatably dry at first, it soon grew sweet in her mouth, more savory than rueberries, sweeter even than beeswax and honey. The trickling of water nearby reminded her that her mother's grotto housed a spring. Thirst overpowered her. With an effort, she rose and followed the sound. The tiny stream at the back of the cave tasted warm compared to the frigid snow outside. In summer, she knew, it would have tasted cool. She drank deep.

"Rest, child," her mother murmured as Tek returned. "You need rest badly now — but do not sleep. You must not sleep until certain herbs for which I have sent arrive."

Sent? Tek scarcely knew what her mother could mean. Had the Red Mare acolytes, as her father Teki now had? All the Vale — herself included — had long believed Jah-lila lived alone, without companions.

"I," Tek started, stopped. Despite herself, her eyelids drooped. Sleep dragged at her. Her womb felt lifeless, her thoughts a blur. "Jan is dead," she managed. "Gryphons killed him. We pledged to one another at courting time. . . ."

"Peace," her mother soothed. "My dreams have already told me. I know that you are in foal to Jan and that the king runs mad for grief. I know that Sa, who sheltered you, is dead."

Tek stared at her, eyes wide suddenly. In truth, her dam's powers must be greater than she had guessed. The magicker smiled.

"Rest easy. Last night's blizzard has sealed the Vale. None of Korr's minions may pursue you now till spring."

Tek felt a surge of relief. A great heaviness had settled on her. Fatigue washed over her in waves. She wanted only to sleep. A sudden smarting brought her out of her doze with a jolt. After a moment's confusion, she realized the Red Mare had nipped her.

"Forgive me," the other said firmly, "but I am in deadly earnest. You must not sleep until the healing herbs arrive. Meanwhile, my dreams have brought me other news which may serve to keep you awake: they tell me that at the grey mare's funeral this day, Korr means to declare himself the Firebringer."

Tek turned to stare at her. "Firebringer?" she exclaimed, her grogginess fading for the moment. "Alma's chosen prophet?"

"Aye, Korr will usurp his son in that office as well — though the marks upon his brow and heel be only smears of white lime."

Despair swept over Tek. What did any of it matter anymore?

"Let him call himself the Firebringer if he will," she murmured dully. "Who shall contest him — Jan? Dead. Sa, dead. Dagg, lost. I and my unborn, forever banished."

"Jan is not dead," Jah-lila corrected gently. "Your mate lives. This, too, have I seen in dreams."

Tek started, stared, heart suddenly pounding.

"What are you saying?" she demanded. "Jan . . . Jan alive?"

The Red Mare nodded. "Alive, but captive — many leagues from here. A race of two-footed sorcerers holds him in the city where I was born a hornless *da* so many years ago."

My daughter stared at me as we lay side to side in the luminous warmth of my ghostlit grotto. The tiers of mushrooms and lichens lining the walls glimmered faintly, casting a moving pattern of light across her rose and black markings. Wild hope and confusion and disbelief played similarly across her face. Her fatigue seemed, for the moment, held at bay by the prospect of learning of her lost mate. I had hoped as much.

"Da?" my daughter murmured, frowning. "What is a da?"

"The daya *resemble unicorns," I told her carefully, measuring her, "though they live much briefer lives. Most are dead by the time a unicorn beareth her second foal."*

Memory of that long-past time and far-off place recalled once more to me the da *dialect of my youth, and I slipped into it now as easily as blinking. Tek lay watching me intently, hungrily.*

"Daya have no horns, nor beards, nor tufted tassels upon their ears," I continued, *"nor fringe of fine feathery hair around their fetlocks. They are mostly dull brown in color. Their manes stand upright along their necks. Their tails are full and silky, their hooves great solid, single toes."*

Still Tek gazed at me. "They sound like what legends in the Vale

*call renegades," she began, "those creatures unicorns fear to become if
we break the Ring of Law, becoming outcasts. . . ."*

She choked to a halt. I nodded.

"Aye, daughter, they sound very much like me, for though I now
bear a horn upon my brow, I've no beard as thou hast, no eartip
tassels, no fetlock feathers. My mane standeth along my neck, and my
hooves are uncloven. Nonetheless, I am a unicorn of sorts. And I was
a unicorn when I bore thee, though not when thou wert begot. Before,
when I lived in that sorcerous City, I was a hornless da like all the
rest, held captive by the keepers of fire."

"Firekeepers?" my daughter answered. "What are they?"

"The enemies of all daya: two-footed creatures something like the
pans in shape —" I saw Tek shudder at the mention of the goatlings
inhabiting the vast woodlands not far from my cave. I hastened to
add, "— though in sooth, pans are as different from firekeepers as
daya are from unicorns. These keepers hold my former people prisoner,
slaves to their treacherous god. . . ."

As succinctly as I could, I described to her the wretched lives of the
city's daya.

"I was able to escape that accursed place," I told her. "Drinking of
the unicorns' sacred moonspring far to the north, I was transformed.
Had I never found my way to that miraculous well and drunk thereof,
I should be a da still."

Tek's face was drawn now with shock, her inner thoughts as plain
to me as though she had shouted them: her dam, not born a unicorn?
Her mother, transformed from some degenerate, hornless freak by the
sacred wellspring that was the birthright of all unicorns — a birthright
I did not share? She shuddered now to realize that the strange, garbled
rumors she had heard all her life must hold some truth after all:
Jah-lila the outcast, the "renegade" — not a true unicorn at all!

"Who knows of this?" my daughter whispered.

"Teki knoweth," I told her. "To Jan once I gave the barest sketch,
on his initiation day. Now thou, too, knowest. And Korr."

"Korr?" The pied mare looked up, astonished. I nodded.

"It was he who showed me to the moon's sacred wellspring — though
such was against all custom and his people's Law."

Tek's eyes grew rounder yet. Clearly she had never thought the black king capable of even contemplating any breach to the Ring of Law.

"After fleeing the City," I said, "I escaped inland. Upon the Plains, I encountered Korr, the young not-yet-prince of the unicorns, a single-horned stallion far more magnificent than any da. His father, Sa's late mate, Khraa, was prince then, and Khraa's mother the queen. Korr, then newly initiated, used to travel alone outside the Vale, on fire to see what lay beyond, burning to contemplate the world.

"Though not strictly forbidden then as they are now, such expeditions were no less frowned upon in his day — but who dared gainsay the prince's son, destined to become prince himself in time? When he stumbled across me during one such youthful sojourn, I was yet a hornless da, wild and desperate from my harrowing flight.

"He mistook me for a renegade at first: one of his own people who had either deserted or been banished from the herd. Of course, thou and a few others well know that such outcasts do not lose their horns, thus ceasing to be unicorns — but Korr believed and still believes the old legends, as many do. Thus he shunned me, but at length I convinced him I was no renegade, that I came from neither his Vale nor the Plain, but from a far and different place.

"Learning of my flight from that imprisonment, he took pity on me at last, telling me of his own proud, free race and urging me to join them. He guided me to the sacred well, where I drank. And when, afterwards, I felt a horn sprouting upon my brow, I trusted that accompanying the princeling Korr upon his return to the Vale, I might find refuge there.

"And yet my strangeness lingered, a strangeness which no new-grown horn could dispel. Our travails in reaching the sacred well — in summer, when poisonous wyverns roved everywhere — had been terrible. Korr's guilt at transgressing an age-old custom began to weigh upon him. He feared for his future as prince, I think, should it become known that he had consorted with a once-hornless 'renegade,' betraying his people's secrets to her.

"In the end, he abandoned me, forbidding me to follow or try to find him. But I did follow, reaching his marvelous Vale. He pretended not to know me then. I called Teki my mate, for propriety's sake, *though we have never sojourned together by the Summer Sea, nor joined ourselves one to another as you and Jan have done by the pledging of eternal vows. Ours has been a partnership of colleagues and companions, not mates.*

"Teki taught me his healer's art, the ways and history of the unicorns, and I shared with him as much of my own lore as I might: starcraft mostly — he is no magicker. Briefly, I shared his grotto, but quickly saw how greatly my nearness, even as the healer's supposed mate, troubled Korr. Though the leaving of his strange, wild folk held much pain for me, I quit the Vale with the reluctant blessing of my 'mate' and settled here, in the hills, to raise thee.

"How sorely was I tempted to keep thee selfishly at my side, for though this life in the wilderness hath its rewards, it is lonely, Tek. In the end, I could not wish such desolation upon thee. The hardest thing I have ever done was to lead thee back to the Vale when thou wert weaned. And until this autumn past, Korr hath always watched over thee, from a distance, hath he not? Even favoring thee highly, for memory of me — and for his guilt's sake at abandoning me upon the Plain. My daughter, at least, hath lived welcome among unicorns, a joy I fear I may never share."

I fell still at last after my torrent of words, and my daughter lay in stunned silence, as though not knowing what to say. A long time passed as we lay there, face to face beneath the warm, shifting glimmer of lichenlight. At last, my daughter found her voice.

"If Teki who raised me is not my sire," she said simply, "then who?"

Her jewel-green eyes were watching me. Dared I tell her the truth? Dared I not? At last, I said: "A renegade — not a Plainsborn unicorn, but a true outcast, one who roved the Plain after quitting the Vale. A Ringbreaker, outside his people's Law."

Her gaze fell. I could not tell now what emotion lit her eye. Could she herself yet tell? Perhaps not. I dared to hope only that in the end, she would not hate me. I glanced impatiently toward the egress of the cave, anxious for the arrival of the restorative herbs my child and her unborn so desperately required. Luckily, she remained alert for the time being — no sign yet of her slipping into dangerous sleep. Nothing *to do but wait. Returning my gaze to Tek, I found my daughter once more watching me.*

"But what of Jan?" she whispered. "You said he lives — a prisoner in that sorcerous place, that city where you were born."

I nodded, relieved to have skirted so nimbly such dangerous ground. Blame my daughter's fatigue — and her overwhelming hunger for word of Jan above even her own history.

"Why did you not bring word?" Tek asked, her voice deathly quiet still. "Why did you not come to the Vale with word Jan was alive?"

I snorted. "And what good is my word in the Vale?"

"Korr has always respected your word!" the pied mare exclaimed.

"Feared it, rather, by my reck."

I saw my daughter's eyes widen. Clearly she had never considered that Korr might be afraid of anything.

I champed my teeth. "In his present state, I much doubt Korr would credit any news I uttered."

Tek fell silent a moment, mulling that. Her eyes flashed suddenly. "You might have come to me, at least," she said savagely, "told me of your suspicions my mate yet lived!"

I sighed. "I dared not. Korr had turned on thee so swiftly, so thoroughly, I feared my presence would only madden him further. And what better pretext to quarrel with thee — even do thee harm — than consorting with an outcast, self-exiled, a magicker, dream-walker, foreigner: your own dam?"

Tek fell silent again, considering.

"If my mate remains a prisoner," she said at length, "then no matter the distance, with or without Korr's help, I must go to him, rescue him!"

Her eyes were on fire suddenly. Vehemently, I shook my head.

"Even were this the mildest of winters, daughter, thou couldst never hope to complete such a trek."

I sensed outrage welling in my daughter's breast. Her thoughts once more showed plain upon her face: was she not a warrior, as fleet as any, and with more stamina than most?

As gently as I could, I said, "Starved as thou art and exhausted by flight from the Vale, thou must needs spend the balance of thy time at rest, recovering thy strength if thou art ever to bring safely to term what lieth unborn within."

To my midwife's eye, her pregnancy was now so obviously precarious that the least misstep might precipitate a miscarriage. Relief flooded me to see her reluctantly admitting the prudence of my words: she must do nothing further to endanger her as-yet-unborn filly or foal. Clearly her unborn's peril was very great. Yet dismay remained on her features for only a moment. Abruptly, my pied child's expression hardened.

"You must go, then, if I cannot." Once more she looked me in the eye. "You know how to reach this city of fire and where within the settlement its sorcerers are holding Jan —"

"I'll not leave thee," I answered sharply, surprised at my own vehemence. My daughter's dire condition had unsettled me more than a little. "Come spring, Korr will send searchers. He cannot but suspect where thou hast fled."

Across from me, Tek shook her head stubbornly. Alarmed, I risked greater candor.

"Daughter, without the herbs I mean to give thee in the coming months, thou wilt surely miscarry — or die in travail. Either may still occur. I must attend thee. I dare not go." Gratefully, I watched her sober. "Be easy," I hastened to add. "All shall be well. It is within my power to aid thine unborn mightily, making up for time and nourishment lost."

Tek lay clearly in a quandary now, her thoughts evident. "What is to be done?" she exclaimed. "Jan must be freed and returned to us — before his mad father destroys us all."

"Jan is safe enough where he is for the present. He's no hope of surviving outside the City till spring thaw, in any case. I am already at work to aid his escape. Once the grass is sprung, we must see which way the wind blows — but enough of this, daughter!"

I stopped myself suddenly, pricking my ears to sounds from without the cave. My pied companion's poor battered frame had begun to droop. It seemed she could keep her eyes open no longer.

"We will talk more of Jan soon," I assured her. "We have all winter

*to plan. Presently I will let thee sleep. But first, healing. Look: the
herbs for which I had sent have now arrived."*

Lifting her sagging head and dragging open heavy eyes, Tek
heard movement in the grotto's entryway. All at once, an unmistakable odor filled her nostrils: salty and goaty. The verges of the
Pan Woods lay not far off. Panicked, the pied mare was just
gathering her limbs to scramble up with a warning cry of "Pans!
Pans!" when her dam snorted, whickering.

"Peace, daughter. These goatlings are come at my request."

From around the curve which hid the entryway, two young
pans appeared, both females, huddled beneath shaggy drapes:
one bearskin, by the smell of it; the other, boar. Tek's nose ran-
kled. She stared at the loathsome, spindly creatures as both
dropped their cloaks by the entrance. Catching sight of the pied
mare, they grimaced, baring their square little teeth — or was
such the pan way of smile? The elder goatling grunted and twit-
tered at Jah-lila, gesturing with hairless forelimbs as she spoke.
The Red Mare replied with similar twittering, incomprehensible
to Tek.

"What," she gasped, "what do such creatures purpose here?"

"They dwell here," her mother calmly replied, slipping back
into the unicorn way of speech, "under my care." Smiling now,
the Red Mare glanced warmly at the young pans. "I found these
starving at wood's edge one day, years past. Their dam had been
killed by a cat and their people fled. I have sheltered and raised
them, suckling them like fillies. The elder already spoke enough
of their odd, guttural speech for me to follow. It is not so unlike
that of the two-footed firekeepers. And I have learned more in
conversing with other goatlings in the wood."

Tek shivered at the thought. Pensively, her mother sighed.

"But since many quirks of the face and forelimb also hold
meaning — and most of these I can at best only approximate —
I fear I still speak Pan but poorly. It has been far easier for these
two to learn Unicorn. They call me 'ama' now, which means

'mother' in their tongue. They are my acolytes: herbalists and midwives. It is they who gathered our grotto's winter provisions. The taller is Sismoomnat, the younger Pitipak. They have been eager to meet you and gladly scoured their home woods this day for the rare and perishable herbs you must take before you sleep."

Eyeing the ugly, upright goatlings, Tek felt her skin tremor. Despite her dam's reassuring tone, the pied mare could scarcely restrain her urge to bolt. Only overwhelming fatigue kept her reclining as the pair of pans approached, laying before her a great clump of ferny, withered fronds. They crouched then, openly curious. The younger one, nearest to Jah-lila, laid one slender forepaw on the Red Mare's neck and stroked her companionably. Jah-lila nuzzled the young goatling easily as one might a filly. All at once, Tek felt her revulsion beginning to fade. She could scarcely catch her breath for wonder.

"Greet-ings, Tek, Jah-ama's daughter," the elder, Sismoomnat, pronounced carefully, her birdlike inflection strangely melodious. "Wel-come to our home. We have brought you ama's herbs. Ama has told us you would find your way to us before the win-ter was out. We are so glad that you have come, and that at last we may behold you. Wel-come, foster sister. Wel-come home."

Sweetmeal
) 19 (

Awakening, the dark unicorn felt sluggish, strangely fatigued, though he was aware he must have slept long and deep. His mouth felt gummy, dry. It was morning now. He remembered vaguely leaving the palace grounds and wandering the city. How long ago? He stirred, trying to gather his clumsy limbs. With great effort, he heaved himself up and stumbled to the water trough, drank — but his head did not clear. All he longed for was to drift. He sensed movement and turned — very slowly. Ryhenna stood in the stall opposite his, her look one of apprehension. Her sisters occupied other stalls.

"How dost thou fare, my lord?" she asked. "Thou didst sleep so late, I had begun to fear. . . ."

The dark unicorn blinked, tongue fumbling over the words. "Tired," he told her. "Very tired."

A hazy memory came to him of green-clad two-foots leading the mares into the warm enclosure. His head nodded, thoughts slipping away. Time passed. A sound at the end of the aisle roused him. The dark unicorn swung himself slowly around to see the *chon*'s purple-badged minion coming down the aisle, carrying a steaming wooden hollow. It bore the delicious fragrance of sweetmeal. Tai-shan moved forward eagerly as the two-foot emptied the steaming meal into his trough.

Followers of the *daïcha* accompanied the male two-foot, but the hollows they carried contained only dry grain, which they poured into the troughs of the other stalls. As Ryhenna and her sisters dipped their noses to the feed, it occurred to Tai-shan to wonder why the mares should receive fare different from his own. He struggled to speak, but the same dulling sense of drowsiness he had suffered the previous evening was stealing over him again. He lay down heavily, numb.

Across from him, the coppery mare lifted her head from her trough. A worried expression furrowed her brow as she gazed at the dark unicorn. Tai-shan's vision blurred. Sleep dragged at him. He would speak with Ryhenna later, ask her about the feed, about what troubled her. Soon. Just as soon as he had rested and his mind grew clear.

Time drifted by. He could not say how long. Weeks perhaps. His injured throat seemed to heal in moments. The dark unicorn was only dimly aware of winter passing, waning. It would be spring again soon. Ryhenna and her sisters remained stabled with him within the warm enclosure, but Tai-shan never mustered energy enough to ask the coppery mare what plainly continued to disturb her. If only he were not so sleepy all the time! Sweetmeal was all the two-foots fed him now.

The *daïcha* returned at intervals to gaze at him, talk to him, stroke his neck. She seemed unbearably sad somehow. Messengers from the *chon* often called her away. The *chon* himself never appeared, though the ruler's purple-plumed minions stood constant watch outside the warm enclosure's egress. They no longer allowed the lady to lead Tai-shan to the yard for exercise along with the mares. The dark unicorn raised no protest. His strange, all-pervasive lassitude made any effort impossible.

But troubling dreams began to invade his sleep: a Vale shrouded deep in drifted snow, winterkilled unicorns lying frozen, others starving. He saw a night-dark stallion, stark-eyed and fanatical, haranguing the cowed, exhausted herd, a crescent-shaped smear of white mud marking his brow. Equally fervent companions surrounded him, their fellows moving in a pack through the crowd: harassing and bullying, demanding answers.

"Where is she, the pied wych? Did you help her to escape?"

About whom were they speaking? The dreaming unicorn could not begin to guess. All he saw seemed familiar somehow — yet memory slipped away from him the moment he woke.

Soon he no longer slept the nights through. Restless, unable to recall what frightening images had tangled through his sleeping brain only moments before, he often remained awake the balance of the night, reluctant to return to the unremembered country of his dreams. Mornings and afternoons, he dozed. Ryhenna, though clearly distressed, seemed hesitant to disturb him. As spring approached, his reveries grew more vivid. Often now he remembered snatches: before him in dreams, the moonbrowed stallion reared.

"I am your Firebringer!" he shouted. "Come spring, we must find and slay the pied wych who seduced my son. Only thus may we gain Alma's blessing for our war against the gryphons!"

The decimated ranks of unicorns groaned. Half looked as though they would not survive till spring — much less make war. Appalled, the dreamer recoiled. If only these dying unicorns had possessed fire, he realized, they could at least have combatted the cold!

Though the fearful images still faded rapidly upon waking, their foreboding lingered. By night, Tai-shan grew increasingly restive, and soon became too restless to doze the day away. Gripped by a vague yet mounting anxiety, he paced his stall for hours, ignoring queries from Ryhenna, whose concern now clearly verged upon alarm. Then, very near the start of spring, a vision came to him: he saw the unicorns' mad ruler ramping before the starving herd.

"By Alma's divine will, I command you — speak! Who among you aided the wych?"

His bullies nipped and harried the silent, sullen crowd. The black unicorn stamped, snorting. Impatiently, he reared — and suddenly his torso began to flatten, shrink. His lower limbs rapidly thickened and changed. For an instant, he stood with the body of a two-foot, moon-blaze white upon the breast, his hornless unicorn's head glaring wildly, teeth bared, hot breath smoking in the cold. Then the head, too, abruptly altered and shrank, becoming the dark-bearded face of the *chon*.

The bullying pack had all sprouted violet plumes from their brows. In another moment, they, too, had transformed into two-foots. The unicorns before them grew bonier, coats colorless drab, manes thinned to bristles, horns broken and falling away — until they had assumed the shape of flatbrowed, beardless *daya*, flinching beneath the bite of the purple-plumes' flails. The dreamer tried to cry out, "Apnor, 'pnor!" *Enough, enough!* in the two-foots' tongue — but coils of vine were strangling his voice.

Without warning, two-foots and *daya* melted from view. The dreamer found himself high on a peak overlooking the Vale. A great storm brewed overhead, black thunderheads churning and roiling. Merciless strokes of lightning flashed like the hooves of an angry god. Before their fury, tiny figures fled — but whether unicorns or hornless *daya*, the dreaming stallion could not say.

The stormclouds swept on, topping the snow-bound crags bordering the Vale and gusting out over the wild southeast hills. Winter snows melted, clearing a frozen pass through the crags. Suddenly, it was spring. Still spilling torrential rains, the stormclouds battered the wilderness, loosing mudslides and flash floods.

Wolves coursed the hinterlands, catching hares, foxes, ptarmigan, deer — even hapless pans foraging the verges of their Woods. The dreamer twitched. The dream wolves shifted, turned into bony haunts hunting down some unseen quarry, crying out above the stormwind in long wailing harks that sounded more like the belling of hounds than the voices of unicorns:

"Where is she hiding? Where can she be? We must track her down at the king's command!"

Still the dreamer had no notion about whom they spoke. On

a cliffside above, watching as they pounded by, stood a roan *da*
mare. The moon lay like a pool of silver at her feet. She bent to
sip from it, and her color darkened, intensified to true cherry
mallow. A black horn thrust like a skewer from her brow. Lifting
her head, she faced the dreamer, gazing at him with her black-
green eyes.

"Little did my former masters guess," she said, "that the fare
whereby they sought to tame thee would only open thy dreams
to my warnings at last. Behold."

The red mare vanished into the rain. Beside where she had
stood, the perfect disk of the moon lay flat upon the ground. It
tipped upright, balanced erect on its edge and became a mare.
Mottled like the moon, her color deepened from ash and silver
to black and rose. Heavy in foal, her sides hugely swollen, she
trotted restlessly, her labor pains begun.

Below her, the circling haunts raised their muzzles, turned.
Baying and whinnying, bones rattling like hail, they bounded
across the meadow toward her. Alarmed, the dreamer thrashed,
struggling to vault down from his mountain fastness and stand
between the bloodthirsty haunts and this unknown mare. But
walls of timber sprang up around him; vines suddenly ensnared him.

"Where is the midwife?" the dark unicorn shouted.

With a mighty effort, he burst the vines and vaulted the wall,
clipping one hind pastern painfully against its rough upper edge.
Plunging down the mountain's side, he found himself running
with ghostlike slowness, floating almost, as though he were swimming. Then he realized he *was* swimming: stormrains had risen
in a furious floodtide. An ocean now parted him from the pied
moon mare.

"Too soon," she moaned, gasping, unmistakably in travail. "Before my time . . ."

"Summon the midwife!" he cried out again. The pied mare
snorted hoarsely, in grave distress. The red one could have aided
her — but was nowhere to be seen. Frantically, the dreamer struggled across the endless watery gulf. In the distance before him,

the moon mare shuddered, collapsing to her knees. Bounding up
the sheer cliffside, her skeletal pursuers closed around her.

"The time of the Mare of the World betides!" the dark unicorn
thundered — and wrenched awake as one hoof struck the near
wall of his wooden stall with a report like a thundercrack.

The warm enclosure around him was all dimness and shadow.
Little white tongues of fire within the lampshells by the distant
egress burned low, fizzing in the silent air. Tai-shan struggled to
his feet, heart racing, the clear memory of his dream hurtling
through him still. Who were the figures he had seen there? He
knew them all somehow — though he could no more recall who
and what they were to him than he could recount his own true
name. Ryhenna, shaken from sleep, peered at him across the darkness from her own stall.

"Moonbrow!" she exclaimed. "My lord, what aileth thee?"

"I must get home!" he cried, staring about him.

He scarcely recognized his present surroundings, the vision still
coursing through his mind. The dream of that faraway Vale and
the unknown mare seemed so vivid, so real, it was the *chon*'s
comfortable stable that felt unfamiliar — unnatural — to him
now. Surely no unicorn was ever meant to be housed in such a
place: fed, groomed, and tended by sorcerous two-foots; head
compassed in silver; mind, will, and energy sapped by luxury.

Across from him, the coppery mare murmured, "Home? My
lord, *this* is thy home!"

Tai-shan shook his head. The adornment slapped against his
muzzle, jingling.

"It isn't," he answered. "My home lies far away from here. It
is a great Vale, I think, nearly surrounded by woods. I must find
it! My people are unicorns, not *daya*. I have stayed too long."

Ryhenna gasped. "Nay, my lord," she protested, "thou must
remain! Thy presence among us is the will of Dai'chon."

The dark unicorn stopped short. That baffling word again.
"Dai'chon," he muttered, cocking his head. "What is this
Dai'chon of which you speak?"

Ryhenna gazed at him blankly a moment, uncomprehending, then gave a nervous nicker. "Dai'chon is the one true god, of course! Master of the celestial fire, all-knowing and all-powerful — it was he that made our keepers and gave them dominion over *daya* and all the world. Why didst thou reck the *chon* keepeth this vast stable? We bluebloods here are sacred to Dai'chon."

The dark unicorn stared at her. "The two-foots' god — 'Dai'chon' is a *name?*"

Ryhenna nodded. The dark unicorn's mind buzzed. Until this moment, he had thought it merely another indecipherable word.

"Dai'chon . . . ," he mused, tasting the syllables on his tongue. Dai'chon had been the first word the *daïcha* had ever spoken to him. "It sounds very close to the name the *daïcha* gave me — Tai-shan." The dark unicorn shifted, suddenly remembering: "That morning in the square — half the crowd cried out 'Dai'chon!' to me instead of 'Tai-shan.' "

Again Ryhenna's nervous laugh. "Not by chance, my lord, for thou greatly resemblest the god. The *chon* is little pleased."

The dark unicorn wheeled. "Resemble —? What do you mean?"

Ryhenna tossed her head and snorted, surprised. "Hast thou not seen Dai'chon's image, my lord — as black of body as thou, but with limbs and torso of a keeper and the head of a *da?* He carrieth the crescent moon upon his breast, as thou dost upon thy brow, and thy tail is unlike the full, silky tails of *daya,* more like a whip or flail."

The dark unicorn felt his limbs go cold. He recalled the image before which the *daïcha* and her followers had bowed that first night upon the beach. He recalled similar figurines seized by the *chon's* purple-plumes in the square as well as the unicorn-headed figurines that had so enraged the *chon.* The coppery mare spoke on.

"When the great streak of fire hurtled out of the sky on the first day of fall, the *daïcha* declared it a sign from Dai'chon and set out in search of the firegod's gift."

Memory welled up in the dark unicorn's mind of standing

soaked and exhausted upon a silvery, windswept beach and seeing a red plume of fire plunge out of heaven.

"Weeks later," Ryhenna told him, "the *daïcha* returned with thee, calling thee Tai-shan. From the first, *daya* and keepers alike have whispered thou art the very image of Dai'chon: his steed, perhaps — or his messenger?"

The coppery mare watched him as she spoke, as though in hope of either confirmation or denial of her words.

"Many," she continued, "even dare to say thou art the god himself, openly calling thee 'Dai'chon' in defiance of the *chon*'s edict and bowing down before images of thee instead of those of the real Dai'chon. Perhaps it is the *daïcha*'s fault in calling thee a name so close to the god's — for now the people have confused the two, and the *chon* is furious." A moment later, as in afterthought, she added, "Furious, too, that thou hast delayed so long in taking up thy duties as First Stallion."

"What do you mean?" the dark unicorn asked again, baffled. He had lost her thread.

Ryhenna snorted, tossed her head.

"The First Stallion exists to get foals and fillies for the sacred stable," she exclaimed. "Yet I and my sisters frolicked daily with thee for weeks, and thou madest not the slightest advance."

Tai-shan shook himself, staring at the coppery mare. "You mean the *chon* intends you — you and your sisters — to be . . . my *mates?*"

Ryhenna stamped impatiently. "Of course. What else might I and my sisters be to thee? The *chon* is anxious for thee to sire more horned marvels such as thyself — not steal the people's worship from their god."

Tai-shan fell back a step, appalled.

"What are you talking about?" he demanded hotly. "Surely the *chon* knows — must guess — I have always meant to depart as soon as spring arrives, to seek my homeland and my people once more. I must leave this place!"

"No! The *chon* considereth thee no more than a strange sort of *da,*" the coppery mare replied. "He will never let thee go."

"Ryhenna," the young stallion told her, "I am no *da* but a free unicorn. How may the *chon* hold me if I mean to be gone?"

"By the same means he holdeth all my race," the *da* mare answered softly. "With ropes and tethers, locked stalls and barred gates. With whips and bits and hobbles — and with tainted feed that taketh away even thy will to rebel."

Her eyes flicked to his empty feeding trough. Following her gaze, Tai-shan felt a sudden chill.

"Tainted?" he said slowly, stupidly. "Tainted feed?"

The coppery mare avoided his eyes, her voice a whisper. "The sweetmeal the *chon* ordered for thee is laced with dreamroot. A healing herb, it speedeth the mending of wounds and numbeth pain — yet it can also induce trance, making the rebellious docile to the firekeepers' will."

The realization reverberated inside his skull like a thunderclap. The black unicorn stood trembling, stunned. The stable around him seemed to grow darker. Wind moaned beyond the warm enclosure's draft-tight walls. He felt buffeted, cold.

"So many times," the *da* mare whispered. "So many times I longed to tell thee — yet feared to rebel against my captors and my god."

Violently, Tai-shan shook himself. "The *daïcha*," he gasped. "The *daïcha* would never . . ."

"The *daïcha* hath no choice in the matter! The *chon* is her master as well as ours." Ryhenna shook her head, speaking more forcefully now. "The dreamroot he ordered lest thou go abroad in the city again, inciting heretical adoration."

Despite his belly's insistent rumbling, the dark unicorn felt his gorge rise. He'd not touch another mouthful of that tainted meal! Tai-shan ramped and sidled, scarcely able to contain his agitation. His mind raced.

"I must find a way to flee this place!"

Ryhenna ignored his protests. "Nay. Escape is impossible. Put it from thy mind. Repent thy rebellion and accept the will of Dai'chon. If thou wilt not, my lord Moonbrow, then I fear for thee in sooth. Even now, it may be too late."

"Too late?" the dark unicorn murmured.

Ryhenna looked at him hard. "I fear Dai'chon's judgment upon thee, my lord! Surely to entice the people's heterodox worship in defiance of the *chon* cannot have been the purpose for which Dai'chon sent thee among us."

"I am no envoy of this Dai'chon," the dark unicorn protested. "The two-foots' confusion of me with their god is none of my doing!"

"Such mattereth nothing to Dai'chon," the coppery mare snapped. "One may hide one's inmost heart from one's fellows, Moonbrow, but mighty Dai'chon recketh all. Twice yearly he cometh to judge the sacred *daya*. None can ever hope to escape his judgment — not even thou! I have seen his vengeance. It is swift and terrible. Dost thou not understand thy peril? The equinox is coming!"

Tai-shan shook his head, not following. "The equinox?"

Ryhenna came forward, pressing against the gate of her stall, her voice urgent. "On that day, every spring and fall," she answered, "a great procession of townsfolk ascendeth at dawn from the sea to the palace gate. Passing within, they proceed to the white clifftops overlooking the sea. In the fall, the priests cut the young foals who are to become geldings and the First Stallion defendeth his harem against all comers. In spring, Dai'chon judgeth the herd and chooseth who must follow him. Those *daya* the priests then drive forth to the kingdom of Dai'chon. . . ."

"Drive forth?" Tai-shan interrupted. "You mean they are exiled, sent into the wilds beyond the city?"

"Not banished," Ryhenna hissed. "*Sacrificed:* herded over the cliffside into the sea!"

The coppery mare fidgeted, unable to stand still.

"A place in that select company is considered the greatest of honors, a glory outshining all. I think the *chon* would rejoice to see thee among that company — for without progeny to redeem thee in his eyes, thou art more trouble to him than thou art worth. Yet the people adore thee. Were Dai'chon to claim thee, however, the folk could raise no protest. It is an *honor* to die for Dai'chon."

The dark unicorn could only stand staring, amazed at her sudden fire. His belly growled again. He ignored it angrily. Ryhenna eyed him with wise, sad eyes.

"My lord Moonbrow, thou hast but one real hope of returning from the white cliffs alive: fulfill thy role as First Stallion. What other choice dost thou have? Even a life imprisoned is better than no life at all! Sire progeny upon thy brood mares. If thou wilt not, I fear Dai'chon will claim thee at equinox."

Tai-shan shook himself. His skin twitched. Fear beat against his heart. "You think this Dai'chon means to kill me?" he breathed.

His stablemate nodded.

"Our dams tell us as nurslings that unlike the common *daya*, those sacred to the god do not truly die — that though our bodies may fall, we bluebloods house within ourselves a spark of Dai'chon's fiery breath that mounteth the sky in triumph and gallopeth rejoicing to the pastures of Dai'chon."

Ryhenna whickered without a trace of humor.

"But last year I glimpsed his chosen rotting on the rocks below the cliffs, food for scavengers. Though I hide it from my sisters, surely Dai'chon must reck my faithless, doubting heart, for I wonder if we bluebloods do not die like other beasts, and have no souls."

For long moments, the dark unicorn could only gaze at the coppery mare. Then slowly he shook his head.

"I'll not lay myself before the mercy of this terrible god," he told her grimly. "Ryhenna, I mean to quit this place ere spring."

"Too late, Moonbrow," the coppery mare whispered. "It is already spring. The procession from the sea hath even now begun. This morn is the morn of equinox."

Only then did Tai-shan note the hour. The little tongues of white fire in the distant lampshells by the enclosure's egress burned pale and wan. Dawn had broken. He had never noticed the darkness greying, the shadows within the stable thinning. He heard Ryhenna's sisters stirring sleepily within their stalls. Ryhenna told him: "This day, Moonbrow, must thou face the judgment of Dai'chon."

Travail

☽ 20 ☾

Standing at the grotto's mouth, the pied mare gazed out over the rolling hills. White snow still blanketed the land — but the smell of spring was in the wind. The two young pans, Sismoomnat and Pitipak, had remained in attendance throughout the winter, making only brief forays at Jah-lila's behest to gather medicinal herbs on the verges of the Pan Woods, barely an hour's lope away. To Tek's delight, a layer of fat had at last begun to sheathe her ribs, and her winter coat had thickened luxuriously. Her dam urged her to eat as much as possible to provide her unborn with all the nourishment she could.

Yet heaving her enormous girth about, Tek wondered at the strange herbs collected by the pans. Surely they did far more than merely sharpen appetite: with spring barely arrived, her belly was already bigger than many mares' near or even past their time. Yet months remained before she was due. Progeny conceived at summer's end never arrived until spring was well underway — unless they came too soon. Tek suppressed a nervous shudder. Earlyborns almost invariably died, often taking the mare with them.

But Jah-lila continued to assure her all was well. Tek herself felt hale and rested, and her young seemed vigorous. Indeed, the pied mare almost suspected her unborn must have two sets of heels, so often did she feel the kicks. Her unborn must be growing crowded in the womb, she realized, eyeing her moon-round belly. Tek groaned. She did not know how much more her sides could be expected to swell. She could barely stagger about as it was.

Nevertheless, her most pressing fears sprang not from her pregnancy, but from the certainty that once the snows of winter melted, Korr would send his Companions through the pass in search of her. Surely he must guess where she had fled. Resolutely, the pied mare thrust such bootless thoughts away. Her mother, she knew, kept careful watch. Tek suspected some of Sismoomnat and Pitipak's foraging expeditions were as much to scout for signs of the king's wolves as to gather bark and herbs.

Whenever the pan sisters returned, Jah-lila questioned them at length in their own tongue, a strange mixture of clicks and hisses, guttural grunts — even gestures that were, in actuality, words. How long had the Red Mare been treating in secret with the pans? Tek wondered. It astonished her how rapidly she herself had come to accept her foster sisters. Their gentle, affectionate natures were much at odds with the unicorns' long-held view of pans.

Before her flight, the pied mare had, like her fellows in the Vale, believed goatlings to be witless, speechless brutes. Now for the first time, she realized that discourse between her own people and the pans might be achieved: a negotiation of safe passage through the Pan Woods during spring pilgrimage and autumn trek, perhaps? Tek had mulled over the possibilities all during the waning months of winter.

And if truce could be reached between races that shared no common tongue, what might then follow between those that did? Perhaps parley — even peace — with species with whom the children-of-the-moon were in conflict: namely, the gryphons? And what of those with whom the unicorns were openly at war: the hated wyverns?

Standing at the entrance to her mother's cave, surveying the far Pan Woods, the pied mare shook her head, unwilling to take her wild musings further. They felt dangerously new and untried, reminding her keenly of Jan. She had always thought him an extravagant dreamer. Only now did she begin to wonder whether his more fanciful speculations might, after all, turn out to be of practical use.

Dusk drew on. Tek watched the gathering shadows travel over the snow-shrouded hills. Far in the distant meadow below, a small band of shaggy boar plowed their way through the deep snow. Tek shuddered, thinking of the wolves that had pursued her across that same meadow, months ago now. She paced restlessly before the grotto's opening, a vague sense of unease nipping at her.

She wondered where Jah-lila could be. After dozing the afternoon away in the warmth and pale glow of the cave's phosphorescent mushrooms, she had awakened only shortly ago to find both her mother and the young pans gone. Surprised, she had strained to her feet and taken up her vigil at the cave's egress.

The burden in her belly shifted, bearing down. The unaccustomed pressure made walking difficult, yet she could not keep still. Clumsily, she lumbered down the path leading from the cave — but quickly lost her breath. Her unborn seemed to weigh against her lungs. She stood lock-kneed for a few moments, panting, before moving on. Twilight deepened. The air grew dank and chill. She saw nothing of either the pans or Jah-lila. The boar in the far meadow had disappeared into the trees.

A ferocious storm was brewing to the northwest, she noted, ambling laboriously along the path. Darkness seethed and roiled over the distant Vale. Blue-white flashes illuminated the rapidly rising thunderheads. Dense and incredibly black, the clouds built with a preternatural swiftness.

The storm was spreading this way, she realized, catching the first whiff of freshening breeze. Stormclouds devoured the setting sun. *Best get underhill,* she told herself, swinging ponderously around. This was sure to be a violent blow. She hoped Jah-lila and her pan fosterlings would return to the grotto soon, hating to think of any beast caught out on such a night. The path back along the hillside's curve seemed steeper than she recalled.

Breathless, heaving, she had taken no more than a dozen steps before a crushing pain overtook her. Tek halted with a sharp outbreath of surprise. The pressure in her belly deepened suddenly into a pang. It passed quickly, but left her weak. Though the evening air was chilling fast, a fine film of sweat pricked her beneath her thick winter shag.

Alarmed, she had managed only ten more paces when a second pang constricted her, forcing her to exhale and drop her head. A low moan escaped her. This pain, too, was brief, though more protracted than the first. The pied mare's thoughts spun. Something must be badly amiss. She and Jan had pledged on the autumnal equinox, only half a year before. Her young would not be full term till near the start of summer, more than two moons away. Cold fear gripped her.

Desperately, Tek staggered toward the distant cave. Her urgency only precipitated another pang, which nearly pitched her to her knees. Wincing, she forced herself on. She must get out of the cold and the coming rain, back to the hidden grotto's shelter and warmth. Doubt chilled her. Could she even reach the cave? The path seemed endless, the grotto nowhere in sight. Another pain.

Rounding a bend in the hillside at last, she saw Sismoomnat, the elder of the pan sisters, standing in the grotto's egress, casting about worriedly, a bundle of newly gathered bitterbark still clasped in her forepaws. Was Jah-lila with her? Tek did not see her dam. Gasping, she managed a wounded warrior's whistle just as another spasm, the most severe yet, swept hard through her. She stumbled, crying out, heard Sismoomnat's answering hail and the rapid two-footed patter of the young pan's heels. A moment later, she felt the other's nuzzling touch as her mother's acolyte surveyed her with a few quick sniffs and glances.

"How goes it with you, sis-ter?" Sismoomnat asked gently, her flat, goatling brow furrowed with concern.

The pressure began to abate, not completely this time. Tek was barely able to raise her head and speak.

"Something . . . is wrong. Sharp pains . . ."

She felt the other's tongue tasting the salt of her sweat — more than a gesture of affection, the pied mare knew. A midwife could tell much by a taste.

"Come," the goatling urged her. "Walk while you may. Storm nears. Jah-ama is not yet home. We must make haste to shel-ter."

Drenched in sweat, Tek stumbled along the narrow path. Its gradual incline seemed almost insurmountable to her now. Though the pain had eased somewhat, she still had to halt, panting, every half dozen steps to rest. The cold wind cut into her coat. Sismoomnat leaned against her, supporting Tek with her own frail goatling's strength.

The cave's mouth loomed. Sismoomnat whistled shrilly through her teeth. Her sister, Pitipak, scampered from the grotto's mouth and hurried toward them. Tek put down her head. Her belly clenched again. She felt as though a relentlessly tightening band encompassed her. She heard the soft guttural cries of the younger pan, felt hairless forepaws caressing her. As she struggled through the cave's entryway, the warmth and windlessness of the ghostlit chamber hit her like a blow. She lost her footing, nearly fell.

"On-ly a few more steps," Sismoomnat murmured.

Pitipak darted ahead, shoving a thick bedding of dried grass into the pied mare's path. Tek collapsed onto it gratefully.

"What . . . what is it?" she gasped, in agony again.

"Birth pangs," Sismoomnat replied calmly.

Panic shot through the pied mare, redoubling the clenching jabs. "No! The foal isn't due . . . for months!"

The two pans had sunk to their haunches beside her, one on either side, buttressing her lest she heel over completely. Tek struggled feebly, but found herself too weak to rise.

"Too soon!" she panted. "I'll . . . lose the foal!"

She stared around her at the grotto full of roots and herbs — if only she had known which ones to take! A healer's fosterling, she held some knowledge of the worts that treated wounds and other ills, but none at all of those used in the midwife's art. Wild with frustration and pain, she half whinnied, half groaned. Where was Jah-lila? If the Red Mare were here, she would know what to do.

"Peace, sis-ter," Sismoomnat soothed, stroking the pied mare's neck and mane. "You need no herb to delay this birth. The pains are ear-ly, but Jah-ama has prepared for this. Have no fear. She will return from her task ver-y soon. Till then, we will aid you. She has instruct-ed us tho-roughly in mat-ters of mid-wifery."

The goatling's nimble forepaws smoothed and kneaded Tek's heaving sides with firm, steady strokes. The ache remained excruciating. Shuddering, the pied mare sensed the younger pan bustling about under her sister's direction, fetching this herb and that. A bundle of bruised and fragrant leaves was thrust beneath her nose. Sismoomnat urged her to breathe deeply to dull the pain. Tek tried futilely to deepen her rapid, shallow panting — but the pangs were coming harder and faster now.

The pains crowded out all else. She felt the unborn within her shifting, shifting with maddening slowness, as though overly cramped within her tightly constricted womb. Tek writhed and rolled, unable to find any position that could relieve the unrelenting contractions. Outside, the downpour grew deafening. Violent flashes of lightning seared her vision even through her clenched eyelids. Roaring thunder rumbled unendingly as though the mountain were preparing to fall.

Her mind glazed, only dimly aware how late the evening had grown. The birth was taking too long. In the Vale, she knew, most mares accompanied the midwife to the birthing grounds in the morning, were safely delivered by noon, then returned before dusk. But this arduous labor had already lasted hours without issue. A monstrous sense of foreboding gripped her. After a time, she realized it was full night.

No moon shone outside. Even without the storm, she knew Alma's heavenly daughter would not have lit the sky — for tonight was moondark, the time of the nothing moon, when the pale moon mare ran paired with the sun on the other side of the world. This was the night each month when unicorns of the Vale huddled underhill, hiding from haunts and spirits: a time of hazard and evil influence, the hour of freaks and miracles.

Superstitious nonsense, all of it, Tek tried to tell herself, contracting and crying out yet again. The young within her, striving so gamely to be born, would not come forth. At last her strength gave out. She could not even moan anymore. *Breech birth.* The realization rolled through her like the thunder. Neither she nor her foal would survive this travail. Mad Korr would have his victory after all.

Hollow hooffalls suddenly, barely audible above the booming of thunder and the clatter of rain. Tek smelled the sweet, spice scent of her dam shaking off in the entryway.

"Daughter!" Jah-lila's voice called, full of urgency and dread. "I came with all speed but could not outrun the storm. Curse the work that called me from you this day. . . ."

The pied mare could not answer, could not even open her eyes. She lay on her side exhausted, unable even to twitch an ear. No curiosity stirred in her to wonder what task had kept the midwife so long from her side. Jah-lila had come too late. Tek knew no herb could save her now. She waited only for death.

"Haste!" her mother was saying. "Sismoomnat, Pitipak — rub your forelimbs with bitterbark."

Someone lay gasping hoarsely nearby. Dimly, Tek realized it was herself and clenched her teeth against the sound.

"Reach, Sismoomnat," she heard her mother saying. "Aye, slow and smoothly — reach deep."

The pied mare felt a sudden pressure moving through her, gliding upward toward the womb. She kicked reflexively, but someone was kneeling on her hind legs, pinning them. She smelled her mother's rain-soaked scent, felt her reassuring nuzzle.

"Peace. Peace, daughter," she murmured. "All will be well soon. Soon."

Tek thrashed feebly, too weak to drag herself away.

"Have you got firm hold, Sismoomnat?" the Red Mare was saying. "Pull, then — pull hard!"

Something slipped struggling from her womb. Tek felt a rush of blood-warm fluid.

"Well done!" she heard Jah-lila exclaim. "Well done, my fosterling. Now, Pitipak, you must do the same: reach deep and pull, exactly as your sister did."

Tek felt again the sliding reach, the clench and pull — and her womb emptied suddenly, the sense of unbearable distention abruptly gone. She felt herself subsiding, her heartbeat slowing, pulse beating fainter, fainter yet. Weariness smothered her. She knew she must be dying now, only distantly aware of the young pans' joyous cries.

"Behold, Jah-ama!"

"So vig-orous — and so well grown!"

"Rejoice, daughter," the Red Mare whispered in her ear. "In thy progeny and Jan's brought hale into the world."

A sensation of warmth stole over her. The pied mare managed a wordless sigh. Her young lived. She had accomplished the task she had set herself in fleeing the Vale: to see Jan's offspring safely born. Her own life scarcely mattered any more. Surely her magicker dam could rear an orphaned filly or foal — even a suckling newborn — as she had the two young pans. Utterly spent, Tek drifted toward beckoning darkness.

The foreboding that had gripped her earlier, she realized drowsily, portended not the stillbirth of her progeny, but only her own end and that of this aged and withered season, now passing with great gnashing and thundering away. Winter's deathgrip was broken at last. By morning, the torrential rains would have battered months of snow and ice into muddy slush. Tomorrow would dawn the equinox, first day of the new and long-awaited spring.

Equinox

☽ 21 ☾

The dark unicorn stood on a vast clifftop. Swept clean of snow, devoid of vegetation, the broad, flat expanse before him lay fetlock deep in straw, withered flowers, and the sweet-smelling shavings of spicewood. Behind, the *chon*'s great timber palace stood. All around, a sprawling press of two-foots stamped and swayed.

"Dai'chon!" they chanted. "Dai'chon!"

The *daïcha* stood to one side of the crowd, flanked by her female companions and her green-plumes. The great crescent of skystuff gleamed silver on her breast. Behind her, the sacred *daya* of the palace milled, coats brushed to gleaming, manes intricately braided. Tai-shan spotted Ryhenna among the rest, her color all coppery fire. She huddled, miserable-seeming.

"Dai'chon!" the crowd shouted. "Dai'chon!"

Tai-shan remembered the arrival of green-garbed keepers to the warm enclosure scarcely an hour before, hustling the *daya* and himself from stable to clifftop through the surging press of celebrants, many of whom had fallen to their knees at the sight of the dark unicorn. Tai-shan cavaled and shook himself as petals and wood shavings, seedpods, and whiskered ears of grain contin-ued to rain down. Even here in the open, the thick, soft carpet of tindery stuff underhoof scarcely muffled the din. The noise on the clifftop was deafening.

"Dai'chon!" the crowd roared. "Dai'chon!"

Before the throng stretched an open space, empty save for a great dais of stone. Offerings heaped its base: provender of every kind, bolts of vivid falseskin, coffers of glinting river stones mixed with little disks of skystuff. Jars of oil and the dark, fragrant juice of crushed berries gave off a sharply aromatic scent. Beyond the platform stretched more open space until the clifftop dropped abruptly away.

"Dai'chon!" ranted the throng, stamping rhythmically. "Dai'chon!"

The *chon*'s purple-plumes held back the crush. Of the *chon* himself, the dark unicorn saw no sign. He stood trapped, purple-badged minions holding twin tethers to the silver halter imprisoning his head. An impassable sea of two-foots surged to one side of him. To the other lay only clifftop and empty air. Stormclouds roiled to the east at horizon's edge, devouring the rising sun.

"Dai'chon!" the crowd thundered. "Dai'chon —"

Without warning, silence fell. The rhythmic stamping abruptly ceased. Two-foots stood panting, covered with sweat in the cool morning air. Tai-shan's ears twitched. The stillness seemed to reverberate. Even the restless *daya* quieted. The only sound upon the clifftop now was that of seabirds and the foaming crash of unseen breakers dashing themselves to spume upon the rocks far, far below.

With one accord, the throng parted. A glittering raft, mounted on poles and borne upon the shoulders of eight brawny two-foots, emerged from the press. Hushed onlookers sank to their knees as it passed. Tai-shan recognized the conveyance as that which he had once seen carrying the *chon* — but the figure now seated upon it bore little resemblance to the firekeepers' king. Drawing even with the dais, the raft's bearers halted. Its occupant rose and stepped regally onto the high stone platform.

The dark unicorn stared at the creature now turning to face the crowd. Garbed all in black, it carried in one forepaw a vinelike flail, in the other a sharpened skewer. A white crescent moon emblazoned its breast. Yet though its body was that of a two-foot, the head resting upon those square, wide shoulders resembled a *da*'s, all black, with fierce, staring eyes and flared red nostrils. Black mane bristled down the arched and oddly foreshortened neck.

Before it, the great crowd of two-foots cowered. Across the open space from him, Tai-shan saw the coppery mare gazing at the dark figure in open terror. Yet despite its fierce appearance, the monster's head seemed strangely stiff, the eyes shadowy hollows. The ears did not swivel. Its lips — pulled back to bare square, white teeth — appeared frozen. The dry, red tongue within the gaping mouth never moved. The neck remained rigid. To turn its head, the dark unicorn saw, the figure had to pivot its whole torso.

At a peremptory gesture from the black-clad figure on the platform, the *daïcha* rose and approached. Tai-shan watched as she collapsed to her knees, folded her forelimbs across her breast, and bowed her head. The glowering godking brandished its skewer and cracked its vine. Lifting her forelimbs, the lady called out to the *da*-headed thing. The dark unicorn could decipher only a few phrases: "Emwe, Dai'chon," *hail, godking.* "Undan ptola," *by your will.* She seemed to be reciting both a greeting and a pledge.

Dai'chon answered nothing, only nodded its stiff, ponderous head. With a low bow, the *daïcha* withdrew, gesturing to her green-garbed followers. One by one, they led the sacred *daya* before Dai'chon. Pulse hammering, the dark unicorn sidled. His breath came in restive snorts. He could not stand still. No opportunity for escape had yet presented itself: his only choices were plunging over cliff's edge or trampling the kneeling crowd.

The parade of *daya* before the godking went on and on. Most passed by without a pause, but every so often, Dai'chon snapped its flail, and the keeper then before the dais halted, allowing Dai'chon to scrutinize that particular mare or stallion more closely. The watching crowd seemed to hold its breath.

Usually, the godking cracked its vine a second time; the *da* was returned to the *daïcha,* and the watchers heaved a heavy sigh. Sometimes, however, Dai'chon pointed toward the halted *da* with the skewer, and the kneeling throng murmured with delight as the *daïcha*'s minion then led his charge to the side of the stone platform nearest the cliff. The half dozen *daya* there pranced gaily, tossing their heads. Their keepers were hard-pressed to keep hold of the tethers. Tai-shan stared angrily, helplessly at the joyous *daya:* all blissfully unaware that they celebrated their own approaching death.

Ryhenna was among the last to pass before Dai'chon. The dark unicorn tensed, heart between his teeth, as the godking cracked its flail, signaling the keeper who held the coppery mare's tether to halt. Ryhenna stood wild-eyed before the platform, so plainly terrified that the dark unicorn half expected her to bolt. But Dai'chon snapped its vine at last and allowed her to pass. Able to breathe again, Tai-shan sighed deep with relief as the coppery mare rejoined the other, unchosen *daya.*

The last of the sacred *daya* was led before Dai'chon. With a snort of surprise, Tai-shan recognized Ushuk, the former First Stallion, whom he had defeated upon their first encounter, months ago. The godking seemed barely to notice the umber stallion, remarking his passage without so much as a crack of the flail. Crestfallen, Ushuk faltered in his gait. The *daïcha,* too, seemed puzzled. Her companions glanced at one another.

With halting step, the umber stallion allowed his escort to draw him on, but he gazed back uncomprehendingly at Dai'chon, plainly unable to believe the god would pass him by. The dark figure on the dais gave him not so much as a second glance. Instead, Dai'chon turned toward Tai-shan. Fixing its strange, shadowy eyes on the dark unicorn, the godking snapped its whip.

The whole crowd started. The purple-badged keepers holding the twin tethers of the silver halter stood riveted, clearly astonished by the godking's summons. Again, impatiently, Dai'chon cracked its vine. Tai-shan saw the *daïcha*'s look of puzzlement change to one of alarm as the *chon*'s minions began to tug him toward the stone platform. The lady took a step forward, as though to intervene, then caught herself. Champing and dancing, Tai-shan suffered himself to be led forward. What choice had he? There was nowhere to run.

His keepers halted before the dais. The lowering face of the godking glared down at him. Cavaling, the dark unicorn laid back his ears. Slowly and deliberately, Dai'chon held out the skewer. The crowd gasped in dismay. A single, bitten-off cry rose from the *daïcha*. Tai-shan saw her standing as though stunned, one hand to her lips. Her companions behind her murmured wide-eyed, some shaking their heads.

Suddenly, the *daïcha* was striding forward. She looked both angry and afraid. Halting before the dais, she cried out to the godking in exhortation and appeal. She seemed to be pleading with the figure above, very vehement. Tai-shan backed and sidled, pulling the *chon*'s purple-badged minions with him. The godking, still clutching its skewer and flail, stood with forepaws upon its hips. Slowly, silently, it shook its head at the *daïcha* and gestured once more with the skewer toward the dark unicorn.

Obediently, the pair of keepers tried to guide their cavaling charge toward the half-dozen chosen *daya* waiting on the far side of the dais. Snorting, Tai-shan braced himself, set his heels. The *daïcha* cried out again, desperately. She looked as though she might rush up the stone ramp flanking one side of the platform to confront the godking face to face.

Angrily, Dai'chon gestured toward a knot of purple-plumes, who started forward as though to pull the lady back from the dais. Drawing their weapons, her own green-plumed followers hastened to intercept them. With a shout, the *daïcha* threw up one forelimb to halt her followers, shaking her head. Both parties milled uneasily, the purple-plumes clearly reluctant to lay hands upon the lady, even at the order of Dai'chon, the green-plumes seemingly unwilling to clash unless their leader were more explicitly threatened. The godking turned once more toward Tai-shan.

"Flee, my lord Moonbrow!" Across the yard from him, Tai-shan saw Ryhenna rear up suddenly among her fellows. "Flee *now* — ere the god ordereth his *chon*'s guard to drive thee over the cliff!"

All around her, *daya* shied in confusion. Startled two-foots scattered. Their cries amid the sudden commotion halted Dai'chon, his skewer and flail half-raised. Ramping and flailing, the coppery mare plunged through the sacred herd. In the same instant, Tai-shan wrenched free of his keepers' grasp and wheeled to face the sacrificial *daya*.

"Run! Run, all of you!" he shouted. "Only death lies beyond the drop. Flee for your lives!"

Between the platform and cliff's edge, the sacrificial *daya* danced anxiously, tossing their heads violently and rolling their eyes. They seemed more afraid of him than of their own captors, the dark unicorn realized in dismay. Two-foot keepers stroked and soothed their skittish charges. At an impatient gesture from Dai'chon, Tai-shan saw his own pair of keepers starting toward him. With a peal of rage, the dark unicorn flew at them. Shouting, they scrambled away through the scattered hay and wood shavings. Behind, the sacrificial *daya* shied. Keepers grasped halter leads in both forepaws, struggling to hold them.

On the stone platform before them, Dai'chon cried out. Tai-shan spun around, startled to hear the godking's voice for the first time. It was low-pitched and strangely muffled, like a cry from deep underhill. The godking gestured with its skewer, and several of the purple-plumes cast aside their staves, rushing Tai-shan with forelimbs outstretched to catch his tethers. The dark unicorn charged them, lashing with his forehooves. The purple-plumes dodged, crying out in fear. Across from him, many of the *daya* around Ryhenna had already bolted. Others now fought their tethers, screaming to break free.

Tai-shan saw the *daicha*'s green-garbed followers striving desperately to hold and calm what *daya* they could. Their lady stood poised, as though uncertain. Then all at once, she rushed to snatch a tether from her minion's grasp. Shouting, she struck the frightened mare across the flank, sending her careening away after

the others that had broken free. Calling sharply to the rest of her
followers, the *daïcha* dashed among the remaining *daya*, waving
her forelimbs and hying the last of the skittish beasts to bolt. The
throng about the palace surged to their feet and erupted in chaos
as stampeding *daya* hurtled through their midst.

Tai-shan circled, making to herd the sacrificial *daya* away from
cliff's edge. Dai'chon's muffled shouts and angry gestures continued. More of the *chon*'s purple-plumes responded, some turning
to chase fleeing *daya*, others coming on toward Tai-shan. At a
shout from the *daïcha*, her own green-plumed guards hastened
to form a line before the advancing purple-plumes to prevent
their reaching the dark unicorn. Ushuk thundered past just as the
green-plumes closed ranks.

"Blasphemer!" the umber stallion shouted, storming toward
Tai-shan. "How darest thou defy the will of the god?"

The dark unicorn ducked and fell back, too surprised at first
to defend himself.

"*Homat!* Ushuk, stop!" Tai-shan heard Ryhenna crying. She,
too, had broken through the *daïcha*'s line of green-plumes. "Did
thy first encounter with black Moonbrow teach thee nothing?
Thou'rt overmatched!"

The umber stallion responded with a growl. "Cursed mare, to
join this *punuskr* — this demon — in defiance of Dai'chon. Thou
shalt share his fate!"

Again he flew at the dark unicorn. Once more Tai-shan dodged
and fell back, sidestepping the abandoned conveyance resting on
the ground before the godking's dais, its bearers long since fled.

"I served the godking joyfully all my days," the umber stallion
cried, his eyes wide and bloodshot, the snorted spray from his
nostrils flecked with blood. "In the end I proved unworthy, and
he cast me aside. Yet still I worship and adore him. *Dai'chon
undan ptola* — the godking's will be done!"

Ushuk lunged, flailing recklessly at Tai-shan. Unwilling to use
his horn against a flatbrowed adversary, the dark unicorn reared
and threw one shoulder against the other. Ushuk's hind hooves
skidded on the soft, slippery carpet of wood shavings. One pole

of the *chon*'s raft caught his legs. Thrashing, the umber stallion toppled. Tai-shan heard the *daïcha*'s horrified cry as, squealing in pain, Ushuk struggled up from the chaff and tinder, one foreleg shattered.

"Himay," he heard the *daïcha* calling. "Ushuk, himay!" *Stand still*.

The dark unicorn recoiled in dismay. The limbs of *daya* must be fragile as deer's! Ushuk staggered, blundering on three limbs back through the ranks of the green-plumes still holding off the *chon*'s purple-plumed guards. At a snarl from Dai'chon on the platform above, purple-plumes surrounded the injured stallion.

"Tash — 'omat!" the lady cried: *No — stop!*

Ignoring her, the godking made a furious gesture. One of the *chon*'s minions lifted a thin slice of skystuff to the great vein of Ushuk's throat and drew the blade across. The umber stallion collapsed with a shriek. He thrashed for a moment, blood spattering the bone-dry tinder. Then he lay still. The dark unicorn stared, stunned, unable to take it in. With a healer's care, Ushuk's limb might have mended! Shaken and sick, Tai-shan backed away.

Behind him, he heard Ryhenna scream. Whirling, he saw Dai'chon kneeling on the platform's edge, Ryhenna's tether grasped in one forepaw. Trembling, the coppery mare tugged and tried to back away — but she seemed almost paralyzed with fright. The godking spoke soothingly in its strange, hollow-sounding voice. It pulled her head closer. Eyes rolling, the coppery mare whinnied shrilly as, crooning, the godking placed the point of the long, sharp skewer to her throat.

"Tash! 'Omat!" shouted Tai-shan, vaulting onto the high stone platform.

He lunged to catch the skewer's length against his horn and bat it away. With a cry, Dai'chon fell back, releasing Ryhenna. The dark unicorn reared. Growling, the *da*-headed creature slashed at him. Tai-shan parried, sweeping his horn to once more knock aside the blade. The godking ducked, dodged. Tai-shan felt his horn strike a solid blow and leapt back astonished — for the other's neck was hard as wood, with none of the give of mortal flesh. The sound of the blow rang hollowly, like a hoof-stamp on a rotten log. Dai'chon staggered. The head upon the creature's shoulders wobbled. A moment later, it fell. Tai-shan cried out. His blow had held neither aim nor force enough to have severed his opponent's gorge — and yet Dai'chon's strange, stiff head toppled with a hollow thump to the dried petals and wood shavings littering the dais. Dumbstruck, the dark unicorn stared at the creature before him. Though beheaded, it still possessed a head: a round, two-foot head upon a squat, two-foot neck. An ordinary firekeeper stood before him, one whose real head had been concealed beneath a hollow artifice of wood. The unmasked keeper glared at Tai-shan, black eyes furious, his own teeth bared as fiercely as the carved teeth of the wooden godhead had been. The dark curls of the other's hair and beard were slick with sweat. An instant later, the dark unicorn recognized him.

"The *chon!* The *chon,*" Ryhenna below him cried. "No god at all!"

Similar screams came from the stampeding *daya*. Shrieks and wails rose from the scattering two-foots as well. Eyes wide with betrayal, faces drawn with shock, the commonfolk of the city scrambled to flee. Yet the two-foots of the palace reacted differently. The *daïcha*'s companions and her green-garbed followers, plumed guards of both colors as well as the *chon*'s purple-badged underlings, while clearly outraged at their ruler's unmasking, did not seem the least surprised to discover their mortal leader impersonating a god. Even the *daïcha*, the dark unicorn realized in astonishment, had known all along.

A stinging welt across one shoulder brought Tai-shan sharply around. The *chon* had lunged at him again, slashing with the skewer and lashing with the flail. The dark unicorn dodged, back-stepping. Ryhenna's cry came almost too late.

"My lord Moonbrow, the edge!"

Wheeling, Tai-shan sprang away barely in time. The *chon* had sought to drive him backward over the stone platform's brink. Shouting, the two-foot ruler pursued him across the dais, cracking the stinging lash. As the dark unicorn ducked, the lash coiled itself about his horn. With a heave of neck and shoulders, Tai-shan jerked it from the two-foot's grasp and slung it spinning off across the clifftop into the empty air beyond. It hung a moment against the gathering stormclouds, before vanishing. Growling with rage, the *chon* redoubled his attack with the blade.

"'Ware the *chon*'s guard!" Ryhenna cried.

Tai-shan glimpsed a handful of purple-plumes breaking through the *daïcha*'s green-plumed defenders to rush the dais. Ryhenna dashed to the foot of the platform's ramp, blocking their path. The purple-plumes fell back in confusion as the wild mare reared and struck at them. Tai-shan returned his attention to the *chon*, countering the other's lunges and blows, parrying each feint and thrust. The nimbleness of this puny, upright creature astonished him. Though the *chon* possessed not nearly the strength of a full-grown unicorn, the sweep and agility of his forelimb gave him great range. Tai-shan had never fenced such a dexterous foe. The dark unicorn plunged, pivoted, ramped, and dodged.

His hooves grew hot. Churning and plunging through the dry stuff strewn about the platform, he felt his heels striking the flinty stone beneath. Flashes of white and amber light leapt from his hooves. More flashes showered down as his horn grated against the skewer of the *chon*. Sparks! Sparks of fire were falling from his horn as it struck against the skystuff — more springing up from his hooves as they skidded on the stone: sparks such as he had once seen leap from the tools of the two-foot firesmith. Now his own hooves and horn were doing the same! Astonished, the dark unicorn stared.

"Look! Look!" Ryhenna below him cried. Many of her fleeing companions had halted, gazing in open wonder at the bright rain falling from his hooves and horn. "Here standeth the true Dai'chon, full of the divine fire!"

Lighting upon the platform's thick carpet of dry hay, withered flower petals, and aromatic wood shavings, the sparks began to smolder. Black stormclouds were fast sweeping in across the sea. A warm, wet wind picked up. Bits of burning chaff gusted from the dais to the open space below, catching in the dried stuff there. A thick pall of smoke rose, filling the air with cinders. Plumed two-foots of both colors tore off their outer falseskins and flailed at the spreading flames.

Choking, the *chon* covered his mouth and nose with one forepaw — yet still he fought. Tai-shan clashed and countered, gasping for breath, until in a furious assault, he drove the two-foot ruler to one knee and disarmed him with a parry that knocked the skewer from his grip and sent it, like the flail before it, spinning away into the emptiness beyond the cliff. The dark unicorn ramped before the defeated *chon,* whose bloodshot eyes glared back at him, full of hatred still.

"Tash! Tash so bei!" The *daïcha* rushed past Ryhenna up onto the platform to interpose herself between the dark unicorn and the *chon.* "Tash bei im chon!"

Tai-shan knew she must be saying, *No, don't kill him. Don't kill my king*.

Fury burned in the dark unicorn. At that moment, he wanted nothing other than to skewer the treacherous two-foot ruler — but the *daïcha* stood suppliant before him, and he owed her his life. Forehooves touching the ground once more, Tai-shan shook himself. A kind of silence fell around him. With great difficulty, summoning all the agility of lips and teeth not made to frame such speech, he strove to pronounce clearly the words of the firekeepers' tongue.

"Undan ptola, daïcha," he told her. *As you wish*.

The other's eyes widened. She gazed at the dark unicorn as though unable to believe her ears. The purple-plumes below the dais stood halted in wonder. The green-plumes, too, had heard. They stood staring. Beyond them, the *daïcha*'s companions sank to the ground, two of them weeping. On the dais, ashen-faced, the *chon* shook his head.

"Tash," he gasped. "Tash — ipsicat!"

Tai-shan did not recognize the second word, but he could

guess its meaning: *No. No — impossible.* The *chon* made as if to rise.

"Tash! 'Omat!" the dark unicorn ordered. *No. Stop.* "Himay." *Keep still.*

The *chon* choked out something else, too fast for Tai-shan to follow. What was he saying now, the dark unicorn wondered, that *daya* — even miraculously horned, outland *daya* — ought not be able to speak?

"Jima 'pnor!" *That's enough,* the dark unicorn commanded, cutting the *chon* off as he spoke. "Asolet." *Silence.* Again the other made to rise, but the dark unicorn stopped him with a feint of his horn. "Tash bim!"

He did not know the phrase for *Come no nearer* and so had to settle for *Do not come.* Tai-shan stamped angrily, galled by his lack of words.

"Ipsicat!" the *chon* whispered again. *Impossible.* Then, gesturing with his forelimb, he shouted suddenly, "Punuskr!"

Tai-shan recognized the term: *demon.* A string of epithets followed, too rapid for the dark unicorn to decipher. From the other's furious tone, however, it was clear they were dire threats. The *chon* motioned to his purple-plumes, shouting.

"Bei so! Bei so ahin!"

The dark unicorn needed no translation to tell him the *chon* was shouting, *Kill him. Kill him now!* But the purple-plumes at the foot of the dais stood motionless, eyes wide with awe. Several fell to their knees, gasping, "Dai'chon!"

The cry was taken up among the green-plumes, a ragged chant. "Dai'chon! Dai'chon!"

Upon the dais, the *daïcha* sank to her knees as well, bowing her head and crossing her forelimbs over her breast. Below, her green-plumes did the same.

"Emwe," she murmured. "Emwe, Dai'chon!"

Below them, the whole clifftop seethed in confusion. Wildfire leapt and crackled. Stormwind had picked up, fanning the flames. Screaming *daya* dashed madly about. Frightened two-foots cowered or tried frantically to flee, but the passageways beside the palace had become so crowded as to be impassable. The palace itself was on fire now. Heaped about the base of the dais, offerings kindled and burned.

A scream from Ryhenna caused Tai-shan to wheel. Fire from the burning offerings had set her mane alight. With shrills of terror, the coppery mare bolted. The dark unicorn sprang after her, vaulting down from the dais through a veil of fire and smoke. He sprinted behind her, crying her name.

"Ryhenna, stop!" he shouted. "Turn — you'll run over the edge!"

The smoke and cinders grew so thick, he could not see her. Then he caught a glimpse of coppery flank. The smoke parted suddenly — just as the earth vanished beneath his heels. Ryhenna hung in the air before him. He glimpsed realization in her eye, felt horror clutch like a many-toed suckerfish at his own breast.

He tried to wheel, to regain solid ground: far too late. His legs flailed only empty air. Ryhenna plunged helplessly beside him. The roiling white sea dashed upward toward them. A great crack of thunder sounded, accompanied by a bitter odor and a blue-white flash. Lightning had struck the clifftop behind — above them now. They were falling.

So, too, did I fall, a voice whispered to him, *not so long ago. It seemed to take forever — though I fell toward frozen earth, not foaming sea.*

The dark unicorn twisted, astonished, still capable of astonishment even now. The quiet voice was infinitely familiar to him — surely the same that had spoken half a year before to him standing nameless upon the strand.

"Who are you?" he cried out.

Your own granddam, of course, the whisper replied. *Who else would I be?*

Memory stirred in him, hazy and distant still. "Sa? My father's dam?"

The hurtling wind whistled past his ears. *Once I was Sa. I am part of Alma now.*

"You told me to find the fire. But the fire was within me," the dark unicorn gasped. "It was within me all along!"

The sky around him seemed to nod in affirmation. *Ever since your initiation pilgrimage, two years past, when I touched your hooves with fire in the Pan Woods, and then your horn in the wyvern's den.* He remembered suddenly, clearly, standing upon the banked coals of a goatling campfire and later bathing his horn in the firebowl of a wyvern sorceress. The air sighed. *I have been waiting such a long time for you to discover that spark within.*

Falling, he answered bitterly, "I've set the clifftop alight with that spark. They're all trapped. Now two-foots and *daya* alike will perish —"

No one will perish, the voice murmured. *Any moment, my Red Mare's conjured rain will douse that blaze. The fire you have kindled in their minds, however, will burn a long time after this day. Your spark will transform the city. The power of the* chon *lies in ruins now. The* daïcha *will lead the firekeepers from this hour forward, and Dai'chon come to be worshiped in a new and gentler way. It will take time, to be sure, but it will come — because of you, my Firebringer. Did you think it your destiny to dance fire solely among the unicorns?*

Beside him in the air, Ryhenna screamed and flailed. Droplets pelted them. He thought at first they were spray from the frothing waves below. Then he realized they came from overhead: rain — a driving rain hard enough to damp the wildfire raging across the clifftop above. In that, at least, the goddess spoke true: those trapped on the cliff would live, though he and the coppery mare perished.

"Take my life," he besought Alma, "but spare Ryhenna."

The goddess laughed, very gently, as he and his companion plunged. The storm-tossed sea surged up to meet them. *But I already hold your life, Aljan, son of my son, Dark Moon.*

Moondark

) 22 (

The pain had passed. A dim haze of morning light filtered into the grotto, augmenting the wan lichenlight of the cavern's walls. The pied mare lay quiet, unable to focus her thoughts. A delicious drowsiness enveloped her. Her mouth tasted smoky-sweet of rosehips. She had no memory of chewing the herb, only of hours of travail the evening before. She was alive, and the knowledge astonished her.

Warm, dry hay had been heaped around her. Sismoomnat, the elder of her foster sisters, crouched nearby, stroking her neck and crooning in the oddly musical, half-grunted language of pans. The goatling held a clump of dried seedgrass near the pied mare's nose, offering it to her. Tek managed to turn her head away. She had no desire as yet for food.

The young pan vanished from beside her, to reappear holding forepaws cupped before her. Tek's response to the smell of water surprised even herself: slurping the delicious contents of her foster sister's palms in a single sup. Twittering with pan laughter, Sismoomnat brought her another drink, another, and another yet. Dozens of swallows at last assuaged the pied mare's thirst.

The muffled sound of her mother's voice reached her then, muttering low and urgently. A strange aroma pervaded the cave: a faint, slightly bitter savor, as of chewed roots or bark. Tek tried weakly to raise her head, and Sismoomnat helped, lifting the pied mare's cheek to rest on her shaggy flank. Their dam stood across the grotto, in the shadows where few of the faintly glowing lichens grew. The Red Mare swayed, lock-kneed in trance, chanting softly: "Brothers-in-ocean, sisters-in-the-waves: swift-coursers, far-rovers, aid us! Two of our kind are in gravest peril. Dreams speak to me of this."

Tek had no notion what her mother might be doing — petitioning some unseen listener? The Red Mare's chanting continued, endless, monotonous. Tek's perceptions grew foggy. Even the slight effort of resting her head on Sismoomnat's flank exhausted her. She felt herself drifting into sleep.

Something nipped at her, rustling the hay. The pied mare jerked awake, struggling feebly. Her limbs did little more than twitch. Sismoomnat stroked her neck and murmured soothingly, then gently turned the pied mare's head, holding it so that Tek could view her own side and flank. Her belly, relieved now of its months-long burden, seemed oddly flattened to her eye, grown accustomed to the huge swell of her pregnant side. The younger pan, Pitipak, crouched near the pied mare's hindquarters, stroking something which nestled against Tek's belly.

"Seek them for me, my sisters-in-ocean!" Her mother's soft, urgent chanting continued. "Already you are coasting the Summer shore, traveling to the sacred shoals off the Gryphon Mountains to calve. My fellows are struggling not far from you. Aid them, my brothers-in-the-waves."

Tek paid scant attention, gazing instead at the young pan beside her, who sang and murmured while she herself stared blearily, trying to focus her eyes. A warm tide of relief flowed through the pied mare suddenly as she spotted the tiny, newborn unicorn lying suckling beside her. She felt exhausted and euphoric and utterly light. The little creature struggled, shifting the hay. Tek felt its toothless gums again, nipping insistently at the teat. Deeply, she sighed.

Not ill-omened, she told herself. *Miraculous. Full of mystery and joy.*

But was it filly or foal? She could not tell. The heaped straw and crouching form of Pitipak obscured her view. Her nursling seemed to shift and blur. The pied mare blinked. At times her doubled vision saw twin images: one dark, one light, so that she could not be certain of her young's true color.

"Hear me, comrades-of-the-deep," the Red Mare murmured. "My fellows are weary and in need of rescue. Do not let them perish, I beseech you. Buoy them up against the waters that would claim them."

The words continued, urgent, ceaseless — just at the threshold of Tek's hearing. She ignored them, too spent to listen, to puzzle them out.

I must think of a name, she thought languidly. *A truename for my child.*

As dam, she alone could fashion her offspring's secret name and whisper this first and most closely guarded gift into that newborn ear alone, never to be repeated to another unless the greatest of trust lay between them. Jan had told her his own truename — Aljan, Dark Moon — on his pilgrimage of initiation, two years gone.

And that was when I knew, she thought, *knew beyond all doubts and shadows that this young firebrand was the one for me, even if I had to wait years for him. And he was worth the wait. As this moment has been worth the wait, to feel our young suckling at my flank.*

"Unicorns-of-the-sea!   Unicorns-of-the-sea!"   her mother chanted softly, tirelessly. "Fierce, fearless single-horns — you who are also the beloved of Alma and who, like us, also call yourselves children-of-the-moon. Bear my fellows safe to land!"

Tek drifted, as on gentle swells. Sleep was dragging at her. She could not remain afloat a moment more. *Return to me soon, O my love, my Dark Moon,* she found herself thinking, as though her mate somehow floated beside her, able to hear her thoughts. *Return and share my joy in the birth of your heir.* Sleep rose like a wave and overwhelmed her. Unresisting, she let herself slip down, down into the darkest depths, devoid of light and sound and dreams.

Unicorns-of-the-Sea

☽ 23 ☾

The driving rain no longer fell, but stormwind continued to batter. The dark unicorn panted with effort, churning with all four limbs just to keep his head above water. Waves heaved and tossed. Land lay nowhere in sight. He could not tell if the darkness were that of storm alone or of night. It had all come back to him now: his people and their Vale, his title among them — Korr's son, prince of the unicorns. He remembered his journey to the Summer Sea at solstice time, the long months of mock-sparring and wooing. A flush of warmth suffused him as he recalled the courting dance on equinox eve. Memory of Tek blazed up, and wild longing filled him to return to his fellows and rejoin his mate.

Too weary to fight the riptide anymore, Jan lay in a daze as the cold, gusting stormrain began to abate. His limbs felt violently jolted, his ribs badly bruised. After he and Ryhenna had sprung from cliff's edge toward the storm-high surf below, strong ocean currents had dragged them far from shore. Alongside him, whenever the wind fell, he heard the coppery mare's panting breath as she, too, struggled against the fierce, running sea. After a time, her thrashing roused him.

"Don't . . . ," he managed, slinging a wet draggle of mane from his eyes. "Don't fight the waves. Breathe deep, and keep your nose just above water. Use your limbs as little as possible."

Eyes rolling and wide, the coppery mare turned to him with a gasp of relief. "My lord — great Dai'chon — ye stir!"

Jan shook his head weakly. "I am no Dai'chon. Ryhenna, I am Aljan, prince of the unicorns. I have remembered my own true-name at last."

"Alj — Al-jan?" she stumbled, still flailing frantically. "But — I saw the divine fire spring from thy hooves and horn. . . ."

Again the dark unicorn shook his head. Breathing hurt his ribs. He had suffered some injury in the fall. The pain weakened him. "Don't swim so fiercely," he urged her. "You'll spend yourself."

Reluctantly, Ryhenna slowed her vigorous paddle. She seemed fearful of sinking without the constant motion of her limbs.

"Call me Moonbrow, as before, if you wish," he said, snorting cold seawater, "though that is not the name by which my people know me."

The coppery mare gazed at him. "Tell me of thy people, my lord Al-jan, Moonbrow," she whispered, "and whence thou comest."

Jan told her of his people, the children-of-the-moon, and of his life among them in the Vale. He spoke until his voice became ragged, rough. Ryhenna's breathing calmed. Her efforts at re-maining afloat grew more steady. She paddled determinedly now, no longer desperate, and listened, hushed, as he described the free lives of unicorns.

"Ye have no keepers," the coppery mare murmured, awed, "and yet ye do not starve? Ye find your own shelter against the cold and wet, and defend yourselves from harm? And ye follow your own god, this Mother-of-all, this Alma?"

Jan nodded, talked out, spent. His tale had taxed his waning strength. He let himself drift, treading the waves as slowly as possible, saw the coppery mare watching him, trying to do the same. The grey sea had calmed somewhat, though the sky re-mained windblown, dark. Abruptly, she turned away.

"I have no such loving god to watch over me," she murmured

bitterly. "My god was a sham, naught but a mortal two-foot in a mask. Oh, Al-jan — Moonbrow — if only I might see this marvelous Vale of thine and meet thy fellows and know the blessings of thy goddess Alma, I might die content."

Jan stirred uneasily, thinking of his dreams. He remembered only snatches — of killing winter cold and starving unicorns; his own father with a false moon painted in white clay upon his brow, ramping and shouting as one mad; Tek and Dagg fleeing together through driving snow, pursued by haunts or wolves. The dark unicorn shivered. All around, the cold waves heaved and chopped.

"Where are we?" he heard Ryhenna beside him asking, her voice plaintive. Clearly she was beginning to tire. He himself felt drained and chilled, at the end of his strength. How long had they been in the sea — all day? Was it dusk now? Evening? He saw no stars overhead, but the sky was so dark, he was not sure if it were night or only cover of cloud.

"Near the coast still, rest sure," he answered, forcing his own voice to sound reasoned and calm. "The storm can't have taken us so very far from shore. If only we knew what direction, I imagine we could swim it." Seeing her casting about worriedly, he added, "Sooner or later, we're bound to drift back toward land."

He turned away for a moment, fearful to catch her eye, and told himself that his words were not a lie. He had no doubt that eventually they would wash up on shore — but he knew that could be days, even weeks hence: long after their spirits had leapt free of the world to join with the Mother-of-all, leaving only bloated corpses on the waves.

Great Alma, save us! he cried inwardly, fighting his own panic down.

Jan shook himself, paddling as much for warmth now as to remain afloat. He saw Ryhenna scanning the horizon intently. Underneath her seeming composure, he sensed she was terrified still, nearly exhausted. The sea began to grow rougher again. Waves pitched and slapped at them. As darkness deepened, Jan realized that true evening must be falling at last, that the grey dimness encompassing them before had been only storm-shadowed daylight. The wind rose, gusted, but with no sign of rain.

Time passed. Beside him, he heard Ryhenna's sobbing breaths. His injured ribs ached. His limbs hung numb. He felt his eyelids straying shut. Only for a few moments, he told himself: he would rest, then swim on. Part of him knew that he was drowning, beginning to sink — down, the long way down to the soft, silt bottom, where firefish and sea-jells would pick his bones. But he could not struggle, could not swim another stroke. He had lost track of the coppery mare, unsure whether she still drifted beside him. Seawater filled his mouth and nose.

Into your keeping, Great Alma, he bade the goddess silently, *take me and my companion Ryhenna.*

A splash of spray. Something long and sleek broke the surface alongside him. Jan started, choking, jerking his head once more into the air above the rocking darkness of waves. A tumult in the waters all around. He paddled reflexively, blinking, stared at the gently curving back of the large dark form that had just surfaced before him. The blowhole atop its rounded head spouted a spurt of steaming breath.

Similar creatures — nearly a score — crowded around him and Ryhenna, bearing them up. Across from him, the coppery mare floundered, dazed, only half aware of their rescuers. The dark unicorn could only gaze in wonder as he felt the smooth, shifting surface of the ocean creatures' backs supporting him, lifting him partially free of the waves. His own struggles ceased as, in the depth of his mind, he heard a soft, laughing voice gently mocking him.

Aljan, my foolish colt. Did you really think I'd let you drown?

The seabeast nearest Jan turned to look at him with its bright black eye. The creature clicked and chattered through its steaming blowhole. Its fellows did the same. Across from him, the coppery mare's thrashing had subsided. She lay insensate, swooned. Jan felt himself growing light-headed, faint. He seemed to be floating through dark, star-filled sky instead of sea. Burning sea-jells and firefish swirled, surrounded him like stars. The strange, streamlined creature gliding before him through the darkness clacked and chittered still. From its short, blunt snout — he beheld now, staring — grew the long, twisting spiral of a unicorn's horn.

The dream of stargliding endured for a great span before Jan returned to himself, found himself once more in the night-dark sea. For hours, it seemed, he could do little more than lie exhausted against the slick, pliant backs of the unicorns-of-the-sea. They were mostly dark grey, though a few were silvery with great black spots. Across from him, Ryhenna slept peacefully, sprawled across the shifting backs of the obliging sea-unicorns. Much of the cloud cover above him had blown off now, and Jan was able to see stars. The few ragged, scudding clouds that remained threatened no rain. The breeze had turned unexpectedly, mercifully warm.

Not all their rescuers possessed the tusk-horn, Jan noted after a time. Only about half did, most of whom appeared to be the larger males — and yet, among those with the longest, keenest, and most elegant horns swam two that were plainly females with half-grown calves. One of the group even sported a pair of horns, one spiral skewer sprouting from each side of the jaw. The group's leader was evidently the beautifully tusked young male who had broken the surface first. In the beginning, he only clicked and whistled at Jan, but presently switched to the common tongue of unicorns and *daya*.

"Among my folk," he began, "I am know as A'a'a'. . . ." A string of crackling squeals followed, baffling Jan's ears. The sea creature tossed his head, flipping a shower of spray. "But I realize this designation is difficult for your kind."

The young male swam alongside, bright-eyed, smiling. The dark unicorn could not escape the impression that he was being politely laughed at.

"You may therefore call me A'a."

Despite his bone-wearying fatigue, Jan managed a bow. "A'a," he began, "I am called Aljan. My companion is Ryhenna. We are both deeply grateful for your aid. But I have never seen or heard tell of your kind before. What are your people called?"

"We are narwhals," A'a replied: "Moonspawn, blessed of the Great Mother. We are on our spring voyage east along the silver coast to our calving grounds off the Birdcat Mountains."

Birdcat Mountains. Jan grew suddenly more alert. Might such be the name of the Gryphon Mountains among A'a's people? The dark unicorn felt his whole body quiver. If the unicorns-of-the-sea knew of the Gryphon Mountains, then surely they knew of the Singing Cliffs where the seaherons nested, from which he could easily find his way back to the Vale.

"We sing to one another constantly beneath the waves," A'a continued. "My pod was closest to you when our dreamers harkened Red-One's hail entreating your rescue."

Red-One? Jan blinked. All the narwhals in his view were dark silver, mottled grey, or black. "Who is Red-One?" he asked. "Is that one among you now?"

A shower of staccato clicks marked A'a's laughter. "Nay. She is of your kind," he replied, "though once, like your companion, she lacked a horn. Years ago, we aided her flight from the two-footed boat-builders. We curse their kind! They kill us when they can — though we have never offered them the slightest harm. They steal our tusks and dappled skins, our rich fat and strong, supple bones. They would harness us as they do their hapless *daya*, we think, could they but devise a means."

A storm of angry crackles and squeals came from A'a's fellows, evidently signaling agreement.

"Where does this red mare live?" the dark prince asked as the tumult subsided.

"Inland," A'a replied. "She visits us from time to time, coming down to the golden shore in spring when we are passing by. Sometimes she travels with us a while. We tell her of all the realms undersea that we have visited, and she speaks of the drylands she has seen. Several of us have learned her tongue, and she speaks our own tongue a little, too."

The swells rolled dark and warm around them.

"You are fortunate, O friend of our great friend," the sleek sea-rover added, "to have such an ally to intercede on your behalf."

Jan lay silent a moment, thoroughly confused. A hornless *da* mare, having escaped the two-foots, now living as a unicorn? Surely he could not have heard the other right.

"You say this mare once lacked a horn . . . ?" he began.

The narwhal leader clacked and nodded. "Drinking from a sacred pool guarded by white poisontails transformed her," he replied. "A horn now grows upon her brow."

The dark unicorn snorted, shook his head, still utterly perplexed. Could A'a be referring to the sacred wellspring of the moon, Jan wondered, deep in wyvern country?

"But how could this Red-One," he murmured, only half realizing he was thinking aloud, "many miles inland, know of our plight — and send you word?"

The black narwhal laughed. "Red-One glides through our dreams," he answered. "Her spells conjured the storm that raised the sea above the rocks and enabled your escape from the stinking boat-makers. It was surely a mighty leap to fling her powers so far. We are uneasy for her now, having received no further sending from her these many hours since."

Jan felt a stab of recognition now. Could Tek's dam be the one of whom the narwhals spoke? He had known all his life that the Red Mare was a magicker, able to enter dreams and bring weather. He knew she often traveled far from the Vale on mysterious errands never explained. It had been Jah-lila, years past, who had saved him from a wyvern's sting and hinted at origins far stranger than merely being the offspring of renegade unicorns — outlaws of the Plain — as most of the herd believed.

The sea-unicorns bobbed and whistled. Despite the mildness of the air after the storm, all Jan's limbs felt suddenly chill. Had Jah-lila once been a *da* in the city of the two-foots? Could drinking of Alma's sacred pool deep in wyvern-occupied territory somehow have transformed her? For all its healing powers, could that miraculous well truly change hornless *daya* into unicorns? The prospect both disturbed and excited him.

"I believe this Red-One of whom you speak is kin to me," he said to A'a, "being mother to my mate."

The narwhal leader reared back, startled, his speech degenerating into a series of squeals and staccato raps, by which, Jan supposed, he transmitted this news to his fellows. The dark prince nearly slid from the backs of his rescuers as other narwhals joined in their leader's gleeful dither, jostling and chattering.

Across from him, Ryhenna's supporters seemed to contain themselves better than their podmates, so that the sleeping mare only stirred, but did not wake. Eventually, to Jan's relief, A'a calmed himself and restored order with a barrage of deep, rapid snaps and bursts of rising notes. As the narwhals quieted, their leader once more resumed the unicorn tongue.

"We were unaware of your kinship to Red-One," the narwhal replied. "This news pleases us very well."

"I seek to return to my home," Jan told him urgently, "and I would bring my companion Ryhenna with me, but I do not know the way. . . ."

"Do not fear," A'a replied. "You need only travel east along the silver shore to reach the whistling steeps and the golden sands where the blue skimmers flock. From there, you and your companion will be able to find your way inland, will you not?"

Whistling steeps, golden sands, blue skimmers. Quickly, Jan grasped the most likely translations: Singing Cliffs, the shores of the Summer Sea, and the dust-blue herons.

"Aye," he cried. "We can easily find our way inland from there."

"Good," A'a replied. "We are not far from the shallows — though you will need to travel many days along the silver strand before you reach the steeps. We should be within sight of the drylands by morning. Until then, sleep, friend Aljan, unicorn of the land, for I see you are as weary as your companion. It is time both of you slept. Rest now till we put you safe ashore."

Prince's Get

) 24 (

Dagg felt exposed, vulnerable now that he had passed outside the Vale. Tepid sun and cool spring air seemed almost sultry. Grazing as he went, he trotted through the greening hills, admiring the delicious shoots and young buds bursting everywhere. His long winter pelt, grown ragged now, had yet to shed. He found himself sweating beneath the shag. Gnats and midges swarmed in droves. He swatted at a biting fly on his rump.

He could not believe how quickly the season had changed. The violent storm at equinox, little more than a month gone by, had banished the hard-frozen snows in a single sweep. Dagg shuddered, thinking of the desperate winter past: Jan, gryphon-killed; mad Korr ordering his son's innocent mate pursued even in her exile beyond the Vale. Then the storm. Common knowledge called Tek's dam, to whom she had fled, a magicker. Could the Red Mare truly have conjured the deluge at equinox — and all that had ensued?

Uneasily, Dagg shoved speculation aside. Those tragedies were over — nightmares from which the herd must now awake. He trotted across pathless, rolling hills of mixed forest and meadow. Deep in his breast stirred the fear that had dogged him all winter since Tek's flight. Had she been able to find her mother, the elusive Red Mare — or had she perished with her unborn in the snows beyond the Vale? Even strengthened as she was by the healer's herb, her desperate run must have cost her much.

A sharp whistle cut through his troubled musing. The dappled warrior halted dead, his nostrils flared. He cast about him with ears and eyes. He stood in an open meadow beside a narrow ravine, gushing now with spring flood. On the cliffside opposite, a figure moved, partially hidden by trees. His heart lifted suddenly as Tek stepped from the forest's edge onto the open hillside.

"Ho, Tek!" Dagg shouted, half-rearing. "Well met!"

The pied mare laughed. She seemed surprisingly hale. Dagg himself was only beginning to recover from the privations of the harsh season past. Despite the recent abundance of sprouting shoots and buds, his ribs still showed. Tek, by contrast, looked sleek.

"Come up," she cried. "I'll meet you."

Wheeling, she vanished into the trees. Dagg splashed across the flooded ravine and started up the rocky trail. A thought struck him just as he reached the trees. Though a tall, strapping mare, Tek had always been lean, slim as a filly, without an ounce of spare flesh. So he recalled her from their years in the Vale, and so she had appeared to him on the hillside above only moments before.

A chill bit into Dagg's breast as he counted the time since the night of courting upon the shores of the Summer Sea. Tek's pregnancy ought to have been far advanced by now, her unborn progeny not due for close to another moon — yet her slender girth made obvious that she was no longer pregnant. Dagg's heart fell. She must have lost the foal.

The sound of hoofbeats along the steep trail made him quicken his pace. Through the trees ahead, he glimpsed Tek rounding the bend. She let out a glad whinny and charged him. Dagg braced, laughing, as she shouldered against him, frisking and nipping. He felt like a colt again, dodging the smarting blows of her hooves and fencing her nimble feints of horn. Panting, the two of them subsided at last, Tek tossing the long black-and-rose strands of mane from her eyes. Dagg marveled at her energy.

"Well, Dagg," she said, a little breathless. "What brings you?"

"You," he answered, chafing against her companionably. "How are you?" he asked her. "How fared you this winter past?"

Tek laughed, stepping back. "As you see. I found my dam and sheltered in her grotto. But you, Dagg —" Her voice sobered. "How fared you and those I left behind in the Vale?"

Dagg cast down his eyes. "So many perished," he answered. "Mainly the old and the very young."

As he thought of Korr keeping huge assemblies standing in the fierce cold for hours daily, sharing only among his favored Companions the secret of where the best forage lay, the dappled warrior's voice grew hard.

"Many starved, who need not have starved. Many died of cold who need not have died. By the end of winter, even the most loyal acknowledged Korr must be mad."

Tek nodded, sobered. "I sorrow to hear of it."

Dagg stamped, pacing restlessly. "Then the tragedy at equinox. That was the final blow. . . ."

The dappled warrior stopped himself, glancing quickly at Tek. He had not meant to mention that catastrophe so soon, to spoil her first joy at their meeting — especially in view of the obvious loss of her unborn. Now the damage was done: he had let the news slip out. Tek's eyes narrowed.

"Tragedy?" she asked him. "Tell me of this."

Dagg scuffed one forehoof. Gnats whined, stinging him. He tossed his mane.

"Come." Tek fell in beside him and started up the slope. "Tell me as we walk."

The hillside steepened, its narrow trail threading through tough, spindly trees. Reluctantly, he began.

"After you fled at solstice time, some expressed hope, saying that with 'the pied wych' now cast out, Alma must once more smile — hah!" He snorted. "But the weather only worsened. Teki and I did our best to foster belief that it must be your exile the goddess found so displeasing. Most conceded that you had had nothing to do with the death of noble Sa and that fear for your life — not guilty shame — had driven you away. Feelings ran even higher in your favor when it became known you . . ."

Dagg hastily bit his tongue, reluctant to speak indelicately in view of Tek's obvious miscarriage.

"That is, when your condition became known," he muttered awkwardly, risking a glance at Tek.

She seemed unperturbed, serene in fact. Dagg frowned. Few mares he knew to have lost their young accepted their misfortune so blithely. Even moons later, he knew, many still mourned. Yet Tek evidenced no such deep-felt grief. Though sober and attentive, her expression was not stricken.

"Go on," the pied mare prompted. Puzzled, the young stallion continued.

"The king raged when he learned of your escape. One Companion who had attacked you broke his leg in the fall. Teki could not save him. The other, so they say, barely escaped skewering by the king after his tale of your bungled arrest. What saved him, I think, was his revelation of your — your pregnancy."

Tek nodded. Abashed, the dappled warrior hurried on.

"The news drove the king into a frenzy. He called your union with Jan unholy, the result of your mother's sorcery. He called your expected progeny 'abomination,' which at all costs must be prevented from birth."

Again, Dagg stopped himself, appalled at how badly he had put it, wishing he could snatch back the words which had just passed his lips. His hide flushed scarlet beneath heavy winter shag. Yet still Tek's expression seemed only serious and inward-turned, not anguished. Sadly, she shook her head.

"I cannot understand what the king could have meant. Perhaps no meaning lies in the ravings of the mad. But go on, Dagg. How did the herd respond?"

"Even some of the king's most ardent supporters acknowledged that he ranted then," continued Dagg, "but all still feared to defy him. Korr ordered his chosen to pursue you at once. Luckily, none knew whither you had fled. Teki was questioned, of course, but he professed bafflement at any suggestions that he had aided you, and his young acolytes backed him, every one, all swearing that they had not seen you in at least a day. Teki insisted on open questioning, before the assembled herd, not some secret interview.

"All the acolytes were let go. Even the king, calling for the blood of your unborn as he was, seemed reluctant to harm them. So many had died by now that the welfare of these young ones was doubly precious to the herd. As for Teki himself, much grumbling ensued among the king's loyalists over the pied stallion's being not only your acknowledged sire, but the mate of a 'known outlaw and magicker' — but the healer answered that you were a grown and wedded mare, responsible for your own actions now, and had not sheltered in his grotto since summer last.

"He also reminded all present that he had not shared a cave with your mother, Jah-lila, since before you were born and could scarcely be held accountable for any actions of a mare who chose to live outside the protection of the Vale and its Ring of Law. And when, he asked, had the Red Mare been adjudged an outlaw? She had never stood before Council or king facing charges for any crime. Strange she might be, a foreigner — but not criminal.

"He further called on all to witness his own long and loyal service to the king. Korr could not very well touch him then. Besides, he and everybody else knew that until his acolytes complete their training — years hence — the pied stallion remains the Vale's only healer. The very survival of many present might well hang upon his skill that winter. At last Korr let him go, but the king vowed that as soon as the weather broke, he would dispatch his Companions to hunt you down wherever you might be hiding, even beyond the Vale, if need be."

"And you?" Tek pressed, brow furrowed with concern. "All this you must have heard at second account. Was your absence marked? I lost track of you that night, in the snow. You fell behind. . . ."

Dagg shook his head. "Nay. When I limped home late the following day, I told my sire and dam I had been caught in the storm and wandered for hours, lost, before spending the night huddled in a small, deserted cave: not far from the truth. If they did not believe me, they said nothing to Korr. Blood ties, it seems, still bind them stronger than fealty to a king.

"All the herd attended the grey mare's funeral, despite the cold. Their grief was unbounded. The loss of Sa seemed to burn in the minds of many as a symbol of all that the herd had lost. Few save his Companions paid heed to Korr's words that day: no outbursts, no open rebellion, but a persistent, sullen, smoldering resentment against the king. Cold and starving, the unicorns were growing weary of being bitten and kicked. Attendance at Korr's rallies fell off sharply after that. We needed all our time and energy just to scout for forage. Most simply did not heed the summons of the king's Companions anymore.

"That pricked him. He dispatched his pack to comb the valley for you as soon as Sa's funeral rites were done. When they could not find you, the king had little doubt you had fled to your mother's haunts in the southeastern hills — though Teki and I kept rumors flying of your having hidden deep in the Pan Woods, or even run away wild renegade onto the Plain.

"Some of our allies swore to glimpsing you — or your haunt — on some distant slope of the Vale, crying out to Alma and the spirit of your princely mate to witness your innocence. More than a few of the king's Companions began to doubt the wisdom of actually finding you. We let them go on thinking you were some sort of wych or sprite. From time to time our sympathizers reported ghostly dreams of you mourning the injustice of your fate."

Warming to his tale, despite its gravity, Dagg found himself nearly laughing now. Inventing eerie sightings with which to confound Korr's superstitious followers had proved the winter's one diversion. Such small, delicious victories, he mused, had often proved the only fodder to chew on during the long, cold, hungry nights. Picking the trail beside him in the warm spring sun, Tek joined his laughter easily.

"You rogues. When spinning tales, neither you nor Teki has ever held the strictest regard for the truth."

Grinning, Dagg shrugged. "When the king has champed the truth all tatters with his 'mouthpiece of Alma' nonsense, I hardly see why others should not join in the feast. At any rate, Korr kept his Companions searching the Vale relentlessly for you all winter. Previously, joining the king had meant ease and privileges, better forage and a bullying self-importance in exchange for little actual toil. Now Korr's constant search parties grew so burdensome that many longed to quit his service, but dared not, lest their former Companions throw the deserters upon the mercy of a resentful herd. They kept to their posts now out of fear, not loyalty.

"As equinox neared, the king let it be known that he intended to send a party into the southeast hills at first spring to hunt you out before your time of bearing came. Yet sentiment had shifted so heavily in your favor by this time that the Companions were openly jeered as they set out. The king ought to use his wolves, so some muttered loudly, to seek out new forage for the starving. Many said that you were surely dead. Others feared that did you live, Jah-lila would doubtless protect you with her sorcery."

He glanced again at Tek, but she gave him no indication one way or another regarding her dam's role in the events of the scant month and a little past, merely glanced at him curiously as they continued up the trail.

"You spoke of tragedy," she reminded. "Some great loss during the mighty storm at equinox? Tell me of this."

Dagg looked away, finding the subject almost too painful to relate. But Tek seemed genuinely puzzled. If Jah-lila *had* precipitated the events of equinox, she apparently had not relayed them to her daughter. With a deep sigh, the dappled warrior said:

"At the dispatching of the Companions, the breaking point seemed to come at last. Korr's mate, Ses, had remained silent all this while. Though clearly not approving, she had spoken no public word against her mate. At equinox, though, Ses declared that if the king sent his wolves to hunt you down, she would leave him.

"Her resolve threw Korr into desperation, partly over the

threatened loss of his beloved mate and daughter — for with
the little filly still suckling, she could not be separated from her
dam — and partly, too, because without Lell under his care, his
claim to regency would be greatly weakened. Should the rem-
nants of the Council of Elders so choose, they could as easily
declare Ses regent as Korr. It was Ses who finally pointed out
that were you, Tek, to bring Jan's unborn heir to term, it would
be that foal, not Lell, to rightfully own the title of princess.

"Korr grew wild then, declaring 'the pied wych' and your child
better dead than left to live. He blamed your dam as somehow
the ultimate cause of all the herd's misfortune, calling her deceiver
and seducer. Ses took refuge in Sa's deserted grotto. Korr sent
his Companions to demand Lell's return, but Ses stood in the
egress of the cave and shouted, 'I'll not rejoin my mate while he
remains in his madness, and if you take my filly from me before
she is weaned, she will die. How will that serve your king?'

"The king's Companions, unwilling to risk injury to either Ses
or Lell, could only return — defeated — to Korr. He was furious,
but what could he do? By day, while Ses foraged, Lell sheltered
in Teki's cave with his acolytes. Public sentiment was now such
that Korr dared not risk removing her in Ses's absence. The herd
might have been moved to open rebellion then.

"Instead, Korr threw himself into planning the expedition to
track you down. He dared not leave the Vale himself — for his
position was now so precarious he feared his absence might lend
the Council opportunity to declare another regent. On the eve
of equinox, he sent his Companions out. In place of the traditional spring pilgrimage to the Hallow Hills, Korr ordered this
quest for vengeance instead. Indeed, we'd few uninitiated colts
and fillies left by then, and those too sickly for any trek.

"The Companions were to cross into the southeastern hills
through the snowbound pass the moment enough snow had
melted to make the way passable. Then they were to disperse,
combing every inch of wilderland until they found you. My parents were among them, but even they, I think, had begun to

scent which way the wind was blowing. Those Companions who remained behind with Korr were mostly old, injured, or sick.

"Great storms had been building in the southeast for days, the end of winter finally in sight. A violent deluge broke at last on equinox eve. Snow-locked mountainsides turned suddenly to muddy slush. Despite the downpour, so my parents tell, the Companions climbed struggling toward the pass. All at once, near the trail's highest point — between one heartbeat and the next — a vast wall of mud hurtled down upon them. The slope above had given way beneath the weight of melting snow and torrential rain.

"A scant few, among them my sire and dam, gained shelter beneath a jutting overhang of stone. They watched in horror as their fellows were swept away. Not one that had been caught by the slide remained to be found. The survivors, fleeing for their lives, returned to Korr and told their tale. Many who listened concluded it must have been a sorcerous storm, conjured by the red wych Jah-lila to punish Korr for seeking her daughter's life. Some are even calling your dam a prophet of Alma now, and Korr the false, blaspheming raver."

The trail had leveled out, threading along the side of the cliff. Dagg spotted the meadow and ravine far below. The pied mare paced silently, thoughtfully beside him.

"I knew nothing of this," she said at last. "If my dam indeed conjured that storm, she has not told me so. Nor has she spoken of the loss of the king's Companions, though I cannot doubt she knows of it. What ensued after the herd received this news?"

"Great mourning," Dagg replied. "Though the king's wolves had been much resented, they were still our blood, warriors of the Ring and loyal to their king — if unwisely so — and kith or kin to many. Their deaths put the herd's loss this winter past at nearly half our former numbers."

"And Korr?" Tek asked.

Dagg shook his head. "The king was devastated, seemed to

regard the calamity as divine judgment. He has been silent since, issuing no proclamations, holding no rallies, making no demands. Many see it as a good sign, the beginning of a return to sanity. He moves about solely in the company of his few remaining Companions — most have dared to desert since equinox, and been accepted back into the herd after fitting penance. Ses still remains in Sa's grotto. Korr has neither called for her nor gone to her.

"Most of the winter's survivors are so relieved at the dispersal of the snows, the early warmth of spring, and the green buds growing that they spend their time foraging ravenously and give little thought to the herd's leadership. Their mood, for the moment quiet, seems to be one of waiting. No word has been heard of you, and though most are anxious for news, none have dared come in search since learning the fate of the king's Companions."

Tek smiled at him. "None till you," she said quietly.

Dagg snorted. "As your shoulder-friend, I doubt your dam would see cause to do me harm. Besides, the snow's long melted, and it scarce looks like rain."

Tek let out a great laugh, and Dagg could not help joining her. They had made good progress up the trail. He spotted a cave suddenly, a narrow slit in the cliff's side — it looked like a mere crease in the rock, not the entrance to a grotto.

"Come in; come in," Tek told him, entering. "My mother set out foraging early this morn. I doubt that she is yet returned, but we can wait within, sheltered from gnats and the cool spring wind."

Dagg hesitated, unease gripping him suddenly. He did not relish meeting the Red Mare face to face. Her veiled powers, her foreignness and mystery unnerved him. Lashing his tail, he followed the pied mare reluctantly into the cave. Its upper walls and ceiling clustered with glowing lichens and fungi in rose, ghost blue, saffron, and plum. Their faint light seemed to brighten as his eyes adjusted. Tek threw herself down in one corner of the cave. Small heaps of last year's herbs and grass lay about. The pied mare nodded to it.

"A little of the forage my mother laid in remains, even yet. Eat, if you will."

But Dagg shook his head, settling himself opposite Tek. Though weary, he felt no hunger pangs. He smelled the absent Red Mare now, her unmistakable scent like roseships and ripening cherries. She had always carried about her that spice fragrance of the magical milkwood pods. The substance of them, so it was said, was in her very bones, imparting the unique brilliant mallow color to her coat.

But though the Red Mare's scent was strong, she herself was not in evidence. Dagg allowed himself a relieved sigh. A respite, then, before he met the magicker. He caught as well an unmistakable whiff of pan: salty and sharp, an odor he had loathed since having been ambushed as a colt by pans for trespassing their Woods. He could only conclude that this cave must have been used as a den by the fetid creatures before the Red Mare chased them out. Politely, he ignored the stench.

"You spoke of the herd's mood of waiting," Tek said, her own mood lifting suddenly. Indeed, she seemed almost ebullient now, in sharp contrast to her gravity of only moments past. "Well, they need not wait long now. Though I am by no means my mother's confidante, she has imparted to me this much: Jan lives and at this moment journeys homeward. He will reach the Vale in ten days' time."

Taken wholly unprepared, Dagg started, restraining himself just short of springing up. He stared astonished at the pied mare across from him. Had Tek, too, run mad? His mentor and shoulder-friend watched him expectantly, eyes bright. She seemed to relish his startlement.

"What . . . are you saying?" Dagg stammered. "Jan is not — he was killed by gryphons. . . ."

Smiling, the pied mare shook her head. "None of us saw. We could only surmise — wrongly, it seems, for my mother has seen by her sorceries that he was taken and held captive in a far place by a strange, two-footed race. Now that he has slipped their grasp, he will be home soon."

She spoke with such anticipation, such confidence that Dagg was loath to contradict her. Yet clearly what she was telling him could not be so. He shifted uneasily. The pied mare watched him amiably, her expression calm.

"You don't believe me," laughed Tek. "Well enough. Were I you, I, too, would doubt. I will let Jah-lila convince you when she returns. But I tell you now that learning of my mate's imminent return has sustained me this last moon and some. I can scarcely wait to show him our union's fruit, which will surprise even him, I think."

Dagg blinked. "Fruit . . . ?" he started, stopped. "But —"

Again Tek laughed. "I bore my young at equinox. Can you not see I am no longer in foal? And such young! Such miraculous progeny as never before seen among the unicorns — Jan will be delighted, as I hope you will be, and indeed all the herd. I must return to the Vale with my prince's get as soon as may be, that we may greet my mate at his homecoming."

Tek spoke quietly, yet with unmistakable excitement. Snorting, the dappled warrior shook his head. Wild dreams of reunion with her perished mate and young obviously comforted the mad mare, he thought desperately. The very notion made his skin crawl. He had always believed in facing the truth head-on, even if truth were a shrieking gryphon. Jan was dead, and Tek had obviously miscarried long before term. Sighing, his companion shook herself, seemingly from sheer joy.

"You will see," she told him gently. "As soon as Sismoomnat and Pitipak return, you will behold my prince's get."

"Sismoo— Piti—" Dagg stumbled over the unfamiliar names. "Who . . . ?"

"My sisters," Tek replied, so that Dagg could only stare anew. Sisters? He had never heard the pied mare speak of sisters — yet even in Jah-lila's self-imposed exile, he knew, Teki had not forsworn the Red Mare: neither healer nor magicker had ever taken another mate.

"Ah," the pied mare said suddenly, pricking her ears. "I hear them."

Dagg turned his head toward the cave's entryway. He heard a strange fluting and twittering mixed with hisses and grunts. The sound sent slivers of ice along his ribs as a salty rankness filled his nose. He smelled pans! That was pan-chatter he heard! Tek continued to lounge at ease. Was her madness so deep she did not realize their danger?

His limbs tensed, preparing to vault him to his heels just as a slight, upright figure ducked through the grotto's egress and called a greeting to Tek. The pied mare whistled back the same phrase. The pan child — for it was a child, only a small thing, not nearly full grown — was followed by other figures, one of which was two-footed like herself.

For a moment, Dagg lay frozen, staring at the pans — and then his eyes turned in even greater astonishment to what had followed these goatlings through the entryway, stepping on delicate hooves as docilely as deer. What dream was this? Dagg could do little more than gape. He had never seen such a thing. What stood before him in the entryway beside the pans could only be Tek's progeny, given form perhaps by the Red Mare's sorcery, or by Teki's miraculous herb? Born under the dark moon of equinox — touched by Alma surely, but in blessing or curse?

"Behold," Tek proudly bade, rising to nuzzle her young. "Behold what Jan and I have made: my prince's get, heir to the leadership of the unicorns."

Enemies

) 25 (

Jan trotted eastward along the silvery strand, the direction he and Ryhenna had been traveling since their rescuers, the unicorns-of-the-sea, had set them ashore many days ago. It had been hard going at first. In the beginning, he and the coppery mare had done far more grazing than traveling, plucking every green shoot and bud they could set teeth upon. Soon enough their pace picked up as his companion's flanks hardened, her wind improved, and Jan's own bruised ribs healed.

Ryhenna grew bolder by the day. Skittish at first, she had started at everything: crabs scuttling across the sand, diving seagulls, beachrunners nimbly skirting the incoming waves. Her years imprisoned in the City of Fire had robbed her of all knowledge of the world outside. Now she took it in with the wonder and eagerness of a filly.

Yet despite her innocence, her youth, Jan reminded himself, she was no filly, but a young mare just coming into flower. A beauty, too. Her odd, coppery pelt flashed in the sunlight, so unlike the hue of any unicorn. Her exotic, upright mane — badly singed at equinox — had since regrown. Now it once more bristled the slim, elegant rise of her neck.

Early on, Jan had managed to chew through the chin strap of her water-logged halter and tug it free. His own, fashioned of silvery skystuff, proved impossible to remove without the nimble digits of two-foots to unfasten its closure. The dark unicorn could only snort and shake his head in frustration while the hard, linked loops clapped at his cheeks and muzzle, chafing him.

Though the spring days warmed, nights along the windswept beach remained bitingly chill. Most evenings he and the coppery mare managed to gather a stack of grey driftwood dry enough for Jan to set alight with a spark made by striking the tip of his horn against one heel and large enough to smolder the night through once the flames died down. He and Ryhenna rarely needed to seek shelter in the scrub beyond the dunes.

Ryhenna asked him constantly for tales of the Vale, her appetite insatiable. Jan told her the old lays, the history of his people: how, four hundred summers past, treacherous wyverns had driven the unicorns from their rightful home, the Hallow Hills, far to the north across the Plains. He told her how the princess Halla and her weary band of refugees had first stumbled across the deserted Vale and claimed it for their new home in exile — only to be attacked each spring by marauding gryphons: savage predators with great wings of green or blue.

He did not speak of the rest of the legend, of Alma's Firebringer, prophesied to deliver the unicorns from exile by restoring to them their ancestral lands and driving the hated wyverns out. Questions! His heart was full of questions still. The voice of the goddess had been silent since equinox — yet he could harbor no doubts now it was her own divine spark which burned in him.

He found himself sometimes dreaming of the City of Fire, of its two-footed sorcerers and their mysteries. Yet each day they fell farther behind him. More often he dreamed of what lay ahead: the Vale and all his kith, especially Tek. Memory of their joy on the night of courting more than a half year gone and of the pledge that they had shared made each day he remained parted from her an agony.

Memory, too, of the confused and disordered dreams Jah-lila had managed to send him in the City — of Korr's madness, the herd's starvation, and the pied mare's flight — filled him with unease. How much of their message did he — dared he — understand? No such visions came to him during his and Ryhenna's trek homeward along the silvery shore.

Three half-moons to the day after equinox, Jan noted a change in the beach along which he and the coppery mare trotted. The pale, ash-colored sand began gradually to mix with particles of yellow amber. Barely enough at first to warm the cool silver into dove, before long the shade had strayed into dun, and then to deep, true gold. Jan tossed his head, whinnying, his pace accelerating to a flying canter. Startled, Ryhenna kicked into a run beside him.

"What is it?" she cried.

Alongside them the waves had changed from grey to green. Jan laughed, tossing his head.

"The sand, Ryhenna. It's gold!"

His companion half shied, shaking her mane. "Then, truth, the Singing Cliffs cannot be far! How I have longed to see the groves where thou and thy fellows danced court, the spot where ye were set upon by gryphons, and the beachhead where thou wert swept away. . . ."

She whickered in delight, spurred, pulled ahead of him.

"I scarce can wait. O Moonbrow, let us run!"

Laughing, Jan sprinted to close the gap. He nipped at the coppery mare's flank. She kicked playfully, veered into the foaming surf to cast up spray after spray of shining droplets, then charged back onto the ribbon of golden beach again. Jan pounded after, heart racing, drew even and crowded her back toward the waves.

With a gay shriek, the coppery mare twisted free of him, and halted stiff-legged, panting. Jan wheeled and also plunged to a halt, breathing heavily. His companion stood looking at him with her bright, brown eyes. She laughed again, pawing at the sand with one round, solid hoof, swished her long-haired, silky tail against one flank, her beardless chin held up impertinently. How like and yet unlike a unicorn she was!

Laughing, he shouldered against her. She nipped him lightly, a playful champ — then started back with a cry of alarm as the shadow of some winged thing in the air above fleeted over them. Jan, too, looked up, then wheeled and stared. A blue-pinioned shape was diving toward them out of the cloudless morning sky.

"Get behind me, Ryhenna!" the prince of the unicorns cried, dodging in front of the hornless mare.

Above them, the winged figure banked suddenly, rearing back. Its elongated pinions stroked the air as it touched down with a spindle-shanked, gangling grace on the golden sand. Jan stared. Though all over dusty blue — the color of a gryphon formel — the creature before them was much smaller than a wingcat.

It stood upright on two lanky, coral legs. Its slender neck crooked, head tilting from side to side, examining him and Ryhenna first with one salmon-colored eye, and then with the other. Fanning its rosy crest, the figure before them trilled happily, a hollow cooing from deep in its throat. Red chevrons beneath its pinions flashed as it folded wing. Ryhenna crowded against Jan, her voice hushed, terrified.

"What is it, my lord?" she whispered. "Is it a gryphon?"

Jan whickered with relief. "Nay," he cried, euphoria filling him. "No enemy, but a friend. Greetings, Tlat, queen of the seaherons. Well met!"

The queen of the wide-roving windriders nodded, mincing toward them across the sand. "Greetings!" she shrieked. "Greetings, Jan-prince! Welcome, welcome. We feared cat-eagles had seized you. We feared you lost!"

Jan fought the impulse to rush forward and rub shoulders with Tlat as he would with one of his own people. The delicate herons, he knew, were ever wary of being knocked down or trampled by the heavy hooves of unicorns. The young prince restrained himself, keeping his heels planted and still.

"Not lost," he assured Tlat. "Not seized by gryphons — though I was pursued by them. A terrible storm swept me out to sea. It has taken me all this time to find my way back."

"Ah!" cried the heron queen. "So the cat-eagle spoke truth after all. We thought he lied to save himself. But who is your companion? What is this odd, hornless one that stands beside you?"

Jan blinked, lost for a moment. The darting thoughts of herons shifted like the winds. Tlat stood craning and eyeing Ryhenna. Jan moved aside to allow her a better view. The coppery mare shifted nervously as the other approached, stabbing her bill into the air and fluttering her folded wings with growing excitement.

"Color of sunsets! Color of burning!" the heron queen exclaimed. "Such a hue among unicorns we have never seen. And round feet — not pairs of half-moon toes, but only single ones: solid as a mussel shell, round as the ripe egg of the moon. Amazing! Where is your beard, burning-colored mare? Where is your horn?"

Ryhenna seemed disconcerted, at a loss for words. "I . . . I am no unicorn, as my lord Moonbrow is," she managed. "I am only a *da* from the City of . . . of Two-foots, far to the west."

"Two-foots? Two-foots?" cackled Tlat. "My tribe know something of these. They glide the waves in great hollowed-out tree-fish. Sometimes we see their windwings on our journeys, but we veer clear lest they hurl their hunting sticks at us. They eat our kind and steal our feathers. They are our enemies, as the cat-eagles are! If you have shared nest with our enemies, non-unicorn mare, then you, too, must be our enemy! Be off!"

The heron queen's agitation grew even as she spoke. Her crest fanned in anger, not welcome, now. Bill cocked, she danced grimly before Ryhenna, ready to fly at her. Hastily, Jan stepped between.

"Peace, great queen of the windriders," he soothed. "Ryhenna's people are prisoners of the two-foots, as was I this winter past. When spring arrived, she aided my escape. Now we are grateful to have come once more among our fast allies, the noble herons, instead of among our common enemies, the two-foots or the gryphons."

"Ah!" clucked Tlat, ruffling. "Ah! I see. My apologies, fiery-colored mare. I spoke in haste. Prisoners! Yes. Did the two-foots steal your horn?"

Ryhenna cast about her helplessly. The other's brash manner had clearly unnerved her. Quickly, Jan addressed the heron queen.

"The two-foots' captives grow no horns," he began, but Tlat's raucous cries interrupted him.

"No horns? How misfortunate — useless! Crippled. Like a broken wing! My commiserations, imperfect mare."

The dark prince saw his companion's face fall, her frame droop. She seemed utterly crushed at the heron queen's screeches of sympathy. He drew breath.

"Indeed it is a great pity, but it cannot be helped. But tell me, Tlat, what has passed since the storm separated me from my band this autumn past. Has word reached you of how the unicorns fare?"

The heron queen bobbed, her gaze turning once more to Jan.

"No word," she cried. "Badly, we fear. Winter here was harsh. Too stormy to risk flying far from our cliffs. Many deaths. Our Mother-the-Sea did not yield much fish. Much courting this spring, though! Each hen has chosen her mates and begun to lay. Soon a great hatching will follow: a great squeaking and crying from the squabs just pipped from their shells. Then will the flock of the herons be renewed! Then will we forget the deaths and sorrows of this winter past."

Her words sent a chill through Jan.

"But no word from the Vale?" he asked. "You do not know for certain how my own people fared?"

Tlat wagged her head, beginning to dance again, her tone dolorous. "No word. Though the winds have moderated since equinox, we have been too busy replenishing our lost numbers to think of travel. We fear your people wintered as poorly as did we, but we have sent no envoys to inquire. Scouting for cat-eagles and fishing to feed my mates, I spotted you upon the strand. Great will be the rejoicing among the herons when I bring word of your return!"

Her words, shrieked and croaked in heron fashion, warmed Jan.

"I am grateful, great Tlat, for the ardor of your welcome. Truly the far-ranging herons are the invaluable allies of the unicorns. May your consorts be many and your nests bountiful. I would stay longer, enjoying your company, but I dare not. I must return to my people. Already I have been absent too long."

Tlat started with a cry, flapping her wings. Ryhenna half shied.

"Too long! Yes! I, too, have been gone a great while. My mates hunger, their warmth dwindling. Each now sits his nest, incubating one of my rosy eggs. Soon the hatchlings will pip! I must return. Having fished, my crop is full. But first, come. You must not depart our shores until I show you the thing we have been keeping all winter. It put us to great trouble, but we persevered out of loyalty to our allies, the unicorns. We knew that you would want us to. I had planned to send fliers to your Vale soon to alert your people of its presence upon our shores. The cat-eagle we captured. One of those who attacked you this autumn past."

Now it was Jan's turn to half shy in surprise. Captured a gryphon — one of the raiders that had harried him and his fellows upon the strand more than a half year gone? He marveled the gracile seaherons had managed to capture such a formidable enemy, much less hold it prisoner for over half a year. But before he could so much as draw breath to question Tlat, the heron queen had spread her wings to the stiff sea breeze and risen into the air. In another moment, she was out of earshot. Earthbound below, Jan and Ryhenna could only follow.

The windrider flew high and slowly, circling back from time to time. Jan and the coppery mare cantered along the damp, gleaming road of sand between wet green wave and dry golden dune. They passed along the sandstone canyons of the Singing Cliffs. Ryhenna cocked her head to the sweet, weeping soughing of breeze through their odd formations, sculpted by centuries of wind and tide.

They came to a familiar stretch of beach and cliff. Jan recognized the break in the cliff wall, the half-submerged rocks, the deep, uneven trough in the sand where, at high tide, the surf washed through with treacherous force. Here was the point at which, last autumn, he had emerged from the cliffs, felt the gryphon's claws along his back, then been swept away by the furious sea.

He remembered the gryphon — a green-and-gold male — overwhelmed by the same vast wave that had claimed Jan. He remembered glimpsing the other's limp form floating on the waves afterward, seeing it cast back up on shore — perhaps *not* dead. Had the wingcat survived? Something moved upon the rocks just above the waterline ahead. Jan halted, staring at the creature as yet unaware of his gaze, while overhead Tlat veered and circled. The creature's dull golden pelt was sandy and scabbed, his foreparts a mass of shabby green feathers: a gryphon on the brink of starvation.

Jan shook himself. Beside him, Ryhenna pressed against his flank, peering over his back at the wasted predator. The lionlike haunches were sunk in, his rib cage showing starkly through thin, patchy fur. One wing lay folded against his side. The other dragged awkwardly across the rock. The wingcat lay in a heap above the swirling tide. One eagle's claw reached down into the sea. From time to time, the gryphon jerked his submerged forelimb from the water, talons clenched — but always empty.

The wingcat was fishing, Jan realized, as with a weak but triumphant cry, the gryphon at last hefted into sight a small, struggling fish. With one snap of his hooked, razor-sharp bill, the fish disappeared down the raptor's scrawny gullet. A moment later, the wingcat returned to scanning the water, foreclaw once more extended beneath the surface of the tide. How many fish could he hope to catch thus in a day? Jan wondered. Surely not enough to keep himself alive. Overhead, Tlat dipped, cawing and feinting at the fishing gryphon.

"Haw! Cat-eagle! Enemy!" she shrieked. "Look up! Look up!"

The tercel hunched, ignoring her, but she persisted, swooping just close enough to scatter any fish. At last the starving gryphon raised his head.

"Take yourself off, you accursed seabird," he rasped. "Has your kind not taunted me enough?"

"We feed you!" cried Tlat. "Our generosity kept you alive this winter past."

"I never asked for your food!" the gryphon snarled, swiping at her with sudden, unexpected vigor. Tlat hovered flapping in the air above him, merrily out of reach.

"You never ask," she shouted, "but you always eat what we bring. Without us, you would be dead!"

"Better death," the gryphon spat, "than to live, starving and maimed, on the leavings of arrogant sealice."

With a caw of delighted contempt, Tlat alighted upon a stone just barely within the gryphon's reach. Her gorge heaved. Had she given him time, he could have lunged and caught her, but in less than an eyeblink, she had disgorged three large fish and darted away into the air again. Jan watched appalled as, driven by hunger too great to deny, the wingcat snatched up Tlat's gifts and wolfed them down.

Yet the gryphon's own look of disgust told Jan he hated himself for accepting, for living as a prisoner of the mocking seaherons. *As I once lived a prisoner of the two-foots,* Jan could not help thinking. A disturbing sense of empathy touched him. Angrily, he shoved it aside. This tercel, along with companions, had sought to kill him and his band half a year ago. Beside him, Ryhenna stood shuddering.

"You do not keep me alive for charity," the wingcat shouted after Tlat, who now circled overhead, chattering derisively. "I know that well enough! But your taunts cannot move me, who destroyed the unicorns' black prince. Surely now my flock will drive the hated intruders from Ishi's sacred Vale. My life no longer matters, already sacrificed to the wind-god's almighty glory. I pray only for an end to my misery."

"Kah! Haw! Nonsense!" screamed Tlat. "The first storm of

autumn battered your companions to bits. None survived to report the outcome of your raid. Your flock will assume you failed — as indeed you *have* failed. Behold! The prince of unicorns returns, alive and hale, unscratched by treacherous cat-eagle claws."

She wheeled to circle above Jan and Ryhenna. Turning, the wingcat started, green cat-eyes wide. An instant after, they winced, grimacing at the pain his sudden movement had caused his injured wing. Cautiously, Jan moved forward, careful to remain well beyond the wingcat's reach. After a moment's hesitation, Ryhenna accompanied him, still peering with fascination and terror at the wounded gryphon. Jan snorted, lashing his tail.

"What Tlat, noble queen of our allies, says is true, wingcat," the prince of the unicorns flung at him. "Your raid did not succeed, though the sea washed me far. It has taken me a long time to return to the spot where last we met, enemy."

"Great god of winds," the gryphon exclaimed. "It *is* you, cursed prince of trespassers. The sea has not been kind to deliver you back unharmed, while mangling me beyond repair. Have you come merely to mock, as this harridan seabird does, or will you kill me at last and end my shame?"

"I go!" cried Tlat from above. "My mates hunger and my unborn chicks grow cold! I leave you to do with this predator whatever seems good in your eyes, friend Jan. Do not forget it was your allies, the seaherons, who preserved his worthless life to await your vengeance."

"I will never forget your invaluable service, Tlat!" called Jan. "May your flock ever increase!"

Overhead, the queen of the dust-blue herons wheeled, winging swiftly toward the Singing Cliffs. A moment later, she was lost against the hot, flame blue of the cloudless morning sky.

Peacemaking
☽ 26 ☾

J an stood eyeing the wounded gryphon, who despite obvious
weakness and pain refused to cower. The prince of the unicorns
had no idea what to do with him. Surely prudence demanded
that he kill this savage foe. To attack any grounded wingcat
on sight had always been the practice among his people. And
yet —

"So, unicorn," the tercel snapped, "did you come merely to
gawk? I am Illishar, of the nest of Shreel and Kilkeelahr, kin to
great Malar, matriarch of all my clan. I fear no unicorn!"

Were he one of my own people, Jan mused, *we would call him
brave.*

The young prince snorted with frustration. Why was it so hard
for him to despise this enemy as he should? The tercel's fellows
had attacked Jan's peaceful band. This very wingcat's talons had
scored his shoulders to the bone. Yearly, the gryphon's kind
raided the Vale to steal away the unicorns' newborn fillies and
foals.

"Well?" the wingcat taunted hoarsely. "Have you nothing more
to say before you end my life, prince of thieves? Or do you mean
to take the coward's way and simply leave me? The herons are
done with me. Without their fish to add to my own meager catch,
I'll quickly starve."

Jan stood silent, considering. The gryphon shifted painfully, hissing. The dark prince felt Ryhenna huddled against him.

"Come, my lord," she whispered urgently. "Let's depart. His hate-filled words frighten me."

"Have you lost your tongue?" the gryphon Illishar shrieked. Jan felt the coppery mare start, flinch. "Or has that silvery chain now clamped shut your jaws? Kill me now, invader — infidel — or else be off! I've little leisure to spend arguing with unicorns."

"Moonbrow," Ryhenna urged him, "let's away."

Jan nodded abruptly and turned. "Aye, Ryhenna. I've long promised to show you all our haunts along the Summer shore. I'll do so now while I ponder what's to be done with this foe."

He started off across the sand, and with a relieved sigh, the coppery mare fell in beside him. Glancing back, Jan glimpsed the tercel sagging as though only anger had kept him upright to challenge Jan. Once more the young prince champed his heart tight against pity. Marauding wingcats deserved none! Quickening his trot, he led Ryhenna away from his injured enemy, eastward along the shore.

For the better part of the morning, Jan showed the coppery mare the beaches along which he and his fellows had galloped that half year past, the cliffs under which they had sparred, the sparse coastal woodlands in which they had foraged and bedded and sought shelter against mild summer storms. He described for her his people's alliance with the dust-blue herons and spoke of how he and Tek had courted and pledged. Ryhenna harkened, rapt, but as she walked through the vast courting glade, he heard her soft and bitter sigh.

"Why do you sorrow?" he asked, puzzled.

The coppery mare tossed her head. "I think on the day, not long distant now, when we shall join your herdmates in the Vale."

Jan frowned, moving to stand in front of her. "Ryhenna, I had thought you welcomed the prospect!"

The coppery mare refused to meet his gaze. "I do," she murmured, "and yet I dread it. What will become of me among thy people, Moonbrow? Will I ever dance court in this sacred glade?"

Jan cocked his head, trying to see her better. "Ryhenna, such is my dearest wish," he told her, "that one day you may find in this glade that same joy which I so lately found with Tek."

His companion sighed again, as though swallowing down some hard little pricking pain. "Who among your people would want me?" she said heavily. "Hornless — crippled. Useless. *Imperfect.*"

The dark prince fell back a step at her quiet vehemence. "You must set no store by Queen Tlat's thoughtless words. . . ."

"Even though they be true?" Ryhenna finished, turning to meet his gaze at last. "O Moonbrow, dost think I have not always known that while I might one day walk among thy people, I can never be one of them?"

The dark unicorn stared at her, astonished. He shook his head vigorously. The halter of silvery skystuff clinked and chinged. "Nay, Ryhenna," he told her. "You are wrong."

The breeze off the golden strand stirred the trees surrounding the glade. Ryhenna's coat gleamed fiery copper in the late morning sun. Jan looked away, at the seabirds gliding overhead, at distant herons winging home to the Singing Cliffs from fishing in the bay.

"The sea-unicorns told me — and Jah-lila herself once told me a thing which leads me to hope our rescuer's tale may be true — that my mate's dam was once hornless as you are, born in your City of Fire, but fled and, joining our company, became a unicorn."

The coppery mare's gaze changed, intensified, grew full of such wild longing suddenly that he found it difficult to meet.

"Surely this is but an old mare's tale thou hast spun to keep my spirit up," she breathed. "My own dam used to do the same, but I pray thee to have done. I am no filly to be made docile so."

Again Jan snorted, shaking his head. "I pledge to you, Ryhenna: my mate's dam is a powerful sorceress; if any among the unicorns has power to make you one of us, it is she."

He saw the coppery mare flinch, shuddering. "And if not?"

"If not," the dark prince told her, "then you will be no less welcome among us, admired for your bravery, your counsel, your beauty." The silver halter jingled as he spoke. He made himself say the words: "A horn upon the brow — it is not the world, Ryhenna."

The coppery mare turned away suddenly. He followed her.

"Moonbrow," she breathed, "I fear this above all else: that rejoining old friends in the Vale, thou wilt forget me."

"Ryhenna," the young prince cried. "How could you think it? Such shall never come to pass."

The coppery mare turned again to face him. The breeze sighed through the trees. "Thy mate will reclaim thee," she said bluntly, "and thy duties as prince. I am not thy mate —"

Jan shook his head. "Nay."

"Among *daya*," she offered, "a stallion may have many mates."

Again the dark prince shook his head. "But not among unicorns."

She gazed at him, lost. "In the City," she whispered, "I was called thy mate, if only from courtesy. What am I now to thee — what can I be — if not thy mate?"

Her voice was tight, her tone desperate. He moved to stand next to her. "My shoulder-friend," he answered her, "she to whom I owe my freedom and my life. Those among the unicorns who love me, Ryhenna, will love you as well."

"I shall never love any as I love thee, Moonbrow!" she cried.

He nuzzled her, very gently. "Nor I you, Ryhenna," he said. "Tek is my mate. I love her. You are my shoulder-friend, and I love you. I love you both, but differently. And when in a year or two years' time, you dance court within this glade, it will be with one whom you love in a way entirely other than the way that you love me. I am your companion, your friend, Ryhenna, just as you are always and ever mine. Stand fast with me," he said, "and no foe shall ever part us."

The pain so plain upon her features all at once subsided. She whickered low, and champed him lightly once, a comrade's nip, no more. "Well enough then, my shoulder-friend."

He shrugged against her laughing, relieved. Sun overhead was climbing toward noon. He shook himself, snorting.

"So tell me, Ryhenna, what should I do with this gryphon?"

The mare beside him shuddered. "Leave him," she answered. "Leave him to his fate."

Jan sidled uneasily. "By rights, I ought to kill him," he murmured, "as a sworn enemy of the unicorns."

He heard Ryhenna gasp. "Too perilous," she answered quickly. "Weak and starving as he is, Moonbrow, he nonetheless might do thee harm."

The dark unicorn nodded. "Aye. And skewering a crippled foe scarce seems honorable — yet simply leaving him to starve smacks hardly more noble. . . ."

"He frightens me," Ryhenna whispered, "and yet —"

"Yet?"

"I pity him," she finished, glancing at him, "hobbled by his broken wing as surely as a firekeeper's tether once hobbled me. Captive of the herons — and now of us — as truly as once we two were captives in the City of Fire."

Jan stamped, frustrated, lashing his tail. He longed now only to quit the Summer shore and begin the last, short leg of the journey inland toward the Vale. Yet the gryphon's fate stymied him.

Great Alma, guide me, he petitioned silently. *Tell me what to do.*

The air around him hung utterly quiet, silence broken only by the whisper of breeze, the soft sigh of Ryhenna's breath, and the faint, far cries of seabirds fishing. Herons winged swiftly overhead, crops heavy. Some carried more fish, silver gleaming, in their bills. The prince of the unicorns sighed. His goddess remained mute still — or else spoke in words he could not reck.

"We'll feed him until I can decide, Ryhenna," he muttered, trotting across the glade toward the trees and the shore beyond.

He and Ryhenna spent the early afternoon gathering food for their captive gryphon. Well aware that the tercel needed meat to survive, Jan searched the tide pools for trapped fish. Two of the six he managed to skewer with his horn were of hefty size. Ry-henna meanwhile, at his direction, pawed the wet, golden sand for the fluted clams and rosy crabs that burrowed there, stamping them with her hard, round hooves to crack their shells.

A dead skate, newly cast up by the tide, rounded their haul into a fair-sized catch by the second hour past noon. Jan set about devising a means to transport their gryphon's food to him. The two-foots, he recalled, carried all manner of goods in wheeled carts. Though he and Ryhenna possessed no carts, he mused, they could still drag.

Eventually, the dark unicorn hit upon tangling fish and shellfish in a mat of seaweed and dragging the whole contrivance back to the gryphon on the rocks. Ryhenna suggested that if she lifted the other end of the seaweed clear of the ground, the pair of them might carry it with greater speed. Jan laughed through his teeth, marveling at their innovation as, trotting side to side, he and the coppery mare brought their prisoner his meal.

Despite obvious hunger, the tercel accepted their offering with little grace: screaming and hissing. Ryhenna refused to approach, so Jan pulled the food-laden mat within a few paces of the shriek-ing tercel by himself, then sprang away to stand with Ryhenna as the wingcat hauled himself laboriously near enough to snag the seaweed and draw it to him.

He fell upon its contents with savage relish. Jan watched, fasci-nated as the gryphon's razor beak made short work of the skate, slicing and swallowing down the tough cartilage along with the flesh. Strong yet amazingly nimble talons picked lacelike bones from the fish, pried open shellfish, and plucked strings of flesh from the crabs' hollow limbs.

At last, the seaweed mat completely pillaged, the wingcat sub-sided with a heavy sigh, green eyes half shut. Plainly it had been the most sumptuous meal he had eaten in more than half a year. Behind the dark unicorn, Ryhenna twitched nervously, anxious to be gone, but Jan lingered. Slowly, carefully, he approached the tercel, halted just out of reach. "Earlier this day," he said, "you called my people trespassers. What did you mean by that?"

The tercel stirred, obviously annoyed at Jan's proximity — his very presence — but too sated and contented to raise further protest.

"I called your people what they are, unicorn: thieves," he answered, almost amiably. "The great vale we call the Bowl of Ishi was ours long before you unicorns came."

Jan stared at him. "Yours?" he cried. "How so? No gryphons ever dwelled in our Vale. It was deserted when the princess Halla first claimed it, forty generations ago."

The wingcat's eyes snapped open, then narrowed angrily. "Deserted? Pah!" he scoffed. "It housed the sacred flocks of goat and deer Ishi gathered for my people's use: to provide first meat each spring for our newly pipped hatchlings. But you vile unicorns drove away the tender flocks, profaning the Vale with your presence. Now the formels must hunt your bitter kind in spring, though we prefer the sweet flesh of goats or deer."

The prince of the unicorns stood dumbstruck. The Vale of the Unicorns — claimed by gryphons as a sacred hunting ground? He had never heard of such a thing. Yet ever since the first attacks upon the princess Halla and her followers, gryphon raiders had returned to the Vale every spring. At last, after forty generations of conflict, Jan had learned the reason why.

"Four hundred years have we sought to drive you out," the wounded gryphon rasped. "My own parents died on such a mission two springs past. They flew to kill the unicorns' black prince. Not you, the other one — the one before you. But they failed. Their names were Shreel and Kilkeelahr."

Jan cast his mind back, two years gone, to the time just before his pilgrimage of initiation, when his father Korr had still reigned as prince and a pair of gryphons had nearly succeeded in assassinating the then-prince Korr, his mate and son. The memory was bitter, tinged with bafflement and fear.

"My people slew your father and mother," he told Illishar.

"How well I know that," the gryphon snapped. "When they did not return, we knew they must have perished."

"They came near to killing my sire and dam," Jan added, remembering still. "And me as well."

"Yes!" Illishar replied angrily. "Had they succeeded, they would have been called heroes, perched high in the pecking order once more. Queen Malar would have rewarded them with a prestigious nesting site, a ledge close to her own upon the Cliffs of Assembly, first pick of the kill. A glorious mission. But it failed.

"Thus was I orphaned as a half-grown chick, disinherited by powerful factions within my clan: my parents' enemies. I grew up a nestless beggar, though I am well-born, kin to the matriarch herself. My father was her younger nestmate — but he fell out of favor. That is why he and Shreel were desperate enough to undertake so daring a raid, to win the glory that would buy them back their pride of place. For what is a gryphon without honor? Only a pecked-upon squab. Now I, too, have failed in my bid for glory. The proud line of my parents ends with my death."

Jan let him talk, scarcely daring to interrupt. It had not occurred to him how lonely the gryphon must be. The dark unicorn shook himself. He, too, had spent the winter as a prisoner among strangers. When guarded queries did nothing to stem the gryphon's words, Jan grew bolder, questioning the tercel about his life before the raid, among his own people. Illishar spoke freely, proudly, of the customs of his flock, of their wars and religion, of the constant struggle both within and between the clans.

No single leader ruled, though Malar, the matriarch of the largest clan, was the most ruthless — and therefore the most respected — leader. She was evidently some sort of cousin — possibly an aunt — to Illishar. Jan could not determine quite which. The wingcats counted kin differently from unicorns.

As the afternoon drew on, Ryhenna grew more fidgety, and Jan sent her back to the beach to forage again while he stayed with the gryphon — careful always to remain out of reach of the raptor's beak and claws. She returned as dusk drew on, dragging the ragged tail of a large grey shark, badly picked at by seabirds.

Illishar fell on it with ravenous appetite, while the coppery mare grimaced and spat the fetid taste of fishskin from her tongue.

As evening fell and the air grew chill, Jan collected driftwood and struck a fire. The gryphon reacted first with alarm, then awe, and finally delight, drawing close enough to the blazing driftwood to warm himself. On opposite sides of the fire, he and Jan talked on into the deepening dark. Ryhenna hovered nervously, afraid to approach because of the gryphon.

Jan sang Illishar the lay of the princess Halla, of his people's long-ago expulsion from their own sacred lands, the Hallow Hills, by treacherous wyverns, of their long wandering across the Plains until they reached the Vale, seemingly deserted and unclaimed, of their settling for the winter into their new home in exile only to be forced to defend themselves the following spring — and every spring thereafter — against raiding gryphons.

Illishar grew silent, sobered after Jan's recounting. The dark prince lay staring into the smoldering coals of driftwood, flameless now, but still shimmering, red with heat. Ryhenna whinnied uneasily in the darkness behind him. He heard her muffled hooffalls above the calm sea's wash: trotting, pacing. She had not yet lain down.

"A great pity, Illishar," Jan murmured, "that neither of our peoples ever sought converse before: no envoys exchanged, no explanations offered or sought. Much spilling of blood might have been spared, I think, had we chosen to speak before exchanging blows." He sighed sleepily. "My people long only to depart the Vale, though it has housed us well for many years. We wish to reclaim our own lost lands by driving the hated wyverns out."

Wearily, the gryphon nodded, chewing at a stem of seaweed, his crippled wing propped against a stone. "Perhaps you are right, unicorn," he muttered grudgingly, "much though it pains me to admit that one I have long held my greatest enemy might have a point."

A little silence then. The breeze lifted. The waves plashed, lapping. The coals of the dying fire shimmered. Unseen, Ryhenna trotted, circled.

"Greater pity, yet," the wingcat added at last, "that with my wing healed wrong, I can never return to my flock to tell them what I have learned. Nor will your people be eager to believe any word you might speak if such word go against their customed hatred of my kind."

The tercel's words trailed off, his breathing deepening, nearly snoring now. Across the coals from him, the young prince sighed again. "Aye," he murmured. "Unicorns are a boar-headed lot."

He dreamed a dream of gryphons and unicorns sharing the Vale without rancor, wingcats perching the cliffs above, his own people grazing the valley floor below. Here and there, on the slopes between valley floor and cliffs, he glimpsed odd creatures, seemingly half wingcat, half unicorn. Their limbs, torsos, and hindquarters were those of unicorns; shoulders, necks, and heads plumed and pinioned like gryphons. Stroking their great wings, they galloped across steep, grassy slopes and, vaulting into the air, took flight.

He awoke with a start. Ryhenna stood over him, pawing at him with one round forehoof. The embers before him lay cold. Across them, Illishar lounged at ease — alert, awake, but resting. The mat of seaweed lay before him, oddly heaped and twisted. The coppery mare glanced nervously at the gryphon, then pawed Jan again. Cold dawn greyly lit the beach.

"Wake, Moonbrow," Ryhenna hissed. "'Tis morn."

The dark unicorn rolled stiffly, gathered his limbs under him, but did not rise. Still eyeing the gryphon tercel, the coppery mare backed off.

"All night, I watched," she told him, "to guard thee. Thy foe is hungry still."

Illishar said nothing, watched them, rustling and twisting between his talons the mat of seaweed before him. Jan staggered to his feet, shaking himself. The silver halter rattled. He had not meant to sleep.

"My thanks, Ryhenna," he told her sincerely. "You guard me better than I guard myself."

The coppery mare tossed her head, bleary-eyed. "I go to the glade to sleep," she told him. "Come fetch me when thou wilt."

Jan nodded, watched Ryhenna lope away along the beach toward the grove. The rustle of seaweed drew his attention back to Illishar.

"Your hornless mare would have been little hindrance to me, had I sought to steal upon you unawares," he murmured to Jan.

Walking around the remains of the fire, the young prince drew closer. "You underestimate Ryhenna," he answered. "She held off a troop of two-foot warriors on the white cliffs of the City of Fire. She would make no easy match for you. But if — as you say — it were so easy a task," he asked, "why did you not kill me this night past when you had the chance?"

The tercel shrugged painfully. "What use, Jan of the unicorns?" he asked. "My wing is bent past repair. I will die soon regardless — why prolong my life a few more days on your bones?"

The seaweed rustled. Jan cocked his head, eyed Illishar's nimble digits twisting and plaiting it. "What do you fashion?"

"A net," the tercel replied, spreading it so that the dark unicorn might better see. "To help me fish. Perhaps after you and your mare tire of me and depart — if you do not kill me outright — this net may enable me to live a little longer."

Jan met the gryphon's eye, and for the first time, Illishar looked away. Jan allowed himself the ghost of a smile. "I see you have not yet despaired of your life as wholly as you pretend," he told the gryphon. "Perhaps you yet dream of returning to your people?"

"Vain dreams!" the tercel exclaimed, casting the seaweed net from him angrily. "The bone set wrong. I will never fly again."

Jan lay down on the rocks, still out of reach, but closer to the injured wingcat than he had ever dared to come.

"Among my people," he told Illishar, "when one of our number breaks a limb, our pied healer, Teki, plasters it with mudclay to keep it stiff until the bone can heal. If it begins to heal wrong, he breaks it again. I have seen him do this."

He thought back to the preceding spring, Dagg cracking one forelimb in a slip on a crumbling slope. He remembered Teki's ministrations; himself, Tek, and others flanking the injured warrior by turns, keeping him upright, walking him three-legged, bringing him forage. The memory made him shudder. Even in the warmth and abundant provender of last spring, Dagg easily could have died.

"It was horrible to watch," Jan told the gryphon who lay before him in the rocks, "but my companion survived, and the bone knit strong and straight. Now he runs again as fleetly as before, as though the limb had never suffered ill."

"Why tell me this?" the gryphon cried, spitting a twist of seaweed from his beak. "To torment me? What use for me to hear of unicorns' legs? It is my wing that is broken — my wing! Tell me what good you can do my crooked pinion, unicorn."

The last words were a snarl, full of bitterness.

"I could rebreak your wing, Illishar," Jan said to him, "bring mud to plaster it. You must keep it very still, three half-moons or more, until it heals."

The tercel stared at Jan. "Our two peoples are sworn enemies," he whispered. "You would not do it."

"Call me your enemy no more," Jan bade him, drawing nearer. "I grow weary of our being enemies. The scars your talons left upon my back this autumn past are old scars now, long healed. Time to heal this ancient rift between our peoples as well."

"No!" cried Illishar, shifting as though to drag himself away from Jan. "Even if you spoke the truth and could reset my wing so that it might heal, do you and your mare intend to remain all spring upon this shore? Who would feed me while my pinion mended? The accursed seaherons have given me over."

Jan shook his head. "I will speak to Tlat and entreat her to continue to tend you. Now that spring has returned, the tidewaters teem with fish. The herons can provide for you without hardship. I think they will do so if I assure them you mean to return to your flock and speak for peace not only between gryphons and unicorns, but between gryphons and seaherons as well."

"I have made you no such pledge," Illishar protested angrily, "to speak for peace among my flock on your behalf."

"Think, Illishar," the dark prince urged, "of the glory to be gained. More glory in merely killing an enemy and arousing his people's hatred against yours all the more, or in taming and allying with him, adding his strength and that of all his people to your own? What more glorious tribute could you possibly lay before your leader, Malar, than the prospect of this great peacemaking?"

Illishar twitched unhappily, pondering. His bill clapped shut. "You have a point, unicorn," he managed, unwillingly. "Perhaps — *perhaps* — peace may be possible between our peoples. But the seaherons! Shrieking pests, they have tormented me all this winter past. Their kind has always been a bane to mine. . . ."

"Peace with the herons as well as the unicorns," Jan answered firmly. "Such is my price."

The gryphon tercel sighed, snapping his beak shut once more. At last he muttered, "As you will."

The dark prince whickered, tossing his head. "One more thing I would ask of you," he added, "one more part to my price."

The silver halter jingled. Illishar eyed him suspiciously.

"Remove this halter," he entreated the gryphon. "Surely your talons are dexterous enough to undo the fastening. Bear it back to your people in token of the bargain we have made."

The tercel's green-eyed gaze grew wide, astonished.

"You would trust me so close?" he asked.

The dark unicorn rose, shook himself, shrugged. "It seems I must. I cannot remove this halter on my own. And if you kill me, who will reset your wing?"

Illishar laughed suddenly. To Jan's surprise, it was not the shrill, raucous bird sound he might have expected, but a deep, throaty, catlike thrumming — almost a purr.

"Your hooves and horn are no less formidable than my beak and talons," the wingcat chuckled. "It seems we must trust one another perforce."

Jan nodded and knelt beside the great raptor, bowing his head to one side so that the other could reach the halter's fastening. Illishar seemed to consider a long moment before Jan felt his sharp, unexpectedly delicate talons picking at the buckle. The halter grew loose about Jan's head, but as he moved to pull away, to rise and shake himself free, the other's grasp gently restrained him.

"Be still," the gryphon said. "I am not yet done."

Surprised, the young prince subsided, felt the careful, meticulous touch of the tercel's claws along the crest of his neck, tugging at his mane. The claws released him, and Jan stood up abruptly. The halter slipped free. With a great whinny of triumph, he shook himself, rearing to paw the air, then fell back to all fours again and ducked to scrub either side of his muzzle first against one foreleg, then the other. His face felt oddly uncluttered, light. He was free.

"Unending thanks to you, friend Illishar," he began.

The tercel before him lay running the links of the halter through his talons, eyeing the crescent-moon shaped browpiece with interest. But as Jan raised his head and turned to speak, his attention was seized by the feel of something both light and stiff against his neck. As he rolled his eyes, green flashed at the far limit of his vision. Snorting, shaking his head, he felt the thing, light as a leaf-frond, caught in his mane.

"What have you done?" he asked Illishar. "What more have you done besides what I asked?"

He felt surprise, puzzlement, but strangely, no alarm. The gryphon looked at him and held the halter up.

"You have given me this," he said, "to bear back to my people in token of our pledge. I, too, have given you a token to carry to your flock. One of my feathers I have woven into your mane. Let none of your boar-headed people dare doubt now that you have earned the goodwill of a gryphon."

Once more, Jan shook himself, tossing his head. He felt elated and untrammeled. He felt like the strange, wild unicorns — wrongly called renegades — who dwelt upon the Plain, unbound by the Law and customs of their cousins of the Vale. They called themselves the Free People, and wore fallen birds' feathers in their hair.

"Go now," the gryphon told him, "and treat with this Tlat of the shrieking herons. I will prepare myself for your return, when I will allow you to break and reset my wing."

Return

☽ 27 ☾

The sky stretched high and blue and clean of clouds. The air was warm, full spring at last. Jan halted, breathing deep. Ryhenna emerged from the trees at his back to stand alongside him. Their three-day passage through the Pan Woods had proved blessedly uneventful: no encounters with goatlings, no ambuscades. The Vale of the Unicorns unfolded below them: rolling valley slopes honeycombed with limestone grottoes. Unicorns dotted the grassy hillsides, grazing.

"So many," Ryhenna breathed. "So many — I never dreamed!"

But to the young prince's eye, their numbers seemed alarmingly scant: almost no colts and fillies, very few elders. Even the ranks of the warriors were thinned. A pang tightened his chest. Eagerly he searched the herd below for someone he knew. Far on the opposite hillside, the healer stood among the crowd of older fillies and foals that could only be acolytes. Jan gave a loud whistle. The pied stallion raised his head, then reared up with a shout, his singer's voice ringing out across the Vale.

"Jan! Jan, prince of the unicorns, returns!"

Jan loped eagerly down the slope, Ryhenna in his wake. Astonished unicorns thundered to meet him as he reached the valley floor. They surged around with whickers of greeting and disbelief, eager to catch wind of him, chafe and shoulder their lost prince. Jan glimpsed runners sprinting off to bear news of his arrival to the far reaches of the Vale. Laughing, half rearing, Jan sported among his people until cries of consternation rang out behind him.

"Look — hornless, beardless. Outcast! Renegade!"

He wheeled to find the whole crowd shying, staring at Ryhenna. The coppery mare stood alone. Jan sprang to her side.

"Behold Ryhenna," he declared, "my shoulder-friend, without whose aid I could never have escaped captivity to return to you."

The crowd fidgeted nervously, then abruptly parted, allowing Teki through.

"Greetings, prince," he cried. "Yonder come your sister and dam."

Looking up, Jan beheld his mother, Ses.

"My son, my son," she cried.

Behind her, Lell eyed him uncertainly with her amber-colored eyes. Jan held himself still as the tiny filly approached, sniffing him over. The sharp knob of horn upon her brow, just beginning to sprout, told him she must be newly weaned. Gazing up at him, she smiled suddenly and cried out,

"Jan!"

Teki began to speak of the winter past. Jan listened, dismayed how precisely his dreams had already revealed to him his people's fate. Sheer madness and bitter waste! Under a sane and reasoned leadership, the herd might have fared the brutal famine and cold with far less loss of life.

"Where is Korr now?" he demanded hotly.

"In our grotto," his dam replied with a heavy sigh. "He grazes only by twilight now, eats barely enough to keep himself alive, though forage is once more plentiful."

Jan bit back the grief and anguish welling up in him. "You say he turned against Tek and drove her from the Vale — why? Why?"

The pied stallion cast down his gaze, shook his head and whispered, "Madness."

"But what has become of her?" Jan pressed. "You say she was in foal?"

Teki's face grew haggard, his eyes bright. "We have no word," he answered roughly. "Dagg, who went in search of her some days past, has not yet returned."

The healer stopped himself, regained his breath. His chest seemed tight.

"We fear she may be dead."

Jan stared at the others, staggered. He turned from Teki to Ses, but his mother's gaze could offer him no hope.

"Nay, not so!" a voice from across the throng called suddenly. "I live!"

The whole herd started, turned. Jan's heart leapt to behold Tek, long-limbed and lithe, her pied form full of energy, loping toward him, flanked on one shoulder by the Red Mare and on the other by Dagg. Others, less plainly visible, trailed them — but the young prince's gaze fixed wholly on Tek.

With a cry, he sprang to her. The press of unicorns had fallen back to let her and her companions through. She stood laughing, no sorrow in her. Her breath against his skin was sweet and soft, her touch gentle, the scent of her delicate as he recalled, aromatic as spice. He nuzzled her, whickering, "My mate. My mate."

She gave him a playful nip, then started back suddenly. "What's this?" she cried. "How came you by this gryphon plume?"

He felt her teeth fasten on it, tugging angrily to work it free, but he pulled back, nickering. "Peace," he bade her. "Let be. I will tell you when you have told me of yourself. How fared you this winter past?"

"My daughter sheltered in my cave," the Red Mare answered, "as safe and warm and well-fed as were you, prince Jan, in the sorcerous City of Fire. You have freed another of its captives, I see, and brought her home with you. *Emwe!* Hail, daughter of fire," Jah-lila called. "Do I guess thy name aright: *Ryhenna?*"

The coppery mare stood staring at Jah-lila. "It is true, then?" she stammered at last. "Ye are the one that erewhile dwelt among my kind?"

Jah-lila nodded. "Born a hornless *da* in the stable of the *chon*. Drinking of the sacred moonpool far across the Plain, I became a unicorn. So, too, mayst thou, little one. Follow, and I will lead thee there."

"I will accompany you!" Dagg exclaimed. He stood transfixed, staring at Ryhenna as though in a dream. Jan watched, taken by surprise, as the other approached the coppery mare. "I am called Dagg, fair Ryh — fair Ryhenna." He stumbled over the unfamiliar name. "The way to the wyvern-infested Hallow Hills is long and dangerous. For all the Red Mare's sorcery, I would feel easier for you with a warrior at your side."

The prince of the unicorns bit back a laugh. Plainly his friend was smitten. After months moping beside the Summer Sea a season past, the dappled warrior seemed finally to have found a mare to spark his eye. The swiftness of it astonished Jan. Ryhenna was now returning Dagg's gaze with shyly flattered interest.

Jan shouldered gently against Tek, nuzzling her, glad to steal a caress while others' eyes fixed on the dappled warrior and the coppery mare. Beside the prince, his mate stood sleek and well-nourished — and plainly not pregnant. Just when her belly ought to have been swollen to its greatest girth, ready to deliver any day, it clearly held no life. An overwhelming sense of loss mingled with his joy at finding the healer's daughter alive and hale.

"Teki told me you were in foal," Jan whispered in her ear. "My love, I am so sorry to see that you have lost it. Later, in a season or two, when you are ready, we can try again."

Shrugging with pleasure against his touch, Tek laughed. "What loss?" she asked. "Nay, Jan. Behold."

Baffled, the young prince of the unicorns turned, following the line of Tek's gaze. It came to rest upon the small figures that had followed her, Jah-lila, and Dagg. Two were unicorns, and two — astonishment pricked him as he realized — were not. The latter were pans, young females both, not yet half-grown. Jan felt his spine stiffen — yet surely such young goatlings must be harmless enough. The two stood calmly beneath his scrutiny, the younger pan pressing against the Red Mare, who nuzzled her.

The other two members of the party were infant unicorns, flatbrowed still, hornbuds mere bumps upon their wide, smooth foreheads. Whose progeny were they, Jan wondered? Surely they could not be earlyborns, for though small, each was perfectly formed, surefooted, sound of wind — yet what mares would consent to tryst with their mates so early the preceding summer that they bore their offspring in late winter, before spring forage greened the hills? Madness! The tiny pair gazed up at him with bright, intelligent eyes.

The coloring of them was like none he had ever seen. The young prince shook his head, astonished. The filly was on one side mostly black, with silver stockings and one jet eye outlined in silver. Her other side was mostly silver, black-stockinged, her dark eye black-encircled. The foal was purest white, not a mark or a dark hair on him, and eyes like cloudless sky. The two seemed to shimmer before his gaze: brightening, fading. Tek was laughing at him. He blinked. Slowly, realization dawned.

"Nay," he whispered. "Truth, Tek, these cannot be — not both of them!"

She nodded. "Aye. Born early, by my dam's design — though without my foster sisters' aid, none of us would have survived to greet your homecoming."

"Pans!" Jan exclaimed, turning to stare once more at the young goatlings flanking Jah-lila. "Pan fosterlings?"

The Red Mare nodded. "Aye, prince. Orphaned young, they took me as their dam. Their care has kept me much from the Vale in recent years. Though passing freely among their own kind in the Wood, they know the ways of unicorns as well."

"Emwe," the younger of the pan sisters said to him, gesturing with one hairless forelimb. Jan felt a tremor of recognition. Their speech was like that of the two-foots — more fluting, less guttural — but clearly recognizable.

"Emwe," the prince of the unicorns replied. "Tai-shan nau sho-pucha." *Hail. Moonbrow greets you.*

"Greet-ings," the elder of the two replied, enunciating the words of the unicorn tongue carefully, "great prince of u-nicorns."

All around, nickers of astonishment, alarm from the nervously milling herd — to hear supposedly mute goatlings speak.

"I am Sismoomnat," the young pan replied, "my sis-ter, Piti-pak. Our fos-ter dam, Jah-ama, has taught us u-nicorn speech. We al-so speak in the way of our own folk. We are glad to have come among you at last, fair u-nicorns. Our dam has long pledged to bring us to you when time grew ripe."

Swallowing his astonishment, Jan managed a low bow. Perhaps more treaties than he had hoped could be struck this spring.

"Greetings to you both, pan fosterlings of the Red Mare," he answered. "Doubtless you know of the long enmity that lies be-tween our two peoples. Perhaps time indeed grows ripe to resolve our differences. Would you be willing to act as envoys between your people and my own?"

Happily, the young goatling nodded. "It is the task for which Jah-ama reared us. Glad-ly will we bear words of peace between our two tribes."

Beneath the goatlings' smooth, long-fingered forepaws, the black-and-silver filly and the flawless white foal fidgeted, shoul-dering one another playfully and eyeing Jan with frank, fearless curiosity. The young pans stepped back as the prince of the uni-corns moved forward to nose his daughter and son. The nameless filly and foal frolicked against him, their long, delicate legs tan-gling, their tiny, ropelike tails spiraling with nervous energy. Jan breathed deep, exploring their every curve. Their scent reminded him of Tek — and of himself.

"The foal is Dhattar," Tek told him softly, "the filly, Aiony —"

A low moan cut short her words. Starting up, Jan beheld a dark figure on the near slope. Unicorns fell back, some hissing with disgust. The other did not approach. Moments passed be-fore Jan recognized the haggard stallion. The young prince stared. Could this wasted figure truly be his sire, once the robust and vigorous king of the unicorns? In less than a year, Korr seemed to have aged many.

"Freaks!" he groaned. "Begotten in lawlessness and borne in wychery. They will bring destruction! The goddess's wrath —"

Jan stamped one heel, furious, moving forward to stand between his family and the king.

"What wrath?" he demanded. "Father, what makes my heirs abomination in your eyes? And how is it you claim to know the goddess's will — does Alma speak to you?"

The bony figure stared. "I — nay. I . . . used to think so," he mumbled, shifting uneasily. Then he raised his head, voice growing stronger. "You should never have chosen the pied wych, my son. I warned you sore —"

"My mate is no wych!" Jan retorted hotly. "She is Tek, that same brave warrior whom, before this winter past, you always honored high. Why are you so against our pledge?"

But the dark other only shook his head, muttering. "Nay, it was a long time past, upon the Plain. The wych . . . I never . . ."

As the Red Mare stepped forward, he shied from her as from a gryphon.

"You speak in riddles, Korr." She eyed him steadily.

"Wych! Wych!" the mad stallion cried, rearing, flailing at the air. "See what your wychery has wrought? I trusted you!"

Gazing at him still, Jah-lila never flinched. "My prince," she said, "you and I alone know what befell upon the Plain so long ago, who trusted whom and who betrayed. Honor binds me to hold my tongue until you speak."

"Never!" the haggard stallion shrieked. "Your spells ensnared me once —"

Members of the herd scattered as, for a moment, it looked as though the wild-eyed king might fly at her — but the Red Mare held steady, her gaze fixed upon him square.

"I charge you now," she answered, "for your own honor's sake, speak plain. It is your only hope of peace."

With an inarticulate cry, the mad stallion wheeled, sprang away up the slope. Below, all around Jan the unicorns watched with expressions of anger, or pity, or scorn. Not until the king's form had nearly reached the treeline did the young prince come to himself with a start and spring forward to follow. His dam stepped quickly to block his path.

"Hold, my son. It is himself he flees — and none of us may catch him till he turn and stand his ground."

Jan snorted, dodging, but it was hopeless. His sire's form had vanished into the trees, the thunder of his heels already faded. Restlessly, the young prince paced a circle.

"What maddens him?" he cried.

Ses shook her head. "Only Korr may answer that."

She did not stand aside. The prince's eye fell on Jah-lila, facing him with calm, unfathomable black-green eyes.

"What do you know of this?" he demanded. "Why is my sire in such terror of you? What befell the pair of you upon the Plain?"

The Red Mare's glance flicked after the fugitive king, then turned to rest ruefully upon her daughter Tek. Bitterly, wordlessly, Jah-lila turned away.

That eve was Moondance, the first, so Jan learned, since the sad return of the courting band that fall past. Now unicorns came from all quarters of the Vale to dance in celebration of their newly restored prince and hear his tale. Jan told them of the City of Fire and his captivity there, of his truce with the gryphon and his decision to treat with the pans as well. Finally, he showed them fire. Striking the tip of his horn to one heel, he set ablaze a great heap of deadwood set upon the rocky outcrop of the council rise.

From the far hillside as the flames rose up, one dark and lonely figure watched. Jan recognized the gaunt silhouette against the moonlit sky, but dared not go to seek him yet, lest pursuit drive the mad king entirely from the Vale, where none might hope to find him. With difficulty, the young prince resigned himself for now. Soon, he vowed, he must follow his sire — to the smoking Dragon Hills, if need be — and riddle out the reason for his madness.

Moon reached its zenith in the sky. Jan lay beside his mate and twin heirs. His dam and her weanling nestled nearby. The young pan nursemaids, fallen deeply asleep, sprawled alongside Lell and his own twins. Dagg and Ryhenna, Teki and Jah-lila rested nearby. Casting his gaze out over the slumbering herd, breathing the scent of them and of moonlight and of smoldering fire in the warm spring air, Jan found himself if not wholly satisfied, for the moment at least, at peace. It was good to be back in the Vale and among his people again.

Weariness overwhelmed him. He dozed. *Aye, I have led you a merry round, I know,* the soft, familiar voice within him whispered. *It will not be the last.*

Drowsing, he felt no tremor, no surprise. He floated, suspended as by lapping waves between waking and sleep. Starlight surrounded him. The gryphon feather lifted in the breeze.

Are you willing to accept yet, the goddess murmured, *that you can neither summon nor dismiss me, and that my words must reach you whenever and in whatever form I wish?*

He seemed enveloped by a medium dark as midnight yet infused with light, that was at once both sea and stars, peopled with other travelers besides himself: swimmers sleek and spiral-tusked.

Are you ready to understand that I am the world, Aljan, where all that befalls you is me and my true voice speaking to you — whether I choose the use of words or no? I have not deserted you and can never desert you, prince of unicorns, my Firebringer, Dark Moon.

After

☾

How my tale has rambled, and how late the night has grown! Truth, I had meant to tell you all, as I promised yestereve — yet I have gotten no further than Jan's return from the City of Fire. Bear with me, gracious hosts, I beg, for I am old, more than thirty winters: a good age for any unicorn, and a vast one for daya among whom I was born.

Ah, well. Summer nights are pleasant, and you have been most tolerant of an old mare's champing: you whom the Vale dwellers so long called renegades, but who justly call yourselves the Free People of the Plain. It is always a joy to sojourn among you. Rest sure, I will tell you what remains of my tale, and all in one sitting, if you will but meet with me upon this same spot tomorow eve.

Then will I spell you the rest — all of the rest — of the tale of the Firebringer; how Jan drove the hated wyverns from their stolen dens, thus regaining the Hallow Hills for his people, the children-of-the-moon. Of this and much, much more shall I speak. Come again tomorrow, I charge you. This time, faithfully I vow, you shall hear Jan's story to its end.